Praise for *The Good Sister*

'An utterly compelling emotional mystery, with beautifully realised characters and a delicious dark twist. I loved it!'
Adele Parks, bestselling author of *Both of You*

'Sally keeps getting better and better. *The Good Sister* is the perfect blend of suspense, twists and richly drawn characters that will have you loving or hating them'
Heidi Perks, bestselling author of *The Whispers*

'I was utterly enthralled as I always am with Sally Hepworth's extraordinary novels. I loved the way my feelings for the two sisters grew and changed and twisted throughout the read as I got to know them more and towards the end there was no way I was putting that book down!'
Nicola Moriarty, author of *You Need To Know*

'I absolutely loved *The Good Sister*. Fern is such a wonderful character. The crossover of uplit and psychological suspense is so successful. I found it immensely enjoyable, heart-warming and satisfying. Sally Hepworth is a brilliant writer'
Emma Curtis, bestselling author of *Invite Me In*

'No one writes domestic suspense like Sally Hepworth. *The Good Sister* is the perfect blend of suspense and heart'
Kelly Rimmer, bestselling author of *The Warsaw Orphan*

'A stunningly clever thriller made doubly suspenseful by not one, but two unreliable narrators'
People (Australia), Book of the Week

'Compelling story, plenty of twists and a satisfying ending. Sally is an exceptional observer of people and their relationships'
Graeme Simsion, author of *The Rosie Result*

'Absolutely stunning'
Heather Gudenkauf, *New York Times* bestselling author of *This is How I Lied*

'A captivating story with utterly convincing characters. A sense of threat lurks quietly in the background throughout, making this both a satisfying and chilling read'
Rachel Abbott, bestselling author of *Close Your Eyes*

Also by Sally Hepworth

The Mother-in-Law

The Family Next Door

The Mother's Promise

The Things We Keep

The Secrets of Midwives

THE GOOD SISTER

SALLY HEPWORTH

HODDER

First published in Great Britain in 2021 by Hodder & Stoughton
An Hachette UK company

This paperback edition published in 2021

1

A CIP catalogue record for this title is
available from the British Library

Paperback ISBN 978 1 473 69703 4
eBook ISBN 978 1 473 69705 8

Printed and bound in Great Britain by Clays Ltd, Elcograf S.p.A.

Hodder & Stoughton policy is to use papers that are natural, renewable
and recyclable products and made from wood grown in sustainable forests.
The logging and manufacturing processes are expected to conform to
the environmental regulations of the country of origin.

Hodder & Stoughton Ltd
Carmelite House
50 Victoria Embankment
London EC4Y 0DZ

www.hodder.co.uk

For Eloise and Clementine
For giving me a glimpse into the great wonders and
(greater) horrors of having a sister

THE
GOOD SISTER

• • •

JOURNAL OF ROSE INGRID CASTLE

It's been three months since Owen left. Left, or left *me*—like so many things in the adult world, it's all a bit gray. He took a job in London; a work opportunity, ostensibly. It's not that I wasn't invited, but it was clear to both of us that I couldn't go. That's another thing about the adult world: responsibilities. In my case, one particular responsibility. Fern.

But let me backtrack, because it sounds like I'm blaming her. I'm not. The problems between Owen and me are 100 percent, unequivocally, entirely, my fault. I committed the most cardinal of marital sins—I changed. Overnight, as soon as the clock chimed my twenty-seventh birthday in fact, I went from being a well-educated, empowered woman to one of those pathetic women who wanted a baby with such ferocity it drove my husband away. An ovulation-kit-wielding, sperm-testing, temperature-taking lunatic. In my previous life, I'd scorned this type of woman from up in my (what I presumed to be) fertile ivory tower. Then I'd become one. And I'd pushed and I'd pushed and I'd pushed—until my husband left. Left . . . or left *me.*

My therapist is right, it is a relief, getting these thoughts out of my head and onto paper. In therapy, we hardly talk about Owen at all. Instead, we while away the fifty-minute hours talking about my traumatic childhood. According to him, a good way to process trauma and put it behind you is to write it down. That's why he gave me this journal. I'm not convinced it will help, but here I am. Apparently, the people-pleaser in me dies hard.

The obvious place to start is the night at the river. I was twelve. We were camping. Mum and Daniel had been dating for about six months, but it was the first time we'd been away anywhere together. Daniel brought Billy, much to my and Fern's delight—we'd forever longed for a brother, and all those wonderful traits a brother brought with him: roughhousing, logical arguments, and good-looking friends. And for the first few days, we had a good time. Better than good. It was the closest I'd ever come to being part of a normal family. Daniel taught us to fish, Billy taught us how to play poker, and Mum . . . she was like a completely different person. She did things like remind us to apply sunscreen and tell us to be careful in the river "because the current could be strong." One day, she even rested her arm affectionately around my shoulders as we sat by the fire. She'd never done that before. I'll never forget what it felt like, our bodies touching like that.

On the last night, Billy, Fern, and I went to the river mouth. The heat of the day hung in the air and we spent most of the time slapping mosquitoes from our arms. Billy was in the water, the only place to get any relief from the heat. Usually Fern and I would have joined him, but something was up with Fern that night. She was in one of her moods. I'd wanted to ask her about it all day, but Fern could be volatile when she was upset. I decided it was better to leave it alone.

We'd been by the river an hour or so when nature called. Billy was showing no signs of getting out of the water, so I headed deep into the trees. There was no way I was going to let him see me pee. It was slow going; it was pitch black and I was barefoot—I had to watch every step I took. My fear of snakes didn't help matters. Still, I was gone for five minutes max. Apparently, that is all it takes.

When I returned to the river, Fern was gone.

"Fern," I called. "Where are you?"

It was strange for her not to be in the spot I left her.

It took me a minute to locate her, illuminated by a patch of moonlight in the shallows of the river. She was standing eerily still. Billy was nowhere to be seen.

"What are you—" I took a step toward her and she lifted her hands. Before I could ask what was going on, something rose to the surface of the water beside her—a sliver of pale, unmoving flesh.

"Fern," I whispered. "What have you done?"

FERN

Every Tuesday morning at 10:15 A.M., I am stationed at the front desk of the Bayside Public Library. The front desk is usually my least favorite post, but on Tuesday mornings I make an exception so as to have a clear view to the circular meeting room where Toddler Rhyme Time takes place. I enjoy Toddler Rhyme Time, despite its obvious vexing qualities—the noise, the crowd, the unexpected direction a child's emotions can take at a moment's notice. Today, Linda, the children's librarian, is regaling the toddlers with a vehement retelling of "The Three Little Pigs." Imaginatively, she has chosen to forgo *reading* the book, and is instead acting the story out, alternately donning a fluffy wolf's head and a softer, squidgy-looking pig's head with pale blue eyes and a protruding snout. At intervals, Linda emits an impressively realistic-sounding pig's squeal, so shrill and penetrating that it makes my toes curl in my sneakers.

The children, on the whole, appear enraptured with Linda's recital, the only exceptions being a newborn screaming wildly on its mother's shoulder and a little boy in an orange jumper who covers his ears and buries his face in his grandmother's lap. I, too, am absorbed in the performance—so much so that it takes me several seconds to register the woman with pointy coral fingernails who has appeared at the desk, clutching a stack of books against her hip. I roll my ergonomic chair slightly to the right so I can still see the children (who are now helping Linda blow down an imaginary house of straw), but distractingly, the woman moves with me, huffing and fidgeting and, finally, clearing her throat. Finally, she clicks her fingernails against the desk. "Ex*cuse* me."

"Ex*cuse* me," I repeat, rolling the statement around in my head. It feels unlikely that she is *actually* asking to be excused. After all, patrons are free to come and go as they please in the library, they don't have to ask for the privilege. It's possible, I suppose, that she's asking to be excused for impoliteness, but as I didn't hear her belch or fart, that also seems improbable. As such, I conclude she has employed the odd social custom of asking to be excused as a means of getting a person's attention. I open my mouth to tell her that she *has* my attention, but people are so impatient nowadays and she cuts me off before I can speak.

"Do you work here?" she asks rudely.

Sometimes the people in this library can be surprisingly dense. For heaven's sake, why would I be sitting behind the desk—wearing a *name badge*!—if I didn't work here? That said, I acknowledge that I don't fit the stereotypical mold of a librarian. For a start, at twenty-eight, I'm younger than the average librarian (forty-five, according to *Librarian's Digest*) and I dress more fashionably and colorfully than the majority of my peers—I'm partial to soft, bright T-shirts, sparkly sneakers, and long skirts or overalls emblazoned with rainbows or unicorns. I wear my hair in two braids, which I loop into a bun above each ear (not a reference to Princess Leia, though I do wonder if she found the style as practical as I do for keeping long hair out of your face when you are a woman with things to do). And, yet, I am most definitely a librarian.

"Are you going to serve me, young lady?" the woman demands.

"Would you *like* me to serve you?" I ask patiently. I don't point out that she could have saved herself a lot of time by simply *asking* to be served.

The woman's eyes boggle. "Why do you *think* I'm standing here?"

"There are an infinite number of reasons," I reply. "You are, as you may have noticed, directly adjacent to the water fountain, which is a high-traffic area for the library. You might be using the desk to shuffle documents on your way over to the photocopier. You may be admiring the Monet print on the wall behind me—something I do several times a day. You may have paused on your way to the door to tie your shoelace, or to double-check if that person over in the nonfiction section is your ex-boyfriend. You might, as I was before you came along, be enjoying Linda's wonderful rendition of 'The Three Little Pigs'—"

I have more examples, many *many* more, but I am cut off by Gayle, who approaches the desk hurriedly. "May I help you there?"

Gayle has a knack for turning up at opportune times. She has fluffy blond hair, exceedingly potent perfume, and a thing about bringing me lemons from her lemon tree. I once made the mistake of saying I'd enjoyed a slice of lemon in hot water and since then I've barely gone a day without a lemon from Gayle. I'd tell her to stop, but Rose says people enjoy making themselves useful in these small ways and the best thing to do is to thank them and throw the lemon away. Bizarre as it sounds, Rose tends to be right about these things.

"Finally!" the woman says, and then launches into a story about how her son left his library books at the beach house and then it got fumigated so they weren't able to collect the books until yesterday and now they've incurred a fine and, also, she'd like to extend her loan, but the book has twenty-seven reserves on it! Twenty-seven! As far as stories to get out of fines go, this one is rather benign, I have to say. I spoke with a gentleman recently who explained that his daughter had taken his library copy of *Ulysses* on a trekking vacation to the Andes, where she'd left it in a mountain village with a mother of newborn twins whose husband had recently passed away. I marveled that an Andean village woman could read English so well as to read *Ulysses,* not to mention have a desire to read such a book while single-handedly raising her twins on a mountaintop, but before I could ask him much about either, he shuffled away. (Gayle, of course, waived the fine.)

I work in the library four days a week, plus two Sundays a month. If it's not raining, like today, I walk the thirty-five minutes to work while listening to my audiobook and I arrive at the library a minimum of fifteen minutes before my shift. If it is raining, I catch the bus and arrive at a similar time. I then spend the day recommending books, processing returns, and avoiding questions about the photocopiers. Depending on the particular day, I might also order new books, set up the conference room for author talks or community meetings, or put together book packages for the home library service. I try to avoid conversations about things other than books, although I'll occasionally indulge Gayle in a conversation about her garden or her grandchildren, because Rose says it's polite to do this with people who we like.

I'm listening to Gayle waive the fine for the woman with the coral-colored fingernails when my eye is drawn to a young man in thick glasses and a red-and-white-striped beanie entering through the automatic doors. A homeless person, most likely, judging by his too-loose jeans and the towel draped over his shoulder. He makes a beeline for the shower room. The Bayside library boasts two showers (thanks to its former life as a hospital), so it's not uncommon for the homeless to come in to shower. The first time I saw a homeless person come in, I was affronted, but that was before I worked with Janet. Janet, my old supervisor, taught me that the library belongs to everyone. The library, Janet used to say, is one of only a few places in the world that one doesn't need to believe anything or buy anything to come inside . . . and it is the librarian's job to look after all those who do. I take this responsibility very seriously, except if they require assistance with the photocopiers and then I give them a very wide berth.

I reach for my handbag and follow the man toward the bathroom. He's tall—very tall—and lanky looking. From behind, with his pom-pom bouncing on his stripy hat, he reminds me a little of Wally of *Where's Wally?* fame.

"Wally!" I call as he steps into the small vestibule—an airless, windowless tiled room leading to both the men's and women's bathrooms. I usually avoid this space at all costs, but seeing the man enter, I feel an unexpected compulsion to face my fears.

"Were you planning to use the shower?"

He turns around, eyebrows raised, but doesn't respond. I wonder if he might be hearing impaired. We have a large community of hearing-impaired patrons at our library. I repeat myself loudly and slowly, allowing him to lip-read.

"Yes?" he says finally, his intonation rising as if he is asking a question rather than answering one.

I start to question my impulse to follow him. I have become more wary of vagrants since a man exposed himself to me a few months back during an evening shift. I had been replacing a copy of Ian McEwan's *Atonement* when suddenly, at eye level, there was a penis, in the "Mc" section of General Fiction. I alerted Gayle, who called the police, but by the time they arrived, the man had zipped up and shuffled out of the place. "You should have snapped it in between the covers of that hardback," Gayle had said, which sounded messy, not to mention unwise for the hygiene of the book. When I pointed this out, she suggested I "karate-chop" him, which is neither an actual karate move (I have a black belt) nor something I would be tempted to do, since karate has a pacifist philosophy.

I have been doing karate since I did a trial class in grade two and the sensei said I was a "natural" (an odd comment as there was nothing natural about kata—on the contrary, the movements felt very specific and unnatural). Still, I found I enjoyed it immensely—the consistency, the routine, the structure, even the physical contact, which was always firm if not hard. Even the "Kiai" shouts, while loud, are to a count and expected. So twenty years later, I'm still doing it.

"Well, here you go then."

I reach into my handbag and retrieve the small toiletry bag that I keep in there. I hand it to Wally, who holds it away from himself as if it might contain a ticking bomb. "What . . . *is* . . . this?"

"It contains toothpaste and a toothbrush, a face washer and some soap. Also a razor and some shaving cream."

I'm not sure how I could be any clearer, and yet Wally still seems confused. I study him closely. He doesn't smell like alcohol and both his eyes are pointing the same direction. His clothes, while ill fitting, are all on the correct parts of his body. Still, the jury is out on his sanity.

"Did you just call me . . . Wally?"

There's something pleasing about the man's voice; his words are round somehow, and completely enunciated. It is an unexpected delight in a world where people are forever mumbling.

"Yes," I say. "You look like Wally from *Where's Wally?* Hasn't anyone told you that before?"

He neither confirms nor denies it, so I decide to provide more information.

"You know *Where's Wally?*, don't you? It's a book." I smile, because Rose says that people should smile while engaging in banter (playful exchanges of friendly remarks), and this, to me, feels very much like banter.

Wally doesn't smile. "You mean *Where's Waldo?*"

Wally is American, I realize suddenly, which explains both his accent and his confusion.

"Actually, no, I mean *Where's Wally?* The original book was *Where's Wally?*, published in the United Kingdom in 1987. Since then, the books have been published around the world and Wally's name is often changed in these different editions. For instance, he's 'Waldo' in the United States and Canada, 'Charlie' in France, 'Walter' in Germany, 'Ali' in Turkey, 'Efi' in Israel, and 'Willy' in Norway."

Wally studies me for a few seconds. He seems perplexed. His gaze, I notice, is just to the left of me, as if he is looking over my shoulder.

"Anyway, in Australia, it's Wally," I say.

"Oh. Kay." He looks back at the toiletry bag. "So . . . the library provides these?"

"No," I say, smiling wider. "I do."

Under his glasses, Wally's mossy green pupils travel right to left slowly. "*You* do?"

"Yes. My sister gives these to me whenever she returns from international travel. Do you know they give them out for free on airplanes?"

"I did know that," he says, which makes me wonder about the accuracy of my assessment that he is homeless. I have, in my lifetime, been known to get things alarmingly wrong. I examine him more closely. His jeans are both too loose and too short and appear to have been cut off by hand, judging by the frayed ends. His buffalo flannelette shirt is in better nick, nicely buttoned right up to the neck. And while he has an overall look of grubbiness, I haven't detected an odor, even in this small vestibule. I look at his fingernails, which are clean. Spectacularly clean, in fact. Buffed and pink and round, each cuticle a perfect crescent moon. The man could be a hand model.

"I apologize, I thought you were homeless." I don't smile now, to indicate this isn't banter, but a serious comment. "I'm afraid it was your jeans that gave me that impression. And the hat, obviously."

He stares at me. Not being one to duck away from a challenge, I stare back. A few years ago, I read a book of tips for people who find eye contact difficult. It suggested staring competitions as a form of exposure therapy. To my great surprise, I excelled at it. As it turned out, staring competitions were nothing like the discomfort of regular eye contact. There is no need to wonder how long you must look at someone, when you should look away or how often to blink. With staring competitions, all you have to do is fix your gaze on the person and let your mind wander. I can do that for hours if I feel so inclined. In fact, I once beat Mr. Robertson, a library patron and good contender, at thirty-seven minutes. I expect Wally, younger and wilier by the look of him, to be a better contender, so I'm disappointed when after less than ten seconds, he looks away.

"Amateur."

Wally opens his mouth at the same time as the door swings open, forcing me farther into the vestibule. The boy in the orange jumper from Toddler Rhyme Time pushes his way inside. On his heels are his grandmother and another woman pushing a double stroller. Clearly, Rhyme Time has finished. Outside, the swell of toddler racket intensifies.

"What's wrong with my hat?" Wally asks, as the door opens again and a small girl and her mother file into the small space. It's getting quite cramped in here now. The boy in the orange jumper jumps up and down and announces "I'm busting" to no one in particular. Then he notices Wally. "It's Wally!" he cries, marveling.

Wally looks at me and I shrug—a nonverbal gesture I've seen people use to indicate, *Told you.*

There are a lot of people in the little vestibule now and the acoustics are particularly irritating. I place my hands over my ears. "It's a compliment," I yell over the din. "Wally is universally beloved, even if he is an odd sort of fellow. Though maybe he isn't odd, maybe he just looks that way? Like you!"

Wally pushes his glasses back up his nose and I lip-read him saying, "*Excuse* me?"

"You don't need to ask to be excused," I shout, moving toward the door. "The library is a public space; you can come and go as you please."

The door opens yet again; this time an elderly man, pushing a walking frame, comes through it. I grab the door and maneuver around the double stroller. I'm almost out the door when a thought occurs to me and I swivel around.

"And if you belched or farted, I didn't hear it, so no need to excuse yourself for that either!"

And with that, I give a little wave and take my exit.

When we were five, my mother took my sister, Rose, and me to the library every day for a year. *A better education than school will ever give you,* Mum used to say, and I quite agree. If it were up to me, every child would have a year in the library before they went to school. Not just to read, but to roam. To befriend a librarian. To bash their fingers against the computers and to turn the pages of a book while making up a story from their superior little imaginations. How lucky the world would be if every child could do that.

I was that lucky. These days, researchers seem to be saying that we don't form explicit memories until the age of seven, but I have a number of memories from the year I was five. Memories of Mum, Rose, and me waking up with the birds, scrambling into our clothes and racing out to the bus stop. Because of our eagerness, we nearly always arrived before the library opened, then passed the time by sitting on the bench out the front, or, if it was raining, huddled under the awning finishing our books while we waited for the doors to open. When we got inside, Rose and I took turns sliding our books into the return slot and then racing to select our beanbags for the day (I preferred the cotton ones—the vinyl could get so sticky after a while). Mum never sat on a beanbag, she preferred the armchairs or seats on the other side of the library. Often, we didn't see Mum for the whole day. That was part of the fun. We went to the toilet by ourselves, we went to the water fountain by ourselves. At the library, we were in charge of what we did and when.

We'd been doing this for a few weeks when one of the librarians, Mrs. Delahunty, began taking an interest in us. First, she gave us book recommendations. Then, she gave Rose and me worksheets on which to write the names of all the books we'd read. If we got to a hundred, she said, we'd be gifted a book from the library to keep! It was through filling out that worksheet that Rose and I learned to write. Some days, when we deliberated on what to read next, Mrs. Delahunty would come over and make suggestions.

"Did you enjoy *The Giving Tree,* girls? If so, I think you would love *Where the Wild Things Are.* Sit down and we'll read it together."

Afterward she'd ask us questions. *Do you think Max really went away? What do you think actually happened?* Mrs. Delahunty said that answering questions helped our brains understand what we'd read. As the year went on, Mrs. Delahunty chose more and more difficult books for us, and by the year's end, according to Mrs. Delahunty, we had the vocabulary of twelve-year-olds! Because of this, the following year we skipped prep and went straight into grade one. Mum was very proud of this. Lots of people said things to us like *What a wonderful mum you must have!* and *Your mum must have spent a lot of time reading to you.*

The first time someone said that, I started to point out that, no, it *wasn't* Mum who spent time reading to us, but then Rose tapped her bracelet against mine. Mum had given us our bracelets when we were born—mine was engraved with a fern, and Rose's with a rose. Somewhere along the way, they became our way of talking to each other without talking. Rose always taps her bracelet against mine as a warning. Stop. It's a good system that almost always works. There's only been one time that Rose couldn't stop me from doing the wrong thing and that was a mistake that will haunt me for the rest of my life.

JOURNAL OF ROSE INGRID CASTLE

Today, my therapist and I dove deep on my yearning for a baby. I talked about how it felt physical, like hunger, like pain. Like loss. My therapist thinks this stems from my childhood—a desire to do right what my mother couldn't. An attempt to heal myself. Maybe he's right.

As conversation steered in this direction, he asked me to talk about my earliest traumatic memory. It took me a while to find it—it must have been buried a long way down in the dusty depths of my subconscious—but now that I've retrieved it, I can't stop thinking about it. It is from when I was five years old; the year after Dad left, not that I have any memory of that. My first scraps of memory that I still hold are from the following year, the year Mum took us to the library. Fern had loved that year! She refers to it with such fondness—how the library became her home, how she discovered the hidden worlds within the pages of books, how that year is the reason she became a librarian. It makes me want to scream. Sometimes I wonder if, like those choose-your-own-adventure books that we used to devour, the two of us were living parallel, alternate lives.

Do you know what I remember from the library year? Sleeping on couches that smelled of dog; being dragged from our old flat in the middle of the night and not being allowed to bring any toys, not even Mr. Bear, even when I begged Mum to let me take him; hauling striped plastic bags out of strangers' houses every morning and putting them in the boot of Mum's little car to take wherever we were headed next; waking up every morning with a pain in my stomach, a combination, I realize now, of hunger and fear.

You know something funny? I don't think Fern even knows we were homeless that year. She probably told herself it was an adventure, or a holiday or an experience. Or maybe she didn't tell herself anything at all. She had a gift for accepting life the way that it was, rather than questioning it. Some days—heck, every day—I envy her that.

It was all Dad's fault we were homeless, apparently. After he left, Mum couldn't afford to pay the rent on her own. She said the landlord was charging so much that no honest person could afford it. That was why we had to sneak out of there during the night with only the things we could carry. For the next twelve months, we stayed in the car or on the couch or floor of whomever Mum was friends with at the time. Luckily Mum had a knack for making friends. "Girls, this is Nancy—we met at the hairdresser!" she'd say delightedly. A few days later, we'd be living in Nancy's house and calling her "Auntie Nance." A week or two after that, we would never see Nancy again—but we'd continue to see the clothes and jewelry she'd lent Mum. We always had a roof over our heads though, and Mum was very proud of that. She'd remind us of this each night before bed.

"I'm doing all this for you two, you know that, right? So you have somewhere to live. If it wasn't for you two, I could easily find a place to live. That's how much I love you."

"Thank you, Mummy."

"And who do you love?"

"You, Mummy."

The months wore on. The library during the day, someone's couch at night. It wasn't all bad. There were things about the library I liked. I liked having somewhere to go every morning, so we didn't have to make small talk over breakfast with whomever was hosting us. Even back then, I understood the shame of taking up space in someone else's life. I liked losing myself in the nooks and crannies of the library, imagining it was my home. I liked that the library was a public space, a space where we were safe, at least for a few hours. I liked Mrs. Delahunty too, though not with the same ferocity Fern did. From time to time, while she was reading to us, I would fantasize that Mrs. Delahunty was our mother. I remember the day she read us *Clifford the Big Red Dog*. After she finished reading, instead of asking us about the story like she usually did, she asked us if we'd had breakfast that morning.

"Nope," Fern said. "Two meals a day are enough for anyone, any more and you're greedy."

She was reciting Mum's words, of course, verbatim. I remember stealing a glance at Mum, over by the magazines, and my stomach got a wobbly feeling.

Next, Mrs. Delahunty asked where we'd been sleeping.

"On the couch," Fern said. There was no hint of concern on her face. I remember thinking how nice it must have been, to be so clueless. And how dangerous.

Mrs. Delahunty's expression remained the same, but the pitch of her voice rose slightly. "Oh? Whose couch?"

Fern shrugged. "Depends whose house we are at."

Mrs. Delahunty looked at me. I looked at my shoes.

After a while, Mrs. Delahunty got up and walked over to Mum. I buried my head in my book, too afraid to look. After a few minutes, Mum came over and told us it was time to leave.

"Who told the librarian that we were homeless?" Mum asked, after we had exited. We were on either side of her, holding on to her hands. I remember that detail, because it was unusual. Usually Mum liked Fern and me to hold hands with each other–it made passersby smile at us, and that seemed to make Mum happy.

"Who told the librarian that we were homeless?" she repeated. There was an edge to her voice, and I remember Fern starting to fidget, repeating the word "homeless" in that strange way she repeated things. We turned the corner into a quiet street and Mum asked again. Her fingernails were digging into my palm.

"Mrs. Delahunty . . . she asked us–" I started.

"So it was you?" Mum turned on me immediately.

I peeked at Fern. She was frightened and confused. She hadn't told anyone we were homeless; she hadn't used that word. She didn't know she was the one to blame.

I nodded.

Mum let go of our hands and bent down low. "You stupid, stupid girl. That lady might seem nice, but she wants to take you away from me. Is that what you want?"

I shook my head.

"Do you want to go a foster home, with a horrible woman who doesn't love you? Never see me again?"

Her face was a contorted, terrifying mask of rage. Bits of spittle flew into my face.

"No!" I cried. All I wanted was to be with her. To be separated from Mum was my greatest fear. She was right. I was stupid. "I'm sorry. I'm sorry, Mummy."

"Let's go home, Fern," she said, snatching up Fern's hand. I ran after them, grasping for Mum's other hand, but she put it into her pocket. I scuttled after them all the whole way home, crying. Mum didn't even flinch when I threw myself at her feet, grazing my knee badly in the process.

When we got back to the house—I can't remember whose we were staying at or why they weren't there that night—Mum made dinner for two. When I asked if I could have some, she acted as if I wasn't even there. Afterward, she bathed Fern and read her a story. It was rare that Mum bathed us, and she never read us stories. I clambered onto the couch to listen to the story, but Mum pushed me off so roughly I fell onto the floorboards, banging my bad knee. I cried so hard my stomach hurt, but she just kept reading. When the story was finished, she tucked Fern in and left the room.

I understood somehow that I shouldn't get into the bed, so eventually I fell asleep on the floor. When I woke, Fern was beside me, her skinny arms wrapped around me, her face buried in my hair. She'd brought the blanket and pillow down from the couch and assembled a little bed around us. She held me like that all night.

Most people think of me as Fern's protector. But the truth is, in her own funny way, she's always been mine.

FERN

At 6:15 P.M. sharp, I open Rose and Owen's white picket gate and walk down the red brick pathway. I have dinner with Rose on Mondays, Tuesdays, and Thursdays, unless Rose is traveling or working late, in which case we forfeit. Attempts to reschedule to another night have not gone well, historically. These cornerstones to my routine are what keep me calm and grounded. Rose and Owen have a lovely house, the kind that looks like it should feature in the pages of *House & Garden* magazine, even though the lawns aren't as neat as they were before Owen went away. Owen used to mow and edge the grass every other week during the winter months and weekly during the summer, but he has taken a job in London now. Still, the lawn is the only blight on the place. The verandah is swept and oiled, and there's a wicker basket next to the door for umbrellas. There's also a shoe rack bearing an upturned never-been-worn pair of shiny red gum boots. Rose takes great pride in keeping house, something she says is a direct response to our childhood home, which was chaotic to say the least. I too have adopted a high standard of order and cleanliness in my home, b of keeping my house to the standard of a magazine spread

I take Rose's three front steps in one leap. As I open the door, I'm greeted by Alfie, whom I kneel to pat. Even the dog picture perfect, with his glossy coat and a ridiculous red kerchief collar around his neck.

"Hello, Alfie," I say as he leaps into my lap. When I stand again, he runs along at my ankles delightedly. When Rose and Owen got Alfie, Rose had insisted that he was going to be an outside dog. ("How many cavoodles do you know who are outside dogs?" Owen had whispered to me. "None," I'd replied, "but I don't know *any* cavoodles other than Alfie, so your survey is flawed.")

In the kitchen, Rose squats in front of the oven with two oversize oven mitts on her hands, watching a chicken under the grill.

"I'm here!" I announce.

Rose startles, almost falling forward, into the oven. "Fern! You scared the life out of me!"

She stands, frowning at me. Rose is an excellent frowner. Even when she laughs, two little vertical lines remain between her eyebrows, as if her face is afraid to have too much fun. Owen used to say it was because she's always worrying about everyone. I know she is worried about him. I can tell because whenever she talks about his job in London, she smiles extra brightly and then quickly changes the subject. Rose also worries about me a lot. I once heard her say to someone on the phone that I'd turned her hair gray (even though her hair *isn't* gray and, besides, stress doesn't *actually* turn hair gray, though stress *can* trigger a condition called telogen effluvium, which causes hair to shed up to three times faster, so while I could cause her to go bald, I couldn't turn her hair gray).

"Did you get the milk?" Rose asks me. She's wearing a white

shirt, black leather pants, and bare feet. Rose is always in some variation of black and white, with the occasional flash of tan or beige. (If you ask me, her outfits could use a few diamantés here and there.) Rose is an interior designer, but "the type who designs office spaces, not the type who chooses scatter cushions." I gather from the regularity and conviction with which Rose says this that this distinction is important to her. For this reason, I have never mentioned that scatter cushions are among some of my favorite things in the world.

"The milk?" she repeats when I look blank. "I called you half an hour ago. You said you'd stop at 7-Eleven on your way?"

Interesting. I have no recollection of this. For someone as fastidious as I am, I can be staggeringly absentminded. It's strange. I have a photographic memory for names and faces, I can find any book in the library with only a character name or cover description, but I will regularly walk out of the house in the morning and leave the front door wide open (Mrs. Hazelbury from next door has taken to just closing the door again, after calling me at the library the first few times, in fear that I had been burgled). Rose says my absentmindedness is part of my charm, but I find it highly irritating. I hate the feeling of not knowing my own mind, not trusting myself, even if the fact is that I'm not to be trusted.

"Never mind," Rose says with a smile. "I'll get some after dinner."

Rose retrieves a preprepared quinoa salad from the fridge and places it on the table. "So," she says. "Tell me something about your day!"

I appreciate Rose's choice of words. Most people ask, *How* was your day?, which is so frustratingly intangible. Telling someone *something* about your day, on the other hand, is specific. I contemplate telling Rose about my interaction with the possible vagrant at the library, but as there is a high possibility that this would lead to a flurry of questions, I select a different item to report instead. "I found out who'd been crossing out the swear words in the books," I say.

Rose tosses the salad. "Oh, yeah? Who?"

"Mrs. Millard," I say. "From the retirement community. She's the one with the mole on her cheek with the hairs growing out of it. She returned a book through the slot after their book club meeting and I happened to be standing there. I saw the crosses and confronted her. She didn't deny it. I told her she had to pay to replace that copy and if I saw any more copies that had been scribbled on, she'd have her library card suspended!"

"Good job, Officer Castle."

Technically, she should have said "Constable," but I understand what she means. "No one defaces library property on my watch," I say.

Rose smiles. Rose is very pretty. Petite with a round face, huge eyes, and nut-brown hair. We don't look like twins (lots of people tell us that). I am tall with a narrow face and reddish-blond hair. In fact, the only physical thing the two of us have in common is the color of our eyes. A very pale blue, like seawater in the shallows of a white sandy beach (an old boyfriend of Rose's said that once, and I thought it the best description I'd heard for the color).

"It's nearly ready," Rose says, getting out her lancet device and blood-glucose strip.

Rose has type 1 diabetes, which means her pancreas produces little or no insulin, which the body needs to function. To compensate for her lack of insulin, Rose has to give herself twice-daily insulin injections, test her blood sugar up to ten times a day, and strictly control the type of food she eats as well as the time of day she eats it. It's a lot of work but she never complains. Now, as she prepares to prick her finger to test her blood sugar, she looks up to warn me and, as always, I set off on a lap of the house (blood makes me queasy).

The house feels empty without Owen, even after all these months. I am fond of him despite of his many disagreeable qualities, such as his penchant for throwing an arm around my shoulder at unexpected times, and his refusal to call me by my given name, preferring instead to use uninspired versions of it: "Fernie," "Fernster," "the Ferminator." It's always struck me as one of the great mysteries of life, who you are fond of. As I wander back toward the kitchen, I nearly stumble on the open suitcase on the floor, partially filled with shoes and a folded garment bag. At the sight of it, my stomach clenches slightly.

Rose is going to London on Friday for four weeks to visit Owen. One full lunar cycle. I know Rose is excited about it, so I'm trying to be excited too, but Rose and I haven't been apart for four weeks before—not even when Rose and Owen got married, because they had a destination wedding in Thailand followed by a "group honeymoon" that all the guests (including me) attended. I try not to think about what could go wrong while she's away, and that, of course, makes me think about what happened *that night* and then, suddenly, I can't think of anything else. I don't want her to go.

"Dinner's ready!"

I tuck the edge of the garment bag back inside the case. That's when I notice the bottle. A white pill bottle with a pink label, showing the midsection of a woman, with full breasts and a curved abdomen. I pick up the bottle and read the label: ELEVIT. TO SUPPORT YOU THROUGH THE DIFFERENT STAGES OF PREGNANCY.

"Fern? Dinner!"

I stand. "Are you pregnant, Rose?"

It wouldn't be ridiculous, I suppose. Rose is twenty-eight, which is an appropriate age, more or less. I have watched television programs about the way fertility dwindles after the age of thirty. Apparently, doctors were recommending that partnered women who wanted children should start as early as possible. Once the surprise of it fades, I feel something akin to excitement hit my system. A *child.* I've always been partial to children. Their lack of complexity, their proclivity for speaking directly, without subtext or agenda. Of course, I'd long accepted that I couldn't have a child of my own, but Rose having a child would be the next best thing.

I return to the kitchen and give Rose a once-over. She doesn't appear to have gained any weight. Then again, if common wisdom is to be believed, morning sickness could ward off weight gain in the early months. Perhaps she'd been feeling off-color these past few weeks, having aversions to food she'd previously enjoyed, but keeping it secret, waiting for a special moment to announce it? But Owen had been gone for months. What would it mean as far as he was concerned?

"I guess you found the Elevit," Rose says after a beat. "My doctor advised that if I was going to try to get pregnant, I should start taking them. Unfortunately," she says, "it hasn't happened yet."

"So . . . you're *trying* to have a baby?" I ask.

Rose picks up the plates and carries them to the table. "I didn't want to tell you until, well . . . I hoped I'd be able to tell you when we had something to announce. Turns out, getting pregnant isn't as easy as I'd hoped."

"Oh." I sit at the table. "Because of your diabetes?"

"Actually, no. It turns out I have a condition called POA. Premature ovarian aging."

She offers me some dressing. I shake my head.

"Premature ovarian aging," I repeat. In my mind's eye, I see a row of eggs with gray hair and wrinkles and tiny walking sticks. "What is premature ovarian aging?"

"Basically it means I have the eggs of a fifty-year-old woman," Rose says. "The quality isn't great and there aren't many of them. We could try IVF, but that relies on me having a good egg to harvest. At the moment, they're not sure that the eggs will survive the process."

Now I picture the eggs in a row of hospital beds, their deathbeds. A row of my potential little nieces and nephews. "That's sad."

Rose puts her fork down. "Yes," she says. "Yes, it is, isn't it?"

"So . . . if you have this . . . *condition,* does that mean I have it too? Because we're twins?"

"No," Rose says. "I mean, it's possible, but not likely. You could get tested if you were worried."

But of course I'm not worried. I am in excellent health, something I take very seriously. My personal maintenance routine encompasses an annual checkup with my GP, twice-yearly checkups with the dentist, biennial Pap tests and breast checks. My exercise routine entails walking to work and back each day, a five-kilometer round trip. I also do karate twice weekly. In addition to karate, I do vinyasa yoga for thirty minutes each morning—for its many benefits, which include muscle stretching and a calm mind. So premature ovarian aging isn't something I need to feel concerned about at all. Besides, I have no plans to get pregnant; I've never been pregnant. I've only ever had sex three and a half times (the half was the first time, and half is more than generous). All three and a half times were with the same guy—a medical student named Albert whom I'd dated for four months a decade ago, and only if "dated" meant spending our weekends studying together, playing the odd game of sudoku, and, of course, sex. I will admit I'd been curious about sex before I'd met Albert, but I was disappointed to find it strange and not particularly pleasant. Albert seemed to enjoy it slightly more than I did, but neither of us had reached anything like the euphoria I'd read about in romance novels. Still, I'd enjoyed our games of sudoku and he appeared to enjoy them too, so I'd been confused when, four months in, Albert abruptly stopped returning my calls, and started keeping his head down when I saw him in the library. When I talked to Rose about it, Rose counseled me that men could be fickle, and if American teen television programs were anything to go by, that seemed to be the truth, so I let it go. I stopped bothering with men after that and I certainly never worried about *babies.*

I'm not capable of raising a baby and that's that. I've made peace with it. But suddenly my interest in babies is piqued. If my eggs *do* turn out to be youthful . . . maybe there could be a use for them after all? This could be my chance to pay Rose back for everything she's always done for me.

I don't sleep well, in general. It bothers me excessively. Especially as I've read all the literature about good sleep and applied all the wisdom. I go to bed at the same time each evening, I exercise regularly and avoid screens and caffeine of an afternoon. And yet my problem remains. Like some kind of cruel karma.

I tend to fall asleep all right, it's the waking that's the problem. Once, twice, sometimes three times a night. I wake abruptly, my body rigid and my breathing ragged. Generally, I'm twisted sideways with my hands tangled in the sheets, a death grip, as if I'm trying to strangle them. Usually it takes at least an hour of deep breathing before I can calm myself enough to drift off again.

I never wake screaming like they do in the movies. In a way, the silence is the worst part. It reminds me of that silent night by the river when I was twelve, when I did that terrible thing.

Most days at work, I break for lunch for half an hour, during which time I eat a honey sandwich and a muesli bar at my desk in an attempt to eschew lunchtime conversation with my colleagues (it rarely works). But Fridays are different. On Friday lunchtimes, most of my colleagues at the library go down to the Brighton Hotel for lunch. Today, among the group are Gayle, Linda, Bernadette, and Trevor. The "social ones." One of us is required to stay back to "hold the fort" and, week after week, I happily oblige. I enjoy the peace and quiet. Still, I've come to enjoy the ritual of being asked followed by the quick, unoffended "No worries" that precedes my colleagues vacating the building. All seems to be going to plan today. I offer my usual "No, thank you," but instead of replying "No worries," Carmel says, "You might enjoy it if you came along, Fern."

Carmel is my boss. With a thin stern face, she resembles a humorless boarding mistress from an old English novel. She has coffee breath, and whiskers on her chin, and spends most of her shifts pushing her cart around, huffing at people who ask for a recommendation. Carmel says our job is to stack books and help people with the photocopiers. ("Libraries aren't just about books," Carmel said to me once, and I laughed out loud. At least, unlike boarding school mistresses, she has a sense of humor.)

My old boss, Janet, had a round, smiling face, and an enormous bosom, and resembled a kindly matron looking after soldiers in a postwar infirmary. Janet had read every book in the library and told staff that our job was to be a frontline soldier in the war against illiteracy and lack of imagination. I told Carmel this once and she frowned at me as if she was trying to work out a complicated maths puzzle.

"Fern?" Carmel prompts. "Would you look at me, please?"

I keep my eyes on my computer and start typing quickly, as if I'm doing something so urgent I can't possibly be interrupted, not even to respond to Carmel. This technique is successful about fifty percent of the time. Not great odds, but I do find it cathartic, bashing at the keyboard, filling up the silence and expectation hovering over me. The silence stretches on until Gayle comes to my rescue: "Right! We don't want to miss our booking, do we? Linda, grab Carmel's bag."

I keep typing. In my peripheral vision I see that Carmel keeps watching me for several seconds, but then, mercifully, Gayle sweeps her up in the flurry of people exiting and she is gone.

It is quiet in the library for the next hour, leaving me with some free time to do some research on the computer. I am an avid book enthusiast, but even I can admit that when it comes to research, you'd be hard-pressed to find a tool more useful than the internet. It's been three days since Rose confided in me about her fertility issues, and twelve hours since she boarded a plane for London. I've used that time to conduct a thorough investigation into what is involved in having baby for your sister. As it turns out, there are numerous options available. You can be a surrogate, which means you use your own egg . . . or you can be a gestational carrier, which means you are implanted with an embryo conceived using a donor egg. If you are using your own egg, you can become pregnant using artificial insemination, where the sperm of the intended father is inserted into your body . . . or you can use in vitro fertilization, where the pre-fertilized egg is implanted. In some cases, the surrogate has sexual intercourse with the intended sperm donor, but this is exceedingly rare, which is an enormous relief. As fond as I am of Owen, and as much as he'd likely prefer his own sperm to be used, the idea of having intercourse with him is startlingly unappealing.

After thinking long and hard and making a spreadsheet of the pros and cons of each option, I conclude that the simplest way to have Rose's baby would be to become pregnant naturally by a man who isn't Owen. This method would have no prohibitive costs, no medical treatment, no need for Rose or Owen to be involved at all. In fact, if I were to become pregnant quickly enough, I could even surprise Rose with news of my pregnancy upon her return from her trip to London! What a happy homecoming that would be! I would, of course, require a man to have intercourse with, but that shouldn't be too difficult. By all reports, men are desperate for intercourse. Apparently, they can be found at nearly every bar and club, prowling for women to have no-strings-attached intercourse with. Unfortunately, I don't go to bars or clubs. But surely men congregate in other places too.

I am still researching when the rest of the staff return from lunch, smelling of beer and garlic and talking several decibels louder than before they left. I continue my research a little longer, as, judging by the way everyone makes themselves scarce, they aren't bothered by what I'm doing. Even Carmel and her ever-present cart are nowhere to be seen for most of the afternoon. Thus, I am knee-deep in research about an online dating app called Tinder when a patron appears at the desk.

"I'm having some trouble with the printer."

I hold back an eye roll. Ninety-nine percent of front-desk queries are about the printers and the photocopiers. The photocopier inquiries are the worst, as each patron is required to load up a beastly little card with coins and connect this card to their account, a process that precisely no one, including myself, knows how to do successfully. As such, I prefer not to engage with those kinds of queries. Not only do I not understand them, they bore me in the most indescribable way. Lately, whenever a patron has a query about the printers or the photocopiers, I pretend I hear someone calling me and excuse myself. I am about to do exactly that when I recognize the person's accent and perfect enunciation.

"Wally!" I cry.

He smiles, albeit a reserved sort of smile, and I find myself taken by his teeth. Straight, white, and even teeth. There are no bits of food stuck around the gum line . . . he appears to care for his teeth the way he does his fingernails. If I had seen these teeth the other day, I would never have mistaken him for homeless (though he *is* still wearing the hat and the ill-fitting jeans).

"Still wearing the hat, I see."

Wally pauses, touches the hat, as if checking it's still there. "Er . . . yeah."

His tone indicates mild offense. It's astonishing what can be offensive to people. For example, apparently it is the height of rudeness to ask someone his or her age or weight, which makes absolutely no sense. Why be mysterious about something that is quite literally on display for all to see? And yet, these rules exist, and everyone seems to understand what they can and can't ask. Everyone except me.

"You're American," I say, hoping that this is a) not offensive, and b) a distraction from the hat comment.

Wally merely nods. His gaze, like last time, lands just over my left shoulder. I actually don't mind this. Some people can be so hungry for eye contact, it's a relief to be able to look away.

"What brings you to the land of Oz?" I ask. I'm quite pleased with the casual whimsy of the comment, but Wally does not look charmed.

"My mother was Australian," he says. "My father is American. I'm a dual citizen." He pushes his glasses up his nose. He's quite handsome, in an odd sort of way. It's not a surprise that I've only just noticed—it often takes me a while to realize someone is handsome. Rose laughed herself stupid recently when I commented that Bradley Cooper wasn't bad looking in *A Star Is Born.* ("You've only just noticed this?" she said, wiping her eyes. Frankly, I thought it was far more laughable the way most people made snap judgments without taking time to consider why they felt that way.)

Gayle chooses this moment to arrive at the desk beside me and ask Wally if there's anything she can do to help. Usually I am very grateful when Gayle comes to my rescue, but today I am frustrated, because it reminds the man why he approached the desk in the first place.

"Ah, yes," he says, directing his inquiry to me once again. "The printer."

"Have you tried pressing Print?" I am unable to conceal my boredom.

"Yes."

"And have you checked you are connected to the correct printer? Each one has its number printed on a laminated document on the wall."

"I have."

I toy with the idea of saying *The network has gone down.* It happened a few weeks back and it was the most glorious catchall for every printer or photocopier inquiry that came my way. Sadly, it hadn't remained "down" for long. I am about to give this excuse a go when I notice Carmel hovering nearby, watching us. I sigh. "Fine. Let's take a look, shall we?"

I follow Wally to his computer. The last time I saw Wally I'd thought of him as lanky, but as I trail along behind him now, I notice he is more athletic than I gave him credit for. His stature reminds me a little of those golfers I enjoy watching on the television during the Presidents Cup. Wide shoulders, narrow torso, firm buttocks. I enjoy this view until we make it to Wally's laptop, when, again, I'm instantly bored. I try pressing Print, and when that doesn't work, I fiddle with a few of the settings. I figure I can do this for a few minutes before declaring it a mystery and suggesting he come back tomorrow. In the meantime, in case Carmel is looking, I frown intensely at the screen as if I'm deep in thought. And I am. About Tinder. Apparently, I'll need to set up a profile with a photo, which shouldn't be too difficult. I'll ask Gayle to take the photo. Then I'll have to vet the suitors. Someone handsome would be good, for the baby obviously. Someone with a few brain cells. Good health.

"What on earth are you doing?" Wally asks, which is annoying, as Carmel is still within earshot.

"What does it look like?" I snap. "I'm trying to print your document!"

I press another button, and a document pops up on the screen. "Rocco. Ryan," I say, reading the name printed at the top of the document. I scan the rest of the document. It looks like a proposal of some sort. There is a list of credentials on the screen. I scan them, then turn to him, aghast. "You're a computer programmer?"

"I am."

"And you're asking *me* for computer advice!?"

"I'm not asking for computer advice," he says. "I'm asking about the printer."

"Pat-ay-ta, pot-ah-ta."

"Right." Wally exhales. "I don't think we're getting anywhere here."

Anywhe*rrrr*e. He*rrrrr*e. Despite my irritation, I find the cadence of Wally's voice pleasant. The neutral mouth movements, the distinct pronunciation of each syllable, the way he holds onto his *r*'s—it's lovely. I close my eyes. "Anywherrrrre . . ."

"Excuse me, miss," the old man seated across from us says. "I'm having some trouble with my computer."

I open my eyes. "Don't ask me! *He* is the computer programmer."

The man looks at Wally, who rolls his eyes but then squats in front of the man's computer. Within a minute, the man is thanking him profusely and Wally is saying "Sure thing" in his gloriously American way. *Surrrre. Thaang.* The man beams at him and Wally nods.

The interaction gives me an idea.

"Are you looking for a job? You could work here! Printer and photocopier specialist! Do you live locally?"

He pushes his glasses up on his nose. He seems to do this with astonishing regularity. "I guess."

"You guess?" It will never cease to amaze me the way people understand things in an instant. I, on the other hand, need to take my time, consider the statement from all angles, and if possible, put it back to the person by way of a question to make sure I've interpreted accurately. In the back of my mind, I'm always aware that I can get it wrong, and the consequences of this, I've learned, can be disastrous. "What do you mean *you guess*?"

"I live in my van. Which, currently, is right outside. So . . . I guess that's local."

"You live in your van," I say, taking in this peculiar piece of information. "So . . . you *are* homeless?"

"I'm not *homeless.*"

"But you don't live in a house? Doesn't that make you homeless?"

I feel oddly victorious. I'd been unsettled by the idea that I'd wrongly assumed he was homeless. I know I have a tendency to get things wrong, but if I can spare myself yet another example of my not being able to trust my own judgment, it's a definite win.

"Technically, I'm *house*less," Wally says. "But the van is my home. And for your information, there are many virtues of van living." He uses his fingers to allocate each virtue. "Vans are affordable." (Thumb.) "They have a low carbon footprint." (Pointer.) "They allow for freedom . . ." (Middle.) ". . . travel . . ." (Ring.) ". . . and it means I can work freelance, choose my own hours." (Pinkie. Replaces hands in pockets.) "So thank you for the job offer, but I prefer to do freelance work."

I try to focus on the words he is saying, rather than the accent, but it's difficult. "You mean you . . . choose to live in your van? And other people choose it?"

"Sure. Look on Instagram under the hashtag 'vanlife.' A lot of people my age are doing it."

I frown at him. Wally looks to be about my age, perhaps a few years older. It feels astonishing that a person of around thirty years old—a computer programmer!—would choose such an unorthodox way to live.

"Well . . . what kind of van is it?"

"A kombi. I have a bed, a kitchenette, a table where I can sit and eat. I use public facilities for showers, like here at the library. I use the laundromat for laundry. And I have pump water to clean my dishes. It's really not as difficult as people think."

I am still dubious. "Where do you keep it?"

"Right now, it's in the parking lot outside. At night, I park it at the Uniting Church on Wilson Street, they let people park there all night. During the day, I try to find all-day parking, or I move it every two hours."

"Sounds . . . tedious."

"It's a lifestyle choice," Wally corrects.

"Oh-kay." I nod, making my eyes wide to indicate that I have not been convinced. "Well, I'm afraid I can't be of any help here. Unless you are looking for a book recommendation?" My mood is immediately buoyed. "What do you like to read, Wally?"

He frowns. "Oh. No, thanks."

"No thanks?"

"I don't really . . . read."

I blink. *"You don't really read?"*

I'm aware, of course, that there are people who don't read. There are those who insist they are *far too busy* to read and who instead spend their time watching Netflix and scrolling social media on their iPhones or Androids. Those who say they read so much for work that they *couldn't possibly* come home and read any more. Those who cannot read. But, judging from the document on the screen, Wally can read. Hence my confusion.

"Do you know how to read?"

Wally looks affronted. "I have an IQ of a hundred and forty-one."

"Mmm-hmm."

"I used to read when I was a child," he says, almost thoughtfully now. "I stopped at some point, I guess."

"What were your favorite books when you were a child?"

He appears to think about this. "Let's see, well, I enjoyed *The Outsiders. The Chocolate War. To Kill a Mockingbird*—"

"I have the perfect book!" I say, cutting him off and taking off toward General Fiction, where I snatch up a copy of *Jasper Jones.* "This will reignite your love of reading," I say, upon my return. "It's won several major awards and been short-listed for half a dozen others. And it was made into a film in 2017." I place the book on top of his notebook, which is next to his laptop. "And if you need me to set you up with a library card, I'd be happy to do that."

He regards me for a longer than normal moment. Then something softens around his eyes. "I apologize, I didn't catch your name?"

"Fern. Fern Castle."

"I'm Rocco."

He extends his hand as if to shake mine; I cross my arms in front of my chest.

"Oh, I prefer not to touch people if I can possibly help it. Did you know that we carry an average of thirty-two hundred bacteria from a hundred and fifty species on our hands at any one time? This includes fecal bacteria! If I shook hands with everyone I met at the library, I'd be constantly ill, not to mention contaminated with god knows what." I reach for my travel-sized antibacterial spray, which is attached to my overalls by a handy carabiner, and pump it into my hands. "Would you like some?"

"Oh no, it's okay. . . . Oh, er, okay, thanks," he says, and I administer a squirt to his palm. He rubs his palms together. "So, shall we see if we can do something about this printer, then?"

Carmel is in the children's section now, watching Linda making recommendations to a mother of four sons who look like they'd much rather be kicking a football than be in the library (perfect candidates for Paul Jennings or Andy Griffiths, or any book with "Fart" in the title, if you ask me). As such, I know now is the time to make my exit. I'm preparing to tilt my head, frown into the distance, and declare that I can hear someone calling me when I have an epiphany.

Wally is handsome, in an odd sort of way. If his IQ is to be believed, he has a few brain cells. Which means there's only . . .

"How is your health, Wally?"

The softness in his eyes is replaced with suspicion. "It's excellent. I jog every morning, ten kilometers."

I smile. For once, the library computer service has brought me some good fortune. He smiles back at me a little uncertainly, until I pose my next question.

"Would you like to go on a date with me?"

His smile falls away.

• • •

JOURNAL OF ROSE INGRID CASTLE

My therapist told me I should keep writing while I'm away. Seeing Owen again is likely to bring up some big emotions, he said, about the marriage as well as my desire to have a baby, and it will be helpful if I get them down on paper. And since I've watched all the movies I care to on the plane, here goes!

I'm terrified about this reunion. I want to believe it will go well, obviously. I *fantasize* about it going well. In my fantasies, Owen will be happy to see me. He will explain that the reason he hasn't kept in touch is because it is too painful to talk to me, knowing I'm so far away. But just because I fantasize about it doesn't mean I expect it to happen. I'm not stupid. I've noticed Owen has been lukewarm about my visit. I've considered the possibility that he's invited me to London to end things for good. Maybe I'd even arrive to find him on the arm of a beautiful English rose with an upper-class accent? The funny thing is, if that is the case, part of me will be satisfied. Because it's what I think I deserve.

This, of course, links things back to Mum. Everything, if you dig down far enough, links back to Mum. She taught us early on that love was conditional. To earn it, we had to perform like we were in a concert. Smile, be cute, say something funny. Know exactly what she wanted you to do . . . and do exactly that.

She loved it when people found Fern and me charming, because it reflected well on her. I remember being on an outing with Mum in the city when we were about six or seven. By this time, we had been granted a little public-housing flat just outside of the city, and we'd often take day trips into the city so Mum could get away from our home, which she hated. This day, we were passing a busker playing the trumpet when Fern stopped and started to dance. Mum had been in a hurry, so didn't notice and kept walking. I tugged Fern's hand to keep her walking, but she just grabbed both my hands and spun me around, giggling.

"Hey, look at those little girls," someone said.

"Aren't they adorable!" someone else commented.

After just a minute or two, a crowd gathered around us, clapping and cheering. I'd never had dancing lessons, neither of us had, but even then, I knew there was something magical about Fern—her golden hair, her long limbs, the pure joy in her eyes. She was like an angel.

"Who do these girls belong to?" someone asked. People looked around expectedly. My stomach was already in knots. When Mum noticed we were missing, she'd be livid.

"They're mine," came her voice.

Fern and I whipped around to where Mum was standing, her hand raised. She beamed from ear to ear. "There you are, my little ballerinas! Putting on a show as always." She laughed, throwing the crowd a little eye roll.

"Don't get too mad with them, Mum," someone said. "They've got a big future in front of them."

Mum accepted people's accolades, basking in the attention. Receiving compliments was one of only a few things that consistently made her happy. Even so, I couldn't relax completely. She might be smiling now, but I knew there'd be no applause for us when we got back home. If Fern shared my discomfort, she hid it well. Her shoulders were relaxed, her face was open. I remember being glad for her. Fern always seemed to have some sort of impenetrable boundary around her that made her immune to Mum's reign of terror. I often wondered if that boundary was part and parcel of whatever was different about Fern. But Mum never took her for an official diagnosis. Giving Fern a diagnosis or help would have made her special and Mum was the only one allowed to be special in our house.

But even if Fern wasn't scared of Mum, that didn't mean Mum wasn't a danger to her. I remember one time when we were seven, when Fern drew on the coffee table. That had been a terrifying day. It wasn't an expensive table–it probably didn't cost anything at all, we got most of our furniture from the Salvation Army back then. We were still living in the council flat at the time, and Mum's welfare payments, she regularly told us, didn't stretch to fancy things. It had been an innocent mistake. There had been laundry all over the kitchen table and Fern had asked Mum where she could do her homework. Mum had said, *Do it on the coffee table.* It was impressive really. Mum had been Fern's mother for seven years and *still* hadn't figured out how she would interpret those words. If I had noticed, I would have redirected her myself, but by the time I saw it, it was too late.

"Who wrote on the coffee table?" Mum roared when she'd seen it.

She'd had been in a bad mood all day, but now she was enraged. I would have taken the blame–I was just about to, in fact–but Fern raised her hand before I could. She'd been so carefree about it, so utterly unaware of impending danger. She'd even smiled a little. It was too late for me to tap my bracelet against hers to warn her.

I held my breath. Mum could fly off the handle for the smallest thing–talking too loudly, talking too quietly, not thanking her profusely enough. Who knew what she would do if we actually did something bad? I must have nudged myself ever so slightly in front of Fern, because I remember Mum narrowing her eyes, distracted from the coffee table for a second.

"What are you doing?" she said, her voice changing. She sounded curious, but in a careful, cold way. "Are you trying to protect her?"

She stared at me coldly. It took me a moment to realize my sin. By expressing love for Fern, by wanting to protect her, I'd betrayed Mum. Our purpose, after all, was to love *her.*

"I would never hurt Fern." Mum's voice was like ice. "It's just a silly coffee table. What . . . do you think I'm some kind of monster?"

"No, Mumm–"

"Do monsters feed their children?"

"No."

"Do they give up everything for their children?"

"No."

Dread pooled in my stomach as Mum got right up in my face. "What about these clothes?" she said, pulling at my T-shirt. *"Do monsters buy clothes for their children?"*

It was the first time I thought Mum might hit me. She had never hit me before. It was a source of pride for her. "I've never laid a hand on my kids," she would say to anyone who'd listen. The implication was that hitting your kids was something bad parents did, and she was not a bad mother. But that day, her face was so contorted, so angry. Her breath was so hot in my face. I was bracing for it–almost welcoming it–when abruptly she turned and marched out of the room.

Fern and I hurried after her. By the time we got to her, Mum was already pulling things off the shelves—books, toys, shoes. "Do monsters buy their kids stuffed animals?" she cried, tossing our toys across the room. "Pens? What about plastic seaside buckets?"

Thunk. Crash. Bang. She got hold of our jewelry box, the one that played music, with the little ballerina inside. Our dad had given it to us. Fern and I listened to it each night after lights out. Mum knew this, of course. That's why she'd looked so elated as she slammed it against the wall and cracked it down the middle.

It went on and on until there was a mound of broken things in the middle of our bedroom. As Fern and I watched, I remember thinking that somehow what Mum was doing was worse than hitting. And how I wished she'd just hit me instead.

FERN

When I was a kid, I loved school. There were several reasons for this, most notably:

The routine of going every day.

The timetable, which ensured I always knew what to expect.

The learning.

The reading.

There were many things about school I found troublesome, of course. The people, the noise, the lights, the smells. Still, I became adept at finding solutions. I tried to arrive at school after the bell had sounded, hence avoiding the morning rush. I sat in the front row, where chatter tended to be kept to a minimum. At lunchtime, I ate my sandwich outside and then went to the library to read. After school I went the long way home, so I didn't need to make small talk with any of the kids. Generally, my work-arounds worked well. But there was one day each year that I had no work-arounds for.

Swimming carnival.

For a person with sensory-processing issues, a swimming carnival is what hell would look like. The warm, wet claustrophobia of the building, the cheering and shouting, the garish team colors, the stench of chlorine. I'd composed several compelling arguments in order to persuade Mum to let me stay home, but Mum always declined. *You need to show team spirit, Fern,* she'd say. *It's important to support your peers.*

On the first year, I'd steeled myself. I wasn't required to participate, at least (one upside of attending a school with no mandatory sport.) All that was required was that I stand on the side and cheer. I came prepared with earplugs, but it was the smell that did me in. It was *something else.* It wasn't the mild fragrance of salt water and chlorine like I'd smelled in backyard swimming pools. It was warm and wet; stale and dank. The moment I walked inside, I felt it permeate every pore. It felt like being underwater, but without the wonderful silence. To the contrary, it was the worst kind of loud. *Inside* loud.

Rose had taken my hand as we walked inside, which I knew was supposed to be a gesture of comfort, but it made my skin crawl. It felt like yet another thing coating me, begging for my attention. She led us to the top of the stadium, the second row from the back, and sat me on the floor. From there, with everyone standing in front, the teachers couldn't see us and no one could pester us to cheer. It wasn't ideal, but it was the best I could hope for. I felt like I was drowning. The chlorine stuck to my skin, the back of my school dress, my feet. I tolerated it, just, until Rose went to do her races (Rose, for some unimaginable reason, had signed up for the fifty-meter freestyle and the relay). "Just keep your head down," Rose had said before she left. "I'll be back as soon as I can."

I passed the time by counting backward from a million in nines.

But the time dragged on and on. Just when I thought I couldn't take it another second, Mr. McIntosh noticed me on the floor and shouted for me to stand up. (Mr. McIntosh was the science teacher. He had yellow teeth and smelled of onions and breath mints.) At the same time as he pointed, my team must have won something, because an almighty victorious roar erupted in the stadium. In the row in front of me, a boy I didn't recognize, with long, white-blond hair, picked me up and spun me around, jumping up and down and shouting "YAAAAAAAAASSSSSS." My senses exploded. It was as though I'd slipped into another dimension.

I didn't mean to hurt him. It must have been a reflex. A well-executed reflex that started with an eye gouge and followed with a knee smash to the groin. I was starting to calm down when someone touched me from behind. A reverse elbow strike later, Mr. McIntosh had a broken nose.

During the follow-up meeting, our school principal, Ms. Knight, commented that "the greatest concern is the fact that she hasn't even shown any remorse." I told her that, to the contrary, all I felt was relief, because it could have been so much worse.

I knew that in that moment, I could have killed someone.

I arrive at the Botanic Gardens at quarter to twelve, fifteen minutes before my scheduled date with Wally. I'd planned to use the extra time to secure a spot in the shade, lay out the blanket I'd brought from home, and unpack the sandwiches. I packed honey for myself, as usual, and one honey and one Vegemite for Wally, in case he doesn't care for honey. But as I enter through the east gate, I am alarmed to find that Wally is already here, sitting on a blanket in the shade of a tree, his long legs stretched out in front of him.

"You're early!" I exclaim.

"I always try to arrive a quarter of an hour early, if I can."

"Really?" I say in wonderment. "So do I."

"Who doesn't value punctuality?" he says, shrugging.

"A lot of people, actually," I say. "I think you'd be surprised."

I arrange myself comfortably on the blanket, which is adequately sized for the two of us and not at all scratchy, which is often the case with picnic blankets. Our date had been fairly straightforward to organize, once I'd explained to Wally what a date was.

"You're asking me on a *date*?" he said, after I'd asked him. It was a surprise, since he'd clearly heard, and I couldn't see how he would need any further clarification.

"Yes," I said, as slowly and clearly as I could.

Still, he looked bewildered. So much so that for the barest second, he looked me directly in the eyes. "A . . . date?"

At this point I was starting to doubt his professed IQ. Wally was silent for long enough that I started wondering if he'd had a medical episode. Had I made a social faux pas? The brief research I'd done on the computers had confirmed that girls did this sort of thing nowadays—asked boys on dates—and yet the poor boy seemed utterly perplexed. It occurred to me that it might be the word "date" throwing him off.

"According to Urban Dictionary, a date is where two people get together for an activity when the possibility of romance between them has been broached but not ruled out," I explained.

Wally's face remained blank. I sighed. This was the exact reason I favored planning over spontaneity. Normally, when I did something outside of the ordinary—like competing in a karate tournament or attending a librarians' convention at the state library—I spent a lot of time planning for it. Familiarizing myself with the best route to take, checking the train timetable, making sure the medical provider was running on time. But this day, it seemed, I'd gone off half-cocked. I decided to offer Wally one further explanation I'd sourced from Urban Dictionary before giving up.

"An activity between two mutually attracted people which very often ends in one or both leaving sexually frustrated."

Finally, bizarrely, he laughed. A funny half laugh that seemed like he wasn't sure if he was laughing or clearing his throat. Then he threw up his hands and said, "You know what . . . sure. I'm free Saturday." "Me too, after karate."

He nods. "What would you like to do?"

I realized a picnic was the only real option for our date, considering I don't go to restaurants or shopping malls and the movies can be troubling if the sound is too loud or the smell of popcorn too strong. Wally agreed to the picnic and then, as if the heavens had been smiling upon us (a ridiculous expression, as heaven surely doesn't have a face, let alone a mouth to smile with), the printer burst into life and started working and I was able to excuse myself and dash away before anyone else could ask for assistance.

Now, here we are. Fifteen minutes early.

I notice Wally is wearing the same black-framed glasses and buffalo flannelette button-down shirt with jeans and, of course, that same ridiculous hat. I have to admit, I find the sameness of him soothing. It's always been unsettling to me, the way people change their appearance. Linda from the library, for example, changes her hair with frightening frequency. Not just the color, but the style—some days straight, other days curled, other days scraped back to her scalp and glistening as if wet. Linda, of course, is an extreme example, but most people tend to change, at the very least, their clothes on a daily basis. A new pair of earrings or a brighter lipstick than normal. *A change is as good as a holiday,* the saying goes, but I've never found change or holidays appealing. For this reason, I am wearing my favorite sun-yellow skirt and rainbow T-shirt with comfortable sneakers. My only discomfort is that my lips feel tacky because this morning—after reading online that one should put effort into one's appearance for a date—I'd applied lip gloss. I'd dearly love to remove it but find myself without anything in the way of a tissue or napkin.

"What is it?" Wally says.

"What is what?"

"You're staring at me."

"Am I?" I consider this a moment. Then I wonder how he even knows this, since his gaze appears to be over my left shoulder, as usual. "Staring competition?" I venture. It seems as good an icebreaker as any. But after a promising start where Wally's eyes widen slightly, he just gazes back over my shoulder. I wonder if he has an issue with his eyes.

"Beat you!" I exclaim.

His expression morphs into that funny smile-frown.

"You're no good at staring competitions," I remark, pulling my sandwiches out of my tote. As I offer Wally the sandwich I brought for him, he opens his own bag and pulls out an impressive haul—an artisan loaf, a wheel of Brie, a bag of grapes, even a block of dark chocolate. "My goodness!"

"What?"

"You've brought a veritable feast. Where did you get all of this?"

"All this?" he says, gesturing to the food. "I stole it."

My mouth opens. "You *stole* it?"

He snorts. "Of course I didn't steal it. What kind of person do you think I am? I got it from the supermarket!"

I am skeptical. "Why did you spend so much money, when you can't even afford to live in a flat or a house?"

"It's not that I can't afford a house . . . I live in my van as a . . . a—"

"A lifestyle choice?"

"Yes."

"Uh-huh." I unwrap my sandwich. I feel his eyes and find him watching me with a dull smile.

"Well. You may not believe it, but I enjoy the simplicity of the van. But I do have enough money for food. I'm a freelance computer programmer, remember?" He retrieves a bread knife from his bag and begins slicing the loaf of bread, chuckling.

"Why do you freelance? Surely you could get a permanent job as a computer programmer?"

"I could." He keeps slicing.

"But you don't want to?"

He puts down the knife. "No."

"Another lifestyle choice?"

He grins. "Exactly."

It's an odd choice, but I find myself admiring him for it. I've often thought about the way people blindly fall into the footprints of their forefathers, getting jobs, buying homes, working hard, and then dying.

"Well," I say. "That's very courageous of you, Wally."

"Thank you," he says. "Though my name is Rocco."

"You don't look like a Rocco."

He gives another snort. "And yet that's exactly what I am."

Wally arranges an elaborate-looking sandwich of cheese, sliced ham, and tomato while I tuck into my honey-on-white. The date is going quite well so far, I think. We've made conversation; we're consuming a meal. According to my research, that's pretty much all there is to it. I've dismissed the possibility of getting pregnant today, obviously. Apart from the fact that it would be awkward and quite possibly illegal to have sexual intercourse in a park, I'm not ovulating. I know this because I bought some ovulation testing kits at the pharmacist, which tell me (by virtue of a smiley face in a small window) when ovulation is imminent. The booklet suggested testing around Day 10 of your cycle, with a view to ovulation occurring around Day 14, which, according to my calculations, means I'll need a second date in just under a week to execute that part of the plan.

"So tell me about van living," I say, swallowing a mouthful of sandwich. I'd preprepared the question. Asking questions is a tactic I use when small talk is required—it makes you appear interested while simultaneously putting all the effort of the conversation on the other party. "What do you like about it?"

Wally is lying on the blanket, resting on one elbow. "Many things," he says. "I find the small space cozy, like sleeping in a little cocoon. When it rains, I hear it pelting the roof; when it's windy, I feel the wind up against the car. It's like I'm out in it . . . but protected. What else? I like that I can't have too many possessions, so when I do buy something, I have to consider whether I really need it. It means I only end up with things that are incredibly useful or very precious. I like that I'm not imprisoned by anything. Debt. Weather. Bad neighbors. My home is wherever I am."

"Where is the van now?"

"Down the road. There's a four-hour parking spot about a mile from here."

"Don't you find it unsettling having to move about all the time like that?"

"A little," he admits. "But moving around is kind of cool."

I consider this. "I moved around a lot when I was a child. Not in a van though. I can't say I found it . . . cool."

Wally shifts on his elbow, getting comfortable. "Why did you move a lot? Folks in the army?"

I shake my head. "Honestly, I'm not sure. I would have preferred more permanence but . . . things always came up. Mum lost her job or the landlord needed us to move." Wally is really paying attention to me, which is both awkward and quite nice. Perhaps this is why, on a whim, I add, "My mum wasn't . . . the greatest mum, I guess."

It feels like a betrayal, for some reason. I don't like speaking badly of Mum. It feels wrong somehow. Rose doesn't feel bad about it. She and Mum never got along, even when we were kids. I remember hiding in the closet with Rose when we were ten, after Mum and Rose had argued about something. "Fern, I know you don't understand this," Rose had said. "But Mum isn't a good mum. You have to do what I say, okay, otherwise I can't protect you. She isn't a good mum, okay?"

"Okay," I'd said.

"I'm sorry," Wally says.

"She overdosed when I was twelve, and my sister and I were put into foster care."

Wally sits up. "Wow. Fern, that's awful."

I focus on the remains of the food, the grapes lolling on the chopping board. "I was lucky I had Rose. She's my twin sister."

I half expect Wally to have a reaction to this. Inexplicably, people seem to have such curious reactions when I report that I am a twin. In social gatherings, often all I have to do is mention that I'm a twin and the rest of the conversation is consumed by the twins in that person's family, whether they were naturally or artificially conceived, or how their great-aunt Margaret was a twin but her brother died in childbirth. I enjoy this, because all I have to do is nod and smile, which is infinitely easier than having to say anything myself. But, extraordinarily, Wally appears to be one of the few people on earth who doesn't have anything to contribute to the twin conversation.

"Rose is my person," I tell him.

Wally blinks. "Your person?"

"You know. Your *person.* Your wife or husband. Your child. Your boyfriend. Your best friend. Someone whose name you can put down on paperwork. Someone you can share personal information with. Someone you can rely on."

Wally unscrews the lid off a bottle of water and takes a sip. "Interesting," he says.

Conversation starts to dwindle then, so I decide it is time to proceed to the next part of the date. Astonishingly, I know what this should entail. Last night, in preparation, I'd undertaken a rom-com marathon, watching specifically for tips on the running order of a date. Trying to be scientific, I'd taken copious notes and, upon comparing them, found they had a lot in common. The first stage of each date was either a little dull or an unequivocal disaster where the person arrived late or dressed in entirely inappropriate clothing. The next stage involved each party sharing something personal. The final stage invariably involved a wacky incident such as a bird coming to eat the couple's food or someone spilling a drink all over the other, forcing all parties to escape amid a cloud of hilarity which inevitably turned into a romance later in the show. As such, I determine that the wacky incident is the most crucial of the three stages.

I glance around for a potential wacky incident and, finding none, I open my water bottle and pour its contents over our remaining food. At a loss for what to do next, I throw back my head and laugh loudly.

Wally's eyes boggle. "What the . . . Fern, are you *all right*?"

His enunciation is made particularly perfect by his bewilderment. My laughter dies down to an uncertain giggle. "I . . . don't know."

"You might be the strangest person I've ever met, you know that?" Wally says, shaking his head. And just as I am thinking things aren't going to plan, he laughs. "I can't believe I'm saying this . . . but I like it."

An hour later, as Wally and I pack up the picnic, I feel irritable. I'm trying to figure out the reason why, since the date—at least when compared with some of the disastrous dates from my rom-com marathon—has been an unequivocal success, when I notice Wally waving his hands in front of my face.

"What are you doing?" I ask.

He holds up my phone. "Your phone. It's ringing."

"Oh." That explains why I was feeling irritable. The sound of a phone ringing is among the most crazy-making noises in the world for me. The tinny, repetitive sound of it. The accompanying vibration. Thankfully, my phone rarely rings. Rose sends text messages unless it's an emergency, and if anyone else calls I let it go to voicemail. But when I look at the screen and see it's Rose calling, I feel my heart rate increase. She's *calling*. It must be an emergency.

I press the phone to my ear. "What is it, Rose?"

"Oh, good, you're there. I hope it didn't scare you, me calling like this, but I have just heard from the neighbor and she said Alfie has been barking a lot."

I scan my brain for a reason why Rose might be calling from Europe to tell me this.

"Was she okay this morning when you fed her?"

I start to get a bad feeling. "I didn't feed her this morning."

"You didn't?" Rose says. "Why not?"

"Why not?" I repeat, trying to make sense of the question. But I can't.

"Fern," Rose says, "*tell me* you have been feeding and walking Alfie."

"I . . . I don't understand," I say. "Why do you want me to tell you that?"

There is a long silence, followed by a long, low expletive. I wait, suddenly feeling quite ill.

"Fern! I told you I would put him in a kennel!" Rose has her breathless, flustered voice on—the one she uses when talking to people about packages not arriving or being overcharged for the electricity bill. She hardly ever uses this voice with me. "You insisted! You said you would feed Alfie!"

I have no recollection of this. But if Rose says I did, then I did. I take a moment to consider the ramifications of this. It's been four days since Rose went away. Four days since Alfie has been without food or walks. I search my brain for information on how long dogs can survive without food. But I don't know. I think I might be sick.

Rose is clicking her tongue in that way she does when she is panicking. "What are we going to do?" she says.

I look at Wally, who is watching me intently. "You said your van is down the road?"

He nods.

"Rose," I say into the phone. "I'm on my way to your house."

Wally is very efficient with time management, as it turns out. After I explain what has happened, he offers to run and get his van (and he does, indeed, *run*) while I pack up the picnic. By the time I shove everything into the bags and get to the gate, Wally is waiting for me in an orange vintage-looking kombi van. He opens the passenger door from the inside.

"Where to?" he asks, and I direct him to Rose's house, a fifteen-minute drive from the Botanic Gardens. He leaves the radio off as we drive and does me the favor of not talking, which I appreciate as I need to keep my brain space clear to focus on Alfie. Not that I can think much. I feel wobbly with the anxiety of it all. I wrap my arms around myself, trying to keep myself calm. I will be of no use to Alfie unless I can stay calm.

When we pull up outside Rose and Owen's house, it looks the same as always. Someone must be collecting the mail, because there isn't any sticking out of the letterbox. I wonder why Rose didn't ask *whoever was collecting the post* to feed and walk the dog too—if she had, maybe Alfie would be all right.

Wally gets out of the car first. "Where will he be?"

"In the backyard," I say.

Wally races up the side of the house and flings open the gate while I walk more slowly behind him, arms still wrapped around myself. When I get to the backyard, I see Alfie is lying on his dog bed on the back verandah. He's utterly still. I try to take a step toward him but find myself frozen on the spot.

He's so still. Unmoving. I see him. I feel his skin and hair in my grasp. Wet, dead flesh.

I've done it again.

Wally kneels at Alfie's side. "He's alive. It's all right, Fern, he's alive."

I nod, but relief is slow to come. Alfie's alive. Not everyone has been as lucky.

"His water bowl's dry," Wally continues. "Where can I find the hose?"

I don't reply. Wally looks around and finds it himself.

"We need to take him to the vet," Wally says to me, filling the bowl. When I don't reply, he says, "Fern? Fern, I need you to listen to me, okay?"

This appears to be a circuit breaker, and I snap to attention. "Yes. Okay. The vet."

Wally places the filled water bowl in front of Alfie. When he doesn't drink, Wally cups water in his hands and holds it to Alfie's snout. After he's had a drink, he picks up Alfie as if he were a newborn baby.

"Fern," Wally says. "Can you get the car door?"

I do. Once I'm strapped into the passenger seat, Wally passes Alfie to me, positioning him so Alfie's head is supported by my elbow. The whole process means that Wally is required to touch me several times, and while I am aware of it, I don't recoil.

The vet has thick gray eyebrows. I am staring at them as he tells us Alfie is lucky. He's dehydrated apparently (Alfie, not the vet), but he has been rehydrated on intravenous fluids for hours and he's doing much better now. In fact, most of the vet's concerns are about how the mix-up happened in the first place. He tells us that in these sorts of cases he usually calls the RSPCA, who then check to ensure the dog is in an adequate home, but Wally manages to convince him that Alfie will be fine in our care. He is impressively convincing. By the time he is finished, even I almost believe him.

"I assure you," he says, "it was all a misunderstanding. Alfie could not be in better hands."

I look at my hands. When I look up again, the vet is looking at me.

"Do you work, Ms. Castle?"

"Yes," I say. "I'm a librarian."

"So you're out of the house most of the day?"

"Yes, but—" I say.

"I'll be with Alfie when she's at work," Wally cuts in. "I'm the dogsitter. Alfie won't be alone for a moment."

I look at Wally in surprise. He studiously avoids my gaze.

The vet looks from me to Wally and back again. Finally, he exhales. "He'll need to be given small sips of water every hour for the next few days. I'll also give you some electrolyte powder. If he isn't keeping anything down, give him ice cubes to lick. I'd like you both to bring the dog back in a couple of days so I can see for myself that he's being taken care of. Okay?"

"Okay," Wally and I say in unison.

"Make an appointment at the front desk. Two days."

We both nod. And a few minutes later, reluctantly, the vet releases Alfie into our care.

On the way home, we stop at Rose's to pick up Alfie's food, lead, and water bowl. Then I call Rose. It goes better than I expect. Rose is calmer once she knows Alfie is all right. She apologizes for being frustrated and says she blames herself—she should have checked Alfie into the kennel like she planned. I tell her that I'm taking Alfie back to my flat and will keep him there for the rest of the time Rose is away. I'm not sure why I didn't suggest that when Rose asked me. I wish I could remember.

"How is Owen?" I ask.

"He's great. He says to say hello."

"Tell him I say hello back."

"I will."

"So, you're having a good time?"

"A perfect time. Just wonderful. I'm missing you, though."

"I miss you too."

I wrap up the phone call quickly, partly because I expect that Rose will be busy with Owen and partly because it feels like it might be rude to chat while Wally is sitting right here in the car. When I hang up, though, I'm still feeling heartsick about the whole thing. It could have been so much worse. Just another few hours and . . .

"Stop thinking about it," Wally says.

"I can't."

"The important thing is that Alfie is okay, right?"

"For now," I say.

"For now?" Wally laughs. "Are you planning on hurting him?"

You don't always have to plan it, I think.

"I don't remember Rose asking me. It doesn't even ring a bell. That's what scares me the most."

"Well," Wally says. "maybe *she* forgot to ask? She was preparing for an overseas trip—she probably had a million things on her mind. It probably slipped her mind."

I shake my head. "Rose doesn't forget things."

"Do *you* forget things?" Wally asks.

"Yes. With great regularity."

"That surprises me."

It surprises me too, I think. *All the time.*

"It can be distressing at times," I admit. "Always worrying about what I might have forgotten, or what I might do wrong if left to my own devices." This is more emotional than my typical conversation, and I don't feel entirely comfortable with it. I wonder if it is a side effect of being on a date.

"What makes you think you'd do anything wrong?" Wally asks.

"Past experience," I say as we turn in to my street. I point to my block. "This is my place here."

Wally parks in front. He pulls up the handbrake and then pushes his glasses back up his nose, something that is fast becoming a trademark of his. "How do you live your life with that fear?"

There's no good answer for this. "I just . . . do. What choice do I have?"

"Wow," he says. "That's brave."

I don't know what to say to that. It feels like a good time to change the subject. "Did you mean it when you said you would watch Alfie for me while I'm at work?" I ask.

"I don't say things I don't mean."

"Well," I say. "In that case . . . see you Monday morning? Nine A.M."

Wally agrees and I slide out of the car, Alfie in my arms. As I watch him drive away, I realize I feel something akin to content. It makes me worry for a world where someone like me can feel content after what I did.

I fall asleep quickly, but I wake with a gasp.

I am instantly oriented. There is no buffering period, no momentary confusion. I know where I am. I know it was a dream, even if I can still *feel* the cool wet flesh beneath my hands, the kicking and writhing, my fingers gripping so tightly that they tremble. I also know it wasn't *just* a dream. It was a memory. A warning. Most of all, it's a reminder. Don't get ahead of yourself, Fern. Remember what you're capable of.

As if I could forget.

I glance at the alarm clock. 3:43 A.M. There are still a few more hours until daylight. If I roll over and go to sleep quickly, it's possible I might still get some sleep. God knows I need it. Three more weeks without Rose.

Will I survive it?

• • •

JOURNAL OF ROSE INGRID CASTLE

It's like I woke up in a dream. Owen met me at the airport with open arms–and a bunch of peonies. You know how couples often have a song? Well, we have a flower, and it is peonies. He gave me a bunch on our first date, and I carried them in my wedding bouquet. Over the years–four years this spring–whenever there has been a special occasion–a promotion, a birthday, an anniversary–it was always celebrated with peonies.

After dropping my bags at his Fulham apartment, we went straight to dinner–a really fancy place in Chelsea. When we got back to his place afterward, I checked the medicine cabinet and the sheets in the laundry for scents of perfume. Clear on both counts. It feels too good to be true. Owen said all the things I had hoped for: that he missed me, that he had been miserable without me, that he wanted to try "us" again. We made love the first night, and the next morning, and the night after that. The sex was better in London, we both agreed. Something about the Northern Hemisphere. Everything was perfect.

Except for the Fern situation.

I blame myself. I should never have left her in charge of Alfie. If I'd been thinking clearly, I would have tried to keep things as simple as possible for her—nothing that strayed from her routine. But Fern could seem so high functioning that even I could be lulled into a false sense of security. Still, even with the Fern situation, it's hard to be too upset when things with Owen are going so well. I try not to think about the fact that soon I'll have to go home.

Leaving has always been a trigger for me. Because . . . you guessed it! Mum. From around the time we were eight, leaving was always her threat. It might have been in response to something we said or did—like being ill or being stressed about a test at school (not that we ever admitted to either, we'd learned by then that we weren't allowed to have troubles of our own). Sometimes, it was for no reason at all.

"Looking a bit glum today," Mum would say. "If everything is so bad, maybe I should just leave? I'm obviously making your life terrible."

I knew I shouldn't, but every time she threatened to leave, I cried. Real throat-clogging tears, the kind that came from the depths of my soul. A couple of times, I cried so hard I vomited. Make no bones about it, I was terrified of Mum. I dreamed of her being kinder, more loving, more like other mothers. But I never, not even once, dreamed of her leaving.

"What are you crying about?" she'd snap. "I thought you'd be thrilled to have me gone."

She'd act like she was frustrated, but I think she liked it when I cried. The tears validated her, made her feel worthy. When, after the drama, Mum would agree to stay, I would count it as a victory. I assumed it was my devotion to her that was keeping her around.

But the older we got, the more volatile she became. It didn't take long before Mum's moods began to dictate my day. And it didn't matter what she was feeling—whatever it was, I was terrified. If she was happy, I was terrified I would ruin it. If she was unhappy, I was terrified she'd blame me. If she wasn't around, I was terrified that she had left for good. Any other mood, and I was terrified she was dreaming up some new way to be cruel.

One of her favorite things was to mock me about food.

"Back in the kitchen, Rosie Round?" she'd say whenever possible, a playful look in her eyes. "You know what they say: 'A minute on the lips, a lifetime on the hips.' "

If I had the audacity to look even slightly upset by these comments, she'd say I was being too sensitive, which, in Mum's eyes, was an unforgivable thing to be. It was before I was diagnosed with diabetes, and I was constantly hungry and thirsty. I tried not to eat too much and I certainly didn't want to do anything to invite Mum's criticism, but I couldn't help it. Inevitably, I would end up right back in the kitchen. It didn't matter that Fern ate as much as I did, Mum never said a word to her. Once, I asked her why she never said anything to Fern, and she shrugged as if it was obvious: "Because Fern can afford to eat what she wants, she has my metabolism."

She was right; Fern was a clone of Mum physically. They were both tall and the kind of skinny where a stray elbow could puncture flesh. Fern also had Mum's hair, a crowning glory of tumbling honey-colored waves. It felt unfair to be twins with her. Next to Fern, I felt like a frumpy interloper, even before Mum decided to point it out.

On our ninth birthday, there was another blowup, this time over a cake Mum made us from the *Women's Weekly* cookbook. Mum made us a fancy cake every year—yet another of the contradictions that was our mother. It was a source of great pride for her; she loved anything that made her feel like a good mother. It was always a big production: selecting the cake she wanted to make, shopping for the ingredients, looking for tips and tricks. That year, she decided it was going to be a unicorn cake—the most difficult she'd attempted. In the lead-up, she'd been to three different shops to find the right cake tin and yet another to get the icing and the gold edible horn. It was a nice time for all of us, not because Fern and I cared much about the cake, but because Mum's mood was always buoyed by the cake making.

As usual, we weren't allowed in the kitchen while she made the cake, we were only invited in for the exciting "reveal" when it was done. The unveiling was Mum's favorite part. We were required to squeal with joy, thank her profusely, and ask a million questions about how she did it—even Fern seemed to understand how we were to act. On this birthday, we performed our roles with aplomb and Mum seemed very pleased, which in turn meant I felt torn between being happy and being terrified that something would happen to mess it up.

After we sang "Happy Birthday," Mum took a photo of Fern and me in front of the cake before I was dispatched to get plates. Peering into the cupboard, I agonized over whether to use the "good" plates or the plastic for so long I was sure Mum would snap at me, asking what the heck I was doing. When I finally produced the good plates, she merely nodded her approval. The relief was so great I went weak with it.

It almost went off without a hitch. Almost. But when I reached for my piece of cake, I felt Mum's cold finger poking me in the stomach.

"Not too much now, Rosie Round!" she said with a snigger.

It might have been the fact that my nerves had been stretched taut all day. It might have been that it had been so close to being a good day. It might have been that it was a hard poke, and Mum's nails were sharp.

The tears came in a flood.

"Oh, for god's sake! It was just a joke. Why can't you take a joke, Rose?"

I willed myself to get it together, but the tears showed no sign of abating. I tried looking at the roof, dabbing at my eyes. Even smiling through tears. But nothing worked.

This just annoyed Mum more. "So, I'm a bad mother now, am I? After I've I spent weeks planning this cake for you? Perfect."

"No!" I said, at the same time as a sob escaped. Fern, who'd been obliviously tucking into her piece of cake, paused, her fork halfway to her mouth. I stood beside her, tapping my bracelet gently against hers. She knew this was a warning. *Something is coming.* It was the best I could do.

Mum flung up her arms. "And now you've ruined Fern's birthday too! Great work, Rose. Really great work."

Mum stormed off, leaving Fern and me alone. Five minutes later, when we heard a noise, we crept into the hallway to find Mum was dragging a suitcase toward the door.

"Where are you going?" I cried.

"What's it to you?" Mum hissed. "You clearly don't want me around, even with everything I do for you. You'll be fine without me."

Instantly, I was shaking. "No. We do want you around. We need you. Don't go, Mummy, PLEASE!"

She locked the door behind her. I banged at it, screamed for her to come back, pressed my ear against the door to listen for movement. When it became clear she wasn't coming back, I sat in the hallway. Fern sat beside me, silent but serious.

I quickly figured out that we couldn't call the police—if we did that and Mum returned, she'd be furious. We couldn't go to the neighbors for the same reason and, besides, Mum didn't like us talking to strangers. We couldn't do anything. We just had to wait.

After a couple of hours, I went to the kitchen and checked the cupboards, determining that we had enough food to last us a week or so if we cooked the pasta and rice and defrosted the frozen food. If Mum wasn't back by then, I'd have to make a new plan. I kept making plans well into the night, long after Fern was asleep, her head lolling against my shoulder.

Eventually I must have fallen asleep too, because when I woke up it was light outside, Fern was sprawled on the floor beside me, and Mum was there, standing over me. It took me a few seconds to put everything back together–what happened, where we were, what day it was. When I realized she was back, I flew into her arms so fast I nearly knocked her over. Of course, I burst into a fresh flood of tears. But this time, when I cried, it didn't seem to upset Mum. To the contrary, she fell to her knees and held me, rubbing my back in rhythmic circles.

"Shhh. Mummy's here now," she said. "Shhh. Everything is going to be all right."

FERN

On Monday morning, I help a woman wanting a book recommendation for her introverted twelve-year-old daughter who wants to become a writer (I give her a copy of *I Capture the Castle* by Dodie Smith); I set up chairs for a Toastmasters group in the function room; and I ask a man who has been in the bathroom for over an hour if he requires any assistance (it turns out he dropped his wedding ring down the sink, and Tom, the maintenance man, has to search for it in the S-bend). I fold and restack the newspapers and lie on the floor to read a book to a little boy who doesn't want to sit on a chair in the kids' area. So more or less a regular day at the library.

I handed Alfie off to Wally at 8:45 A.M., as planned. When Wally arrived outside my building in his orange kombi van, I will admit to being relieved to see him. Yes, we'd made an arrangement, but people can be fickle with arrangements. Sometimes, for no apparent reason, plans can be canceled, postponed, or even just deemed to be an idea rather than an actual plan (as is often the case when coffee is involved, I've found—"Let's have coffee," people will say, but then seem perplexed when I get out my diary to determine when we will drink it). So I was pleasantly surprised when Wally showed up.

I was all ready for him, naturally. I had packed up Alfie's lead, his food, his water bowl (and two large bottles of tap water, so Wally could fill it up even if he couldn't find a tap or hose). I'd also given Wally a wad of plastic bags for dog poo, and a tennis ball. Wally took it all eagerly, which was quite nice. I'd always found there was something agreeable about people who liked dogs and something untrustworthy about those who didn't. The night before, I'd considered telling Rose that I was outsourcing Alfie's care for the day, but after careful consideration, I'd decided against it. After what had already happened with Alfie, I wanted to spare her the additional worry of a stranger looking after her dog (even if, judging by the text messages Wally has been sending from the dog park, Alfie is receiving a vastly superior level of attention than he would receive in either Rose's or my care).

Midmorning, I'm looking at one such text message—a photo message of Alfie, sitting on Wally's lap at a café drinking from a bowl shaped as a coffee mug labeled PUPPY-CINO—when I am intercepted by Carmel and her cart.

"Fern, I'm glad I ran into you," Carmel says, even though she was not running and nor had we made physical contact. She is wearing a bold yellow dress that suits neither her skin tone nor her personality. "I notice you haven't put your name down for the staff bowling day."

She pauses expectantly, as if waiting for an answer, even though no matter how many times I replay her comment, I can't find the question. Once, years ago, Rose told me that conversations were simply a series of questions. One person asked a question, the other person answered, and it went back and forth like this until the questions ran out. This explanation has assisted me through countless episodes of small talk. But lately, it feels like more and more people are opting for statement-to-statement types of conversation. Which generally leaves me at a loss. I am still searching for an appropriate response when Carmel continues.

"Cat got your tongue?"

The expression isn't as ridiculous as it sounds. I googled it several years back and established there were two possible origins: one, referencing a whip used by the Royal navy called the cat-o'-nine-tails (apparently the pain this whip inflicted was so severe that it caused the victim to stay quiet for a long time), or two, derived from ancient Egypt, where liars' and blasphemers' tongues were cut out and fed to the cats.

"I am able to speak," I confirm. "And you are correct that I haven't put my name on the list for the bowling day."

Carmel's eyes narrow. Her eyelashes are short and sparse and could do with a coat or two of that volumizing mascara that Rose wears. "Fern, these team-building events are important. Getting the team together in a social environment helps make for better communication in the workplace." Almost as an afterthought, she adds, "It's a company-sponsored event, so you don't have to pay."

Again, no question has been posed. I look around and let out a long sigh—attempting to send out a nonverbal message that I am tiring of the conversation and she should speed it up.

"Fern, are you planning to put your name down?" Carmel says snippily, which frankly is a little annoying as I'm the one who is being put through this pitiful attempt at conversation. But at least she's finally asked an actual question.

"No," I say. "I don't like bowling."

Now Carmel is red in the face. "Well, I'm sorry to hear that. But it is a compulsory event for all staff."

"It is?"

"Yes, it is." Carmel seems surer of herself now, nodding with each syllable. Yes. It. Is.

"Then why have a sign-up sheet at all?"

"Well, because . . ." Carmel drifts off, less certain now.

I wait.

At lunchtime, I am in the staff room, tapping away at my computer, when Gayle appears at my desk. She has what looks like a bit of spinach caught in her teeth and unusually wide—excited—eyes. I'm relieved it's not Carmel. I've made a mental note to avoid Carmel until this bowling function is over or until her conversation skills improve, whichever comes first.

"There's someone here to see you," Gayle says, once I have pointed out the spinach.

I frown. The only time anyone comes to see me at work is on my birthday, when Rose comes to take me out to lunch at the sandwich place I like. That is always planned in advance, of course, because I don't like surprises. But today is not my birthday and I don't have anything planned.

"Who is it?"

"It's the man from the other day. The one who was having trouble with the printer." Gayle lowers her voice to say this and waggles her eyebrows up and down. It makes her look quite bizarre.

"Where is he?" I say, getting up.

"Just outside the door," she whispers excitedly.

Sure enough, when I come to the staff room door, Wally is standing there. Alfie is by his side, on the lead.

"Hello," I say, then frown at Gayle, who is still standing there. She shuffles away sadly.

When I look back at Wally, the first thing I notice is that he's not wearing that atrocious hat! He looks different without it. He has quite lovely hair—thick and black and swept, with the slightest curl to it. I study it admiringly before noticing the rest of his clothes are different too. Instead of the jeans and shirt, he's wearing a business suit . . . with a tie! There's something else different about him too . . . something to do with his face. I can't quite put my finger on it.

"I'm so sorry to do this, Fern," he says, "but something has come up and I won't be able to watch Alfie for a couple of hours. I could have left him at your place, but I knew you'd worry so I brought him here. It's a . . . an interview of sorts. It just came up and I . . . I . . ."

For someone who is usually so eloquent, Wally seems to be struggling to string a sentence together. It's almost as if he's nervous. I look him up and down again—the suit, the tie. Suddenly I realize what is different about his face. "You shaved!"

He rubs his face and smiles at the floor. "I did."

"For the meeting?"

"Yes. It's with a former colleague of mine. We worked together a few years back and there's a chance we could do something together again."

He holds out Alfie's lead and I'm grabbing hold of it when I hear Carmel's cart rolling toward me.

"Fern! There you are!"

"Who's that?" Wally asks.

I gauge the distance between Carmel and me and deduce that it's too late to make a run for it. "My manager. She wants me to go tenpin bowling. I have a company-sponsored bowling night on Wednesday."

"Really?" Wally says. "Funny, because I'm an excellent tenpin bowler."

"Would you like to be my guest?"

"Sure," Wally says. "Why not?"

Carmel rolls to a stop in front of us, staring at Alfie.

"Put me down for two for the bowling, Carmel," I say.

Carmel glances up from Alfie. "Pardon?"

"Two. For the bowling. Me and Wally."

"Rocco," Wally corrects, shooting me a frown. He extends his hand to Carmel. "Rocco Ryan."

I think Carmel is going to protest, but instead she takes his hand. "Rocco *Ryan*?" She stares at Wally for a moment, then shakes her head. "I, er, fine. I'll put you both down. But Fern, the dog has got to go."

I pretend not to hear her. "Good luck with the meeting," I say to Wally.

Carmel and I both watch Wally walk away. He looks nice in his suit. I get the feeling, from Carmel's odd behavior, that she has noticed too.

"I'll look forward to bowling," I call after him on a whim, realizing, despite the multitude of reasons I shouldn't, that it's true.

I have a secret at the library that no one knows about, not even Gayle. I found out about it several years ago, while Janet was still the manager. I'd been at the front desk that day, because Linda and Gayle had both been off work with a hacking cough that had done the rounds of the library staff (which I'd escaped due to my disinclination to shake hands). A council meeting had taken place in the circular meeting room that afternoon and, afterward, tea and cakes had been served. I hated it when tea and cakes were served to the council workers, because it meant dozens of fat, balding, middle-aged men were hanging around, nursing cups of tea and pieces of cake, and taking up lots of space, physical and emotional, the way fat, balding, middle-aged men did. Their small talk hummed around the building, bouncing off walls and making me feel squidgy. Lots of questions like, *'Scuse me, love, where's the bathroom?* and *You couldn't clear this plate away, could you, darl?*

I'd give them blank stares and scurry away, but wherever I went, there were more fat old men with more questions. Worse, this time, one of them had located the little bell at the front desk that I had hidden in a drawer, and was it pinging every few seconds.

Ping.

"'Scuse me."

Ping.

"Is anyone here?"

Ping.

Ping.

Ping.

It was hard to describe what that particular kind of noise—trapped noise—did to me. It filled my brain like a scream, until tears itched at my eyes and my heart threatened to burst from my chest. I'd been hiding among the travel books at the back of the building when Janet, my old boss, found me.

"Bad place to hide," she whispered. "These guys all fancy themselves as world travelers—they'll be back here soon, looking for books about Egypt so they can point out all the places they went on their last vacation."

"Crochet section?" I asked.

"I've got a better idea," Janet said. "Follow me."

I followed her to the very back of the library, the older part beyond the archive area. There, in the red brick wall, was a door that I had not noticed before. Janet opened it with a key.

"This is a little treasure I found a few years back," she said, opening the door to a tiny windowless room filled entirely by a shabby armchair and a small side table. It had a slanting roof where the stairs went overhead. "I call it the secret cupboard. I use it sometimes to make phone calls, or go through payroll, or do something where I don't want to be interrupted. But I think perhaps you could use it more than me." She handed me the key. "This is the only key that I know of. It's yours now."

I looked at the small gold key.

"Use it whenever you like. But don't ever tell anyone of its existence. It's too precious to be shared."

I agreed. Far too precious.

I had been in the secret cupboard earlier this year when Janet had a massive stroke in Junior Nonfiction. Dead before she hit the ground, apparently. *A perfect place for her to die,* people said later. *Surrounded by books, in the place she loved most.*

All these months later, I can't figure out if I feel guilty for being in the secret cupboard when it happened, or glad.

I spend most of the afternoon in the secret cupboard with Alfie. He is very happy. I set up some newspaper and his water bowl and he remains there cheerfully even during the short periods when I have to dart out and be seen by Carmel on the floor. I am doing one such trip when Gayle spots me.

"Fern, there you are! There was a man here to see you earlier, but I couldn't find you."

"A man?" This is most peculiar. "Wally?"

She shakes her head. "No. A different man."

I frown. I don't know many men and, apart from Wally, I don't know any who would pop in randomly to see me at the library.

"Well . . . what did he look like?"

Gayle thinks about it. "Good-looking. Thirties, probably. Clean-shaven and nicely dressed."

I'm stumped. "Are you sure he wanted to see me?"

"He asked for Fern. He said he was a friend."

I assume it must be a mistake. He probably asked to see someone else. Or maybe wanted to borrow a book on ferns. "Did he leave a message?"

"No. He said he'd come back another day."

"Oh. Well, then I expect he will." *If* he *was* actually looking for me.

I'm distracted from the clean-shaven mystery visitor when I spot Wally walking into the library. He mustn't see me, because he walks quickly past me, headed toward the shower room.

"How did the meeting go?" I say, running to catch up to him.

Wally keeps walking. "I can't talk right now."

He pushes through the door into the vestibule and I slow my step. I usually stay out of there in the afternoon, as it tends to get a little stinky. But today, I decide I'll brave it.

Wally whirls around. "Are you planning to follow me into the shower?"

"No," I say. "I thought you'd stop before we got there. And you did." I grin. "How did the meeting go?"

"The meeting didn't happen, okay?"

I frown. "Why didn't the meeting happen?"

"I was going to take the train to the city, but I couldn't find an all-day parking spot at the station. The most I could find was two hours. So I didn't go."

I stare at him. "Because you couldn't find anywhere to *park*?"

He rolls his eyes. "You have no idea how difficult it is to find adequate parking."

"I wouldn't say I have no idea. Such a thing as moving a car around is actually very easy to imagine."

"Are you trying to be funny?"

"No," I say. "Was that funny?" I am genuinely curious. But he doesn't respond.

"Why didn't you just pay for parking?" I ask.

"I didn't have any money."

"I thought you *did* have money. You're not homeless, right?"

He's red in the face now. "I didn't have any *coins,*" He makes a noise like *ugh* and clenches his fist into a ball, like he is angry.

"Why are you angry, Wally?"

"I'm angry that I missed the interview, okay? I'm angry that you're following me when I want to be alone. I'm angry because you keep calling me Wally!"

He's the most upset I've seen him. I think of something Janet said to me once when a borrower had been very angry that a book they had reserved hadn't been returned yet. The borrower said she had walked a long way in the heat to get to the library and she wasn't leaving without the book. She had become quite aggressive indeed. Janet had apologized profusely and offered to personally drop off the book to the woman when it was returned. Then Janet had asked if there was anything else she could help her with. That was the moment the woman broke down in tears and confessed that it was the anniversary of her son's death, and she'd been desperate to escape the day by losing herself in a good book. Janet had driven the woman home via the bookstore, where she'd purchased for the woman not only the one she'd reserved, but also several others.

"Why were you so kind to her?" I asked when Janet returned to the library. "When she'd been so rude to you?"

"Angry is just a pen name for sad," Janet had explained. "In my experience, nine times out of ten if you are kind to the angry person, you will calm them down and find out what is really going on with them."

"You know," I say to Wally. "I have a parking spot, at my place. I'm a five-minute walk from the train station. You're welcome to park there if you have another meeting. Or anytime, really."

He frowns, his expression different again. Not angry, more confused. "That's very generous."

"Not really. I don't own a car, so it just sits there empty."

He appears to think about this for a moment.

"I do have one thing to ask in exchange, though."

Wally crosses his arms. "Oh? What?"

He watches me through narrowed eyes. His eyelashes are long and dark and curled, like an old-fashioned doll's.

"I'd be most grateful," I say, "if I could keep calling you Wally."

To my surprise, Wally throws back his head and laughs. And even though I'm not sure why we're laughing, I laugh too.

I arrive at the bowling alley at approximately six thirty on Wednesday evening. I'm unable to confirm the exact timing due to leaving my phone at home. This oversight is unlike me, and I attribute it to the low-level anxiety I've felt all day at the prospect of visiting a bowling alley. A bowling alley, with its noise and lights and smells, is most definitely out of my comfort zone. Part of me, the rebellious part, feels excited about this. The rest of me is struggling to breathe.

I caught the bus here. Wally had offered to drive me but small talk in cars always gives me a headache, so the bus seemed a safer option. The flyer in the staff room said it was a 6:45 P.M. meetup for a for a 7:00 P.M. start, which would allow everyone time to select their bowling footwear and to collect their meal coupons and tokens for the pinball machines. (Learning about the pinball machines had been a blow. Games tended to be loud and bright and I hate loud bright places.) But I've prepared for it as best I can, and I find myself feeling cautiously optimistic.

I feel pleased to see that I've beat Wally here, even if he arrives just a few minutes after me, at 6:33 P.M., jogging up the ramp, hat bobbing on his head. He's in such a hurry he almost runs past me.

"Wally," I say, as he's about to jog through the entrance.

He slows to a stop and smiles tentatively, his gaze close to my face. Then he begins to speak.

"I'm wearing earplugs," I say. "So I can't hear you."

Wally blinks. Then his mouth moves again.

"I said *I can't hear you,*" I say louder.

He pushes his glasses up on his nose and then gestures for me to remove an earplug. Reluctantly, I do.

"I just inquired as to why you are wearing those," he says, pointing to my eyes.

"The swimming goggles? I find they work better than sunglasses to block out the garish lights at these kinds of places."

The barest of smiles appears at Wally's lips. "I . . . see."

I am aware, of course, that the goggles are a fashion faux pas, but I'd hoped that people might just go with it and assume they were some sort of new trend.

"Listen," Wally says. "While your earplug is out, I wanted to say that I'm sorry for being rude the other day. I hadn't been to this sort of meeting in . . . a while. And you were right, it wasn't about not being able to find a parking spot. I shouldn't have got snappy with you."

You were right. These words remain lodged in my head. *You were right.* And not just about anything! About something in the muddy confusing world of *feelings.* I can't wait to tell Rose.

"Are you feeling better now?" I inquire.

He nods. "As a matter a fact, I rescheduled my meeting to tomorrow afternoon."

I give a little clap that feels quite jaunty and I make up my mind to try it again tonight. "Fantastic news. And you'll park at my place?"

"If you don't mind."

"I don't mind," I say, replacing my earplug. Wally opens his mouth again, but when I point to my earplug, he closes it again and we venture inside.

My senses are assaulted the moment the doors open, even with the goggles and earplugs. The inside of the bowling alley smells like popcorn and hot dogs and cotton candy, a smell that coats my skin and clogs my pores and fills me up from bottom to top, like sand inside my skin. My sneakers stick to the patterned carpet as I walk; the flashing neon lights burn into my retinas. The music blares from all directions—the game machines, the bowling lanes, the overhead speakers—and while the earplugs dull this slightly, it's still overwhelming. I keep my head down and forge through it, wading farther into the wild. Along one wall, about a dozen kids crowd around a long metal table singing "Happy Birthday" to a boy who, according to the numeral on his cake, is eleven years old. Everyone coexists in the space, entirely unperturbed by all of it. Everyone, apparently, except me. On the back wall, I locate a sign that reads BAYSIDE LIBRARY TEAM BUILDING, and usher Wally toward it. Carmel is standing there, wearing a red shirt and a short scarf tied at her throat. Strange as it sounds, she looks rather nice.

"You're wearing a scarf," I say to Carmel.

She studies me curiously, then says something I can't hear. I turn away from her, looking instead at a group of youths standing around a vending machine dispensing Pokémon cards. Their appearance suggests they are around ten or eleven. Rose and I went bowling when we were a similar age. I was apprehensive about it, but when Rose suggested to Mum we stay home, she just became more determined to take us. "*It will be great fun*," she'd said, before she and Rose got into an impassioned argument that only made things worse. Eventually it was clear that we would have to bowl.

When we got there, my strategy was to remain focused on the bowling. I'd read a book about bowling technique and I got three strikes that night. It might have been fun if not for the back-and-forth between Mum and Rose the whole time. "*The food is cold.*" "*My shoes don't fit.*" "*It's not your turn!*" And then, as we waited in line to hand back the shoes: "*You ruined the evening. This is why we can't ever go out. What is wrong with you?*"

Rose cried all the way home.

I look back at Carmel, who is talking animatedly to Wally, frowning and smiling and nodding at intervals. I haven't seen Carmel smile much before. I notice she has a silver tooth, close to the back. As they talk, Wally rummages through a tub of bowling shoes. He catches my eye and mouths, "Foot size?"

"Seven," I reply, and the next thing I know I am sitting on a bench while Wally fits me with bowling shoes. It's bizarre having someone put your shoes on, as if you're a child or a mannequin. I tell Wally it's unnecessary but he keeps doing it, so I let him. It's actually rather nice.

By 6:45 P.M., the whole team has arrived and Carmel gathers the group to deliver some sort of welcome that I can't hear. Then we are divided into teams and Wally and I are placed with Gayle and Linda, who are delighted by Wally's presence, judging by the amount of unnecessary touching of his shoulder, forearm, and hand.

Wally was correct when he said he was quite good at bowling. In fact, it's fair to say that he is an exceptional bowler. He gets three strikes in the first three bowls, and I get two. Gayle and Linda don't hit a pin between them. Carmel, I notice, doesn't bowl at all, instead using the time to wander up and down among the three teams, much like she does at the library with her cart.

At the end of the round, Wally waves his hands in front of my face. I watch his mouth carefully.

"May I get you a drink?" he says slowly.

I *am* thirsty, I realize. I glance over at the bar area, past a horde of squealing children, to see what they might have available. Behind the bar, which is staffed by a woman in a pink-and-white-striped boilersuit, I see a sign that says SPRITE.

"A Sprite would be very nice, thank you, Wally."

Wally nods and wanders off toward the bar, leaving me to ponder how nice it is, having someone inquire after my thirst like this *and then* procure me a drink! Wally is, I realize, an above-average date. Linda and Gayle appear to think the same, judging by the way they appear in front of me the moment Wally is out of sight.

"I can't hear you," I remind them.

They gesture for me to remove my earplugs. I sigh loudly but acquiesce.

"You've been keeping this quiet, haven't you!" Linda exclaims.

"They met in the library," Gayle quips.

"I like his hat," Linda says. "It reminds me of something."

"I know what you mean," Gayle says.

I don't know why they required me to remove my earplugs, since they are only speaking among themselves. I glance around for Wally, to see how he is doing with our drinks, but he seems to have disappeared.

"Where's Wally?" I ask.

"Of course!" Gayle and Linda cry in unison. "*Where's Wally? That's* who he looks like."

Noises ricochet around the room. Someone cheers, and a child cries and a bowling ball hits the polished lane. I wrap my arms around my middle.

"Finished here, ladies?" Carmel says.

"Just taking a break while Rocco gets us some drinks," Gayle says.

I see him now, leaning over the bar, making his order. He glances back at me and for an instant, our eyes meet.

"Remind me again how you met him, Fern," Carmel says.

I open my mouth just as a game machine starts playing a tune, and the sound of collective victory and defeat from a couple of small boys rings in my ears.

"She met him at the library," Gayle says. "Right, Fern?"

Nearby, the token machine releases a stack of tokens. *Clink clink clink clink clink clink clink.* I feel people moving closer to me, making space for a person in a wheelchair who is being wheeled past. "Um . . . what?"

"You met Rocco in the library," Gayle repeats, louder.

Carmel and Linda keep asking me questions, even as the noise continues around me. It's like a ride I can't get off. I put my earplugs back in, close my eyes, and start to rock gently, then more vigorously.

"Fern," someone says. They must be speaking loud because I can hear them through my earplugs.

I open my eyes again. They're all looking at me, glancing at each other worriedly, and then looking back at me. Wally is nowhere to be found.

"What?" I say, but I must say it too loud or too quiet or in a strange voice, because they all appear rattled.

I rock harder. Disco music plays loudly enough for me to clearly make out the tune even with my earplugs in. Several people dance while they wait for their turn to bowl. My breath is high in my chest and my head is aching.

"Drinks!" Wally appears, smiling, carrying a tray of drinks.

I feel like I might scream. Perhaps I do scream, because all of a sudden everyone is gathered around me. It's unbearable.

"Move," I shout, and they all take a few steps back.

Wally places a hand on my wrist but I rip it away. He nods, then says, "Fern. Follow me."

He waits for a moment to make sure he has my attention, then begins to walk. I follow him, a few paces back, through the gap he has created in the crowd, through the building and out the automatic doors into the cool, soothing air, then away from the entrance and out into the parking lot.

"Are you all right?" Wally asks, once we are away from the noise and the smells and the lights.

My heart is still thundering. "I thought I could do it," I say to Wally, or myself. "I thought it would be okay."

Wally nods. "One thing I've learned about facing fear," he says, "is that sometimes, it's just too scary."

• • •

JOURNAL OF ROSE INGRID CASTLE

Yesterday Owen and I took the Eurostar to Paris. It was late when we checked into our hotel room on the Champs-Élysées and when I woke this morning, Owen was at my bedside with strawberries and proper French coffee. Today we spent the day strolling around the streets, eating and drinking and window shopping. There was a particularly sweet moment while we were climbing the stairs to the Sacré-Cœur in Montmartre. A little girl in a red coat had tripped up the stairs and Owen had scooped her up before she even hit the ground and popped her back on her feet. It had made me smile and ache all at once. *That could be our little girl,* I thought. If only I could give him a child.

I tried to put it out of my mind, and I did manage to for a while. But then another thought started to distract me. Fern. She hadn't been answering my calls. She didn't even answer when we agreed on a scheduled time. It was so unlike her. I know she is probably fine. But . . . what if she isn't? That's the tough part. If she were a child, I could call the cops and ask them to go over there and they would. But Fern isn't a child. For heaven's sake, I'm the one always advocating for her to be treated equally, as an adult. But in the real world, she's not like other adults. And she's my sister. And if I don't protect her, who will?

My therapist says I'm a perfectionist, in all things, including sisterhood. That is true enough. Ever since I was a child, I've longed to be perfect.

If I could just be perfect, I used to think, everything would be okay. It became my life's mission. Each night I would lie in bed and plan the perfect day, a day incapable of upsetting Mum. I'd get up early, make my own breakfast, clear the dishes quietly. I'd keep an eye out for things I could do to be helpful. Put on a load of laundry, sort the socks, bring Mum a cup of coffee. Mum loved it when I did things like that. She'd smile and say, "You're a good girl, Rose."

But no matter how hard I tried, I always got something wrong. If I put on the laundry before school, by the time I got home, it had sat there for too long and needed to be rewashed. If I made dinner, I'd accidentally use ingredients Mum had bought for another meal. If I tidied up, I'd always lose something important that Mum had left out intentionally.

It didn't take long before Mum's voice permanently took up residence in my mind. It was clear that something was very wrong with me. I was stupid, lazy, selfish. I didn't pay enough attention to things; I didn't look after my sister properly. I was bad. Sometimes I was bad even when I hadn't done anything.

Before I was diagnosed a diabetic, even my health was a source of great irritation to Mum. I knew better than to complain about feeling thirsty or light-headed, but there were things I couldn't avoid. For example, occasionally I wet the bed. A classic symptom of juvenile diabetes, I found out later, but at the time we didn't know that.

"You wet the bed again, Rose. Again! What is the matter with you?"

I begged Mum to take me to the doctor for months before we finally went. And even after I was diagnosed, Mum still acted like I was making a big deal out of nothing. Every time I tested my blood sugar, she'd roll her eyes. Fern, on the other hand, read up eagerly on diabetes and became an expert, often pointing out what I could and couldn't eat to Mum. It made Mum wild. There was something about us sticking up for each other that set her off.

Like the time we were ten. Fern and I had just got in from school and we were sitting side by side at the kitchen table with our homework books open. Mum usually napped at this time of day, so we'd both been startled when we heard her pottering around. After a few minutes, she came into the kitchen. Immediately, I knew something bad was coming. Her eyes looked strange. They always looked strange when something bad was coming.

"All right," she said. "I know what you've done. If you come clean and admit it, you won't be punished. But if you don't admit it, there will be consequences for you both."

Fern looked at me with a puzzled, questioning look in her eyes. I tapped my bracelet against hers and tried to choose my words carefully.

"What . . . is it, Mum?"

"Don't insult my intelligence, young lady! You know exactly what I'm talking about. Look at that face—all innocent. You think I don't know what a conniving little bitch you are?"

I ran through a list in my head. Had I unknowingly shrunk a piece of her clothing in the dryer? Eaten something she'd earmarked for herself? Been too loud? Too happy? Too miserable? One option was to pick one of those things, but if I was wrong, then I'd be in trouble for two things. I thought until my head hurt. When I couldn't come up with a response, I couldn't help it. I cried.

"Here come the waterworks," Mum said, rolling her eyes. "It's not going to work this time, Rose! We're not leaving this room until one of you admit it."

I knew Mum meant it. Once, she had locked us outside for hours until we confessed to another crime (stealing her jewelry, that time, which she later found behind her dresser). It was the peak of summer and we didn't have sunscreen on, so we'd huddled under the one tree in the communal yard, following the shade as it moved. I remember watching some other kids from the building squealing as they ran through the garden sprinkler. We didn't dare ask to join them, so instead, to pass the time, Fern recounted the plot of the Agatha Christie she'd been reading to me. She was quite good at that, the storytelling. Mum didn't let us inside until after dark, when the mosquitoes had feasted on us and we'd scratched our ankles so hard we were bleeding.

"Right," Mum had said this day. "Well, I'll just have to pick one of you to be punished. Eenie. Meenie. Miney. Mo."

She pointed at Fern.

"It was me," I said immediately.

Fern looked surprised, but Mum didn't. As usual, Mum knew exactly what she was doing. She knew I'd never let Fern get in trouble.

"I'm sorry," I said.

"Go to your room and don't come out until I tell you," Mum slurred.

After an hour or two, the doorbell rang. Pizza delivery. We'd never had pizza delivered before. It smelled amazing. Mum didn't call me for dinner, nor did I expect her to, but I was surprised when Fern hadn't come to bed by 8:00 P.M. I'd been in my room for hours by then, without food and with only half a glass of water that had been sitting beside my bed. I'd been diagnosed with type 1 diabetes a few months earlier and I knew if I didn't eat, my blood sugar would become dangerously low. I searched the room for food—the pockets of my clothing, and Fern's. There was nothing.

Still, Mum didn't come. I waited. And waited. By midnight, I had a headache. By morning, I was shaky, drenched in sweat, and I felt like a sledgehammer was thumping at my temples. The half glass of water was gone. I was freezing, which I knew meant I was hypoglycemic. I needed sugar. Juice, preferably. I needed to test for ketones. I needed to eat.

Around 9:00 A.M. when the door flew open, I didn't even have the energy to lift my head. Mum was standing in the doorway. In her hand was a glass of orange juice. She watched me for a long time. I remember thinking: She's worried. She's realized how sick I am. She'll be horrified by the state of me and she'll rush to my bedside. She might even drive me to the doctor.

Instead, she calmly sat on the bed. But instead of offering me the juice, she placed it on the bedside table just out of my reach and then held out a wad of cash—tens, twenties, even fifties.

"You lied," she said quietly, holding it out to me. "You didn't take the money. I just found it, in my dresser drawer."

At first, I was confused. I'd almost forgotten the reason I was in here. So that was it. She thought I'd stolen her money. The idea, of course, was laughable. *Of course* I didn't take her money! But she already knew that. She'd merely fabricated it to create some drama.

"Sometimes I don't know what is wrong with you, Rose. Why didn't you just tell me you didn't do it? You could have saved everyone a lot of trouble."

"I'm sorry," I said, or at least tried to, but my throat was too dry to project it.

Mum considered this a moment. A long moment. I glanced at the juice.

"Well," Mum said, after an eternity. "I'll forgive you this time, but don't lie to me again, all right?"

I nodded.

"Good." She smiled. "In that case . . . all is forgiven."

Mum held out her arms for a hug, indicating I should hoist myself upright. This, I think, was Mum's favorite part. The forgiving. It made her feel like a good mother, an honorable, noble mother. Her eyes shone with goodness. But the whole time she held me all I could think of was how much longer I would have to wait before I could ask my honorable mother for that glass of juice.

FERN

Wally drives me home. I'm not used to being in a vehicle at night. It's dark outside and the noises are sharper, more delineated. The click of the car's indicator while we wait at the traffic lights. The sound of the steering wheel moving under Wally's hands. It's almost hypnotic. By the time Wally pulls up in front of my house, I'm practically in a trance.

"How are you doing?" he asks when I don't get out of the car.

"Not great," I say. "Pretty embarrassed."

"Embarrassed?" Wally pulls up the handbrake. It's loud in the quiet car. His gaze settles over my shoulder, as usual. "Fern, can I tell you something?"

I nod.

"Before I lived in this van, I developed an app called Shout! with a friend of mine. It allowed people to order food and drinks from their table without having to go to the bar, and it allowed restaurants not to have to employ waiters to take orders, only to ferry food back and forth from the kitchen. There are several apps like it now, but it was the first of its kind. I was the programmer—I designed it, coded it, tested it. And it was a huge success."

"Congratulations."

"Thanks. It was pretty exciting at first. But then I had to start doing other stuff, apart from coding. I had to go to marketing meetings, I had to network with investors, that kind of thing. My partner kept saying things like, 'This is the most important meeting of our careers.' We'd go to cocktail parties and have to talk to people—not even about Shout!, we'd just talk about sport or horse racing or whatever the other person found interesting. I didn't understand what I was doing there, and I hated it." Wally glances at me briefly, then back over my shoulder. "The pressure was enormous. It wore away at me. I stopped going in to work. I stopped getting out of bed. I think my partner would have ditched me, but we were so close to selling. Then we did sell it, and we got this ridiculous amount of money and everyone was ecstatic and I . . . just fell apart. The night after we sold, when everyone else was celebrating, I was in the emergency department, with chest pains. I thought I was having a heart attack. I was referred to a psychiatrist and kept as an inpatient at a mental facility for nearly a month. A full-blown nervous breakdown, apparently. I was so ashamed that when I got out, I left my big successful life behind and moved to Australia!"

"Why?"

He shrugs. "You can't get much further away than Australia, can you? And I had a passport, because of my mom. I thought, over here, I'd get another chance to just . . . be me. One of the reasons I got the van was because I needed to make my life small." Wally shakes his head. "But over the last few months, I've been developing another app. That's what my meeting is about tomorrow. Some investors are interested. My point is that lots of people get in over their heads. It doesn't mean you can't try again."

"Are you suggesting I try bowling again?"

He thinks about this. "Or not. But don't let it scare you off trying things."

Wally looks away from me, at the windscreen. His arms loosely grip the steering wheel and I fixate on the dark brown hairs on his arms, his slender wrists, his long elegant fingers.

"Was it the touch?" he asks.

I wonder if I missed a critical part of the conversation. "Pardon?"

"At the bowling alley. I touched your arm. Before you screamed. Was that what upset you?"

"Oh. No. . . . Well . . . it wasn't *just* the touch. It was the lights, the music, the smells, the staring. *And* the touch."

"I'm sorry," he says.

"It's all right."

"I should have known."

"You should have known that I don't like to be touched? Why would you know that?"

"Because," he says, "I don't like to be touched either. I've learned to do it—to shake hands, to hug, to pat someone on the back—because that's what people do. But I don't like it."

"But just because you don't like it doesn't mean that I won't like it."

"True," he says. "But . . . you are a little bit like me."

I open my mouth in surprise. Alike? I want to cry, "What ways are we alike?"

But then it hits me.

The way that Wally looks over my shoulder.

His commitment to being punctual.

His failing to attend his interview and his frustration at himself afterward.

He doesn't like to be touched.

Wally is indeed a little bit like me. How had I not noticed this? The idea of this brings on a flood of comfort and security. Like I'm being seen and understood. I feel like a foreigner in a new country who, after months of not being understood, has finally run into someone who speaks my language.

"You . . . don't like to be touched?" I ask. "Not at all?"

"Some touching is okay," Wally says. "If I'm expecting it, it's not so bad. And a firm touch is better than a light one—"

"Light touches are the *worst*!" I exclaim. "Light surprise touches."

"I'm okay with my loved ones touching me," Wally says. "Though, usually they know how to do it right."

"Or not do it at all," I agree. "What about sex? Good or bad?"

Wally thinks about this for a minute. "Good. And bad. Depending on many factors."

"I don't really know what the fuss is about," I admit. "It seems a bizarre thing to do, if you think about it. How did people even discover it?"

Wally rests his head against the headrest and frowns. "It's a good question. I guess Adam and Eve must have got bored in the Garden of Eden from time to time. Maybe it was a dare? Or maybe Eve tripped and fell and . . . I don't know, landed . . . on . . . Adam?"

Wally's cheeks are extraordinarily red, I notice. It makes me laugh a little. And after a second, Wally does too. It's magic. People rarely laugh at the same things that I do. Usually when I laugh, other people are silent. And when others laugh, I'm still trying to understand the joke. Before long, we are both laughing so hard that tears appear in the corners of my eyes and I have to wipe them away. Wally wipes tears away too. He steals a sideways glance at me, and we lock in a rare moment of direct eye contact. It's funny what happens then. It's as though there's a change in the atmosphere or something. I have to concentrate on taking a breath, which makes me aware how loud I am breathing.

"Would you like to have sex with me?" I ask.

Wally freezes. It is, admittedly, a sizable deviation from my plan. For one thing, there are at least two days until I ovulate. For another, at least according to the romance novels I've read, when it comes to seducing men, there tends to be very little in the way of ascertaining of the other party's interest. If the novels are anything to go by, sex is supposed to kick off with the hero crushing his lips against mine after doing something to upset me. So I watch Wally's reaction with interest.

His eyes widen slightly and his lips part, but he doesn't speak for some time. I am pleased with this reaction. I suspect I would have felt a little startled by the crushing lips. As he contemplates my request, I settle back into the cozy pod of the van with the darkness surrounding us. I am feeling something approaching relaxed . . . until a sudden pounding on Wally's window sends us both flying off our seats.

"Do you have permission to have your van parked here? This is private property, you know."

I recognize the voice as that belonging to my neighbor, Mrs. Hazelbury. Through Wally's window, I see that she's dressed in her peach candlewick robe, holding it together with both hands at the throat. I can't see from where I'm sitting but I'd hazard a guess she's also wearing her matching slippers.

Wally rolls down his window and she peers into the van.

"Fern!" Mrs. Hazelbury says. "There you are! I've been trying to get in touch with you all night."

This is a surprise. Mrs. Hazelbury never tries to "get in touch" with me. She prefers to wait at her window and call out as I walk by on my way to work. *Have you seen my newspaper? It has gone missing two days in a row! Do you know what is happening to the block of land down the road that has been purchased by developers? Do you think the new people in flat number five have got guests staying?*

"Your sister called twice," Mrs. Hazelbury says, craning her neck to see farther into the van. "Apparently she's been calling your mobile phone all night and there's been no answer."

I feel a shiver down my spine; a sluice of ice water. Rose has called? Again?

What have I done now?

"She wanted me to peek in your window and make sure you weren't lying dead on the floor," Mrs. Hazelbury says. "I have to say, I did notice a small dog in there while I was looking, which I'm certain is against the rules of the body corporate."

"I left my phone at home," I say to no one.

"There was a man hanging around earlier too," Mrs. Hazelbury continues, taking a closer look at Wally. "It wasn't you, was it? No. He was bigger and his hair was lighter."

In the back of my mind, I think of the mystery man who visited me at the library. The same guy? Perhaps I've forgotten to pay a bill and they are sending someone door to door? But I put that thought aside for the moment. "What did Rose want?"

Mrs. Hazelbury throws up her hands. "How should I know? Perhaps you should go and call her back instead of idling in this car all evening, keeping everyone awake!"

After finishing her inspection of Wally's van, she gives us a nod and wanders off. I reach for the door handle. "I'd better go," I say. "Sounds like Rose is worried."

Wally frowns, gazing just over my shoulder again. "Just because she's called doesn't mean you've done something wrong, Fern."

I feel the tingle again, low-level dread, this time in the pit of my stomach. "Unfortunately, in my case, it does."

"She's very . . . involved in your life, isn't she? It feels like she calls every time we're together."

"Rose is protective. She's looked after me all my life, so she knows the . . . situations I find myself in. If it wasn't for her . . . who knows where I'd be? Last time she called she saved Alfie's life, remember?"

Wally doesn't respond.

"Anyway," I say. "I'd better go call her."

I slide out of the car and slam the door. Wally waits until I've made it up the stairs and am safely inside. It's funny to think that only a moment ago, I was asking Wally to have sex with me. Goes to show it really does just take a moment for everything to change.

I have seventeen missed calls, all of them from Rose. There is also a text message: *CALL me ASAP.* I run through a mental list in my head. What could I have done? Alfie is lying contently on the couch. The oven is off. Mrs. Hazelbury didn't report anything out of the ordinary. What else could it be? I am still running through possibilities when my phone rings again.

"Rose."

"Fern! Thank god. I've been so worried."

"Why have you been worried?"

"Because! I told you I was going to call tonight at seven P.M. I wanted to see how Alfie was. I called and called, and you didn't respond."

I wait. "That's it?"

"That's it? Fern, you could have been lying dead in a ditch for all I know."

"What would I be doing in a ditch?"

"Fern!" She exhales exasperatedly.

"I don't remember you saying you were going to call," I say. "What time is it over there?"

"It's two hours after we were supposed to talk," she says. "When you didn't answer, I had to go through my emails to find Mrs. Hazelbury's number and then I asked her to look through your window and check that you weren't dead!"

"I know. She told me."

"I was really worried, Fern."

Rose sounds agitated. I, on the other hand, am flooded with relief. I missed a call. Not ideal for a worrier like Rose. But no one has been harmed. No one has died.

Everything is fine.

"Where were you?" Rose asks.

After everything that's happened, it takes me a moment to remember. "At the team-building night. We went bowling."

There's a short silence. *This* is exactly why I hate phone calls. A silence can mean so many things. Has the call dropped out? Is she taking a sip of her drink? Is she waiting for me to say something?

Finally, she speaks. "You went *bowling*?"

"Yes."

"Why? Is this because of the new boss?"

Rose knows how much I loved Janet. "Yes. It was compulsory for all staff to attend. It didn't go well," I admit.

I hear her exhale. "Oh, Fern. Did you get overwhelmed?"

"A little," I say, deciding not to tell her about the sensory meltdown. Rose worries too much as it is.

"You must be tired," she says. "How did you get home?"

"A friend drove me."

Another pause. "Which friend?"

"Wally."

The longest pause yet. "Is Wally a *guy*?"

There's something about Rose's tone that irritates me. *Of course* she could never just be happy that I have a guy friend! I also feel irritated at myself. Why do I need her to be happy? That's the strangest thing about having a sister, in my opinion. The way you can be mad at them and want their approval all at once.

"Yes. He's a guy."

"Where did you meet him?"

"At the library. He was taking a shower."

"A *shower*?" Rose sounds mad.

"He doesn't have a shower," I explain. "He lives in his van."

I glance out the window and am pleasantly surprised to see the van is still out there. I squint at the driver's seat, trying to spot him. The van is in darkness but it's possible that he's in the back. Maybe he's already gone to sleep? I kneel on my couch to get a better view.

"So let me get this straight. You've been bowling tonight, and you were driven home by a man who lives in his van?"

From my kneeling spot on the couch, I replay the sentence in my head and find it accurate. "Yes."

"Fern, you need to be careful. This man could be trying to take advantage of you. For money or food or even sex!"

I smile at the last part. If only she knew.

There is a knock on the door. I startle and fall off the couch onto the floorboards.

"Fern! Are you all right?"

"Fine," I say, straightening up. "Er, Rose . . . I've got to go. Someone is at the door."

"At this time of night—"

I end the call and get to my feet. Almost immediately the phone starts to ring again, but I ignore it, flinging open the door.

It's Wally.

"I didn't answer your question," he says.

"What question?"

Wally's cheeks turn crimson. "Well . . . we were talking about Adam and Eve? And you said . . ."

He drifts off. I wait. Wally rubs the bridge of his nose under his glasses.

"I said . . . ?"

Wally lets go of his nose and steps into my flat, grinning. "Are you really gonna make me say it?"

"Say what?"

He shakes his head. "You are funny."

I'm not sure why I'm funny, but as he sweeps me into his arms and presses his lips to mine, it seems moot, as I couldn't have answered him anyway.

Sex with Wally is a pleasant surprise. The few times I'd had sex with Albert, it had been with duty, even with curiosity, but each time he crawled his way around my body I could barely think of anything else but the moment it would be over. With Wally, I find myself having a lot of thoughts. Thoughts of . . . *Maybe we could try this next?*, or *What is it that you are doing there and why does it feel so good?*, and *How can I arrange for us to do this all the time?* The fact that I was trying to get pregnant escaped my mind entirely until the moment it was over. When I do remember, I can't find it within myself to care.

"Is it safe?" he'd asked, when we were both naked and he was hovering over me.

An odd question, I thought, but then I supposed it was important that one felt safe when they were in a new environment. I'd taken a few moments to ponder this, finally determining that while it wasn't *im*possible that a madman could burst into my flat at any given moment wielding a handgun, neither was my flat war-torn

Syria. So, after an appropriate amount of consideration, I'd replied, "Yes. It's safe."

And that seemed to be the right answer, because everything commenced rather quickly after that.

Afterward, I couldn't stop giggling. When Wally asked me why, I couldn't explain it. A physical reaction, I decided, was the only explanation.

"I think I had an orgasm," I said. "I mean . . . I'm not sure. How do you know, do you think?"

Wally rolled over so he was lying on his side. "Actually, I'm not sure," he said thoughtfully. "Shall we google it?"

"Good idea."

And so we lay there, in bed, googling orgasms and clicking on articles. After reading eight or nine articles, we determined that it was very likely that I'd had one, but it would be better to try again so we could be totally sure.

Wally leaves before morning, which makes me like him even more. As much as I'd savored the night with him, I am keen to keep my morning routine intact. There's been enough disruption this week, I decide. But as I go through my yoga poses, I find I'm still thinking about him. I imagine telling Rose about my relationship with Wally. Wouldn't that be something? On television and in books, sisters always talk to each other about these kinds of things, teasing each other about boys, confiding secrets. I imagined Rose gasping and giggling and demanding sordid details. I imagine her helping me get ready for a date and begging for details afterward. It would be something I'd quite enjoy, I decide.

I'd hoped for this sort of reaction when I started dating Albert.

"I have a boyfriend," I'd told her, even though Albert and I hadn't specifically used the terms "boyfriend" and "girlfriend." Still,

I'd come to recognize our behaviors as typical of those in that kind of relationship, so it seemed a logical conclusion to draw. "His name is Albert."

"What do you mean . . . you have a *boyfriend*?"

This should have been my first warning. Unlike the vast majority of the population, Rose didn't usually ask questions to which she already knew the answer. She knew I didn't understand it when people did this. But this day, she seemed to have forgotten.

"I mean . . . I have a boyfriend," I replied.

Rose didn't gasp or giggle, but she did ask dozens of questions about Albert, none of them in the least bit interesting. What was his last name? Where did he live? What was he studying? Her lip curled as she talked, as if a boyfriend was something that personally offended her.

"When can I meet him?" had been the last question, something of a surprise given that she'd seemed so disgusted by his existence.

After some prodding, I'd agreed to bring Albert to dinner at her place, where she'd proceeded to ask him all the same questions she'd asked me and more. There was no nudging or winking or giggling. There was nothing fun about it at all. There was nothing fun about it the next day either, when Albert stopped talking to me. So I decide it might be better not to tell Rose about Wally. For now.

At 9:15 A.M., when I'm about to leave for work, Mrs. Hazelbury knocks on my door.

"I'm sorry to bother you so early, Fern, but I wanted to catch you before you went to work. I have a copy of the body corporate documentation here." She holds up a stack of papers and places her eyeglasses on her nose. "Section 4.2 states that no dogs are permitted in the building, and section 15.6 states, and I quote, 'Parking of larger vehicles including trucks, trailers and caravans is strictly not permitted by building bylaws.' " She removes her glasses and looks at me expectantly. "Are you familiar with these bylaws?"

"I am," I say. (In fact, I'd read the body corporate documents very carefully after moving Alfie into my flat, and then done subsequent research on the computers when the library was quiet.) "However, bylaws that have a blanket ban on pets have been found to be contrary to section 180 of the Domestic Animals Act, which advises that 'a bylaw must not be oppressive or unreasonable, having regard to the interest of all owners and occupiers of lots included in the scheme and the use of the common property for the scheme.'"

Mrs. Hazelbury blinks. I take her blank expression to mean she needs further explanation.

"That means that the bylaw can say what it wants, but owners' corporations do not have the legal power to prohibit pets from private properties."

Now Mrs. Hazelbury understands. I can tell because she becomes red in the face.

"As for the van," I continue, "you'll find it is not a caravan or trailer. It is registered as a standard motor vehicle and as such does not breach any of the bylaws mentioned. Anyway, I do need to get going now, Mrs. Hazelbury, or I'll be late for work."

With that, I take Alfie by his lead, walk out, and close the door behind us, leaving Mrs. Hazelbury standing speechless at my front door.

Everyone is especially kind to me at the library today, and I ascertain it is because of the scene I made at the bowling last night. It is also possible it is because there is a dog by my side. With Wally at his meeting today, I had no alternative but to bring Alfie to the library with me. The fact that Carmel is at an interlibrary meeting for the morning is a fortuitous twist of fate, and one I take advantage of.

Alfie is a big hit with library staff and borrowers alike. Even the grumpy old folks who've been bused in from the nursing home cheer a little at the sight of him. Linda uses him as a prop during story hour. Gayle goes out to buy dog treats on her break and feeds him so many that he can't do much more than loll about at my feet while I process returned books into the system. Of course, he chooses the second that Carmel has arrived back from her meeting to poop on the carpet.

"What on earth is going on here?" she cries, as I'm on my hands and knees with a spray bottle and paper towel.

I look up. Carmel is wearing those eyeglasses that become sunglasses when you go outside. Except she's inside and the glasses don't seem to have realized.

"Oh, Fern," she says, softer now. "Hello. It's good to see that you're . . . feeling better, after last night . . ."

She trails off. I get the feeling I'm supposed to say something (I'm starting to get the hang of the strange way Carmel talks), but I'm not sure what. Eventually I try "Mmm," and it does the trick, bizarrely.

"Anyway. As I told you the other day, dogs are not allowed in the library."

"Actually," I say. "Owners of assistance dogs have the right to take their animals into all public places and onto public transport, including buses and trains. The Commonwealth Disability Discrimination Act 1992 makes it unlawful to discriminate against a person with a disability who is using an assistance—"

Carmel frowns underneath her rapidly fading glasses. "So . . . you're saying this is an assistance dog?"

I look at Alfie dubiously. "Yes . . ."

"I see. Then I assume you know it is a requirement that assistance dog owners must provide evidence of their disability when requested."

I don't reply. But Carmel waits, so I throw in another "Mmm."

"So?" Carmel says expectantly. "Where is your evidence of disability?"

I've underestimated Carmel. I've also underestimated her glasses, because in this short time, they've almost returned to clear.

I cross my arms.

"Fern, the dog has got to go."

I frown, looking off into the distance. "Sorry, will you excuse me, Carmel? I think I hear someone calling—"

I rise to my feet and am about to walk off when Carmel says, "Please don't walk away while I'm talking to you, Fern."

"But you'd finished talking. You said the dog had to go, and *then* I walked away."

"But . . ." Carmel looks utterly discombobulated. ". . . you hadn't answered me!"

I place a hand to my brow and close my eyes, breathing deeply, the way women in old-fashioned movies did before they "took to their beds." I've always wanted to try it and it is surprisingly gratifying. "You didn't ask a question, Carmel. How am I supposed to answer a question, if one hasn't been posed?"

Carmel doesn't reply, even though that *was* a question. Like me, she is also breathing deeply. I think she, too, would like to take to her bed.

"Fern, will you please make alternative arrangements for the dog?" she asks after a long silence.

I sigh. At least she has been clear, I suppose. I pull my phone from my pocket to check the time. Wally will have finished his meeting by now. I thumb him a text. Satisfyingly, he writes back almost immediately.

On my way.

"Someone is coming to get him now," I say to Carmel.

"Good," she replies, looking happier. "I trust I won't see him in the library again."

I wait until she finishes the sentence and, not hearing a question, hurry away before she can stop me.

Wally arrives at the library promptly, once again dressed in a suit and tie. The sight of him sends a bizarre, not unpleasant zing through me.

"Hello," I call out from the back of the library (perhaps too loudly given the amount of people that turn to look at me). Alfie and I trot toward him.

"Hello," Wally says when we are closer. We have a frightening moment of eye contact before Wally bends down to pat Alfie.

"How was your meeting?"

"It was a bigger meeting than I expected," he says. "There were a bunch of people there. I gave a presentation."

"Pr*eee*sentation," I repeat.

Wally laughs. "Sorry. Pr*es*entation."

I'm enjoying the interaction so much I decide to experiment with casual touch. I step forward and punch Wally on the arm, the way I've seen people do when they're having a laugh. But I think I do it too hard, because he stops laughing and looks alarmed.

"Sorry," I say.

"That's okay," he says, rubbing his arm.

"So it went well? Your pr*eee*sentation?"

"Yes," he says. "Very well. Maybe I can tell you about it after your shift? It's going to be a nice afternoon . . . maybe we can take a walk."

It is, I decide, the perfect suggestion. No noise, no smells, no unnatural light. Lots of fresh air. There will be small talk, I suppose, but I'm getting used to Wally's small talk. Even becoming fond of it.

"I can't today," I say, handing over Alfie's lead. "On Thursdays, after work, I visit my mother. Then I have dinner with Rose."

"Your mother?" Wally looks bewildered. "But . . . I thought you said your mother died?"

"I said she overdosed," I reply. "I never said she died."

As soon as the automatic doors slide open at Sun Meadows, the smell of casserole and urine starts to seep out. It's a malodorous, tacky smell that clings to me, even hours after I've returned home, showered, and washed my clothes.

Tragically, it is also now my mother's scent.

Once, my mother's scent had been talcum powder and toothpaste and laundry detergent. "Cleanliness, godliness, and all that," she used to say as she hummed around the house. I remember having to hold my breath when I was in the room with her, particularly when she bent down to kiss me at night.

One day she asked me why I was holding my breath, and I told her. "Your smell makes me feel sick."

Mum had looked sad then. "I'm so sorry, baby," she'd said. "I had no idea. If you'd prefer I didn't hug you—"

"It's okay," I'd said, shaking my head. "It's worth it."

At the reception desk, a woman I don't recognize smiles vaguely at me before returning to her paperwork. Security isn't very tight at my mother's establishment. I sign the visitor book, take a badge, and walk past the elevator, which has been screened off and bears a handwritten sign saying, OUT OF ORDR (no "e"). Fine by me. Elevators make me claustrophobic anyway and smells seem magnified in them particularly if I'm sharing the space with other visitors. I take the stairs.

At the top, a man in a brown dressing gown pushes a walker down the corridor, scanning the floor as if looking for something.

"Hi Fern," one of the nurses says. It is Onnab, whom I have determined to be one of the best nurses when it comes to Mum's state of personal hygiene and state of mind. "Your mother is in her room. She is having a good day."

A good day, I have learned, can mean a vast range of things. It can mean Mum is happy to see me and will attempt conversation, or it could mean she is quiet and doesn't say a word. She is rarely aggressive or combative, and I'm grateful, because apparently that isn't always the case with people in this ward.

Mum's door is ajar, and I knock lightly then push it open. Mum is in a wheelchair in the corner, dressed in a pair of gray trousers and a white blouse that is turning a little yellow. Her hair has been brushed and is pinned back, which makes it look very gray around the temples. She's even wearing shoes, the black Velcro ones with white socks underneath. It does indeed appear to be a good day.

"Hello, Fern," Teresa says.

Teresa is Mum's new speech pathologist. She was twenty-seven years old last time I asked. She has a thick brown ponytail, a singsongy voice, and lots of ideas about ways to improve Mum's speech. Today, for example, there is a machine beside Mum's chair, which is attached to a long cord. At the end of the cord is a flat circular object that hovers over Mum's head.

"What's all this?"

"Transcranial magnetic stimulation," Teresa says. "We did it last week too. Your mother is responding very well to it. Watch."

She holds up a flash card showing a picture of an apple.

"A-pple," Mum says.

"Now this one." Teresa holds up a flash card of a lion.

"Lion," Mum says.

I am impressed. Because of Mum's brain damage, speaking is hard for her now. Usually she pauses before each word as if gathering strength, and then her mouth stretches wide around each syllable. Even with all the effort, her pronunciation is hollow sounding and requires extreme concentration to understand. But these words come out remarkably clearly.

Mum looks at me. "Pop . . . pet!" she says, with painful slowness.

Mum started calling me "Poppet" after the overdose. I think it's because sometimes she doesn't remember my name, Mum had never used affectionate nicknames for us before. But a lot of things have changed about Mum. She smiles more now. She is easily delighted, reminding me of a much older lady, or a younger child. She's actually very good company, most days.

Mum's overdose happened sixteen years ago. She took the pills in the evening, and Rose and I didn't even think about it when she didn't get up in the morning. Mum had never been a morning person. At midday, we helped ourselves to lunch. In the afternoon, we toyed with the idea of waking her, but Rose was nervous about upsetting her. She had a point—Mum was always cranky when we woke her up.

It was nine that night when we finally knocked on Mum's door. By then she'd been in a coma for hours. Too many hours, they told us later. I called the ambulance, because Rose was mute with shock.

It was perhaps the only time in our lives when I was the one to step up in a moment of emergency.

We found out later that Mum had overdosed on Valium and alcohol and her brain had been irreparably damaged. A few weeks later, Mum was moved to a permanent care facility and Rose and I bounced around foster homes until we were eighteen.

"Well," Teresa says in her singsongy voice. "I think that's enough for one day, Nina. You should be very proud of yourself."

"You should, Mum," I agree. "I haven't heard you sound so clear in . . . years."

Teresa beams. "If she continues to improve at this rate, she'll be speaking in full sentences by the end of the year. I can't wait to have a good old chitchat with her, hear all her stories."

Teresa removes the round thing from Mum's head and starts fiddling with the machine. Mum looks at me. "Where . . . you . . . sis . . . ter?"

Mum asks this every time. I'm not sure if it's because she doesn't remember that Rose never visits, or if she just hasn't given up hope. In the early days after her accident, it had been a requirement that our foster various parents bring us for weekly visitation, but the day Rose turned eighteen, she stopped coming. ("Mum unsettles me," she said, when I asked her why. It must be one of those things I don't understand, because I never feel unsettled by Mum. To the contrary, our hour of unthreatening, halted conversation is one of the most settled parts of my week.)

"Rose is in Europe," I say.

Mum's eyes widen, which means she is interested.

"I know," I say. "She's gone to visit Owen. He's taken a job there this year and Rose is visiting him for four weeks."

I'm grateful that today I don't have to lie about Rose's whereabouts. Often, when I tell Mum that Rose isn't coming, her eyes fill with tears. Her emotions are unpredictable since her overdose, happiness to tears in an instant. I wish Rose would just come in and visit.

"Owen?" Mum frowns. "Eur-ope?"

"Yes, he's taken a job there," I repeat. "Anyway, Rose is just visiting him. She will be back at the end of the month."

Mum doesn't reply.

Sometimes I am sad that Mum doesn't say much. Sometimes, like Teresa, I'd like to have a full conversation with her and see what she has to say. Sometimes she seems so frustrated by the fact that she can't talk, she clenches her fists and grinds her jaw. Other times, she seems like she's made her peace with her disability, and just sits there and lets my chatter wash over her. During those times, I have to admit, I like the fact that I can talk and talk and never have to worry about making eye contact or talking too much or missing any social cues. It's probably the only place in the world where I feel like I can do that. That, I suppose, is what mothers are for.

"I have some news," I say to Mum on a whim. It feels good, because I never have news. Mum's eyes widen again.

"I've met a boy," I say, and finally I get the gasp I've been waiting for.

When I arrive home from Sun Meadows, Wally's kombi van is parked in my parking spot. It looks distinctive among the maroon sedans and white Toyota Corollas, and it adds some character to the place. I reach the sliding back door and pause a moment. I don't know the proper greeting when arriving at someone's van, so I knock loudly and wait.

"Hello," Wally says, poking his head out of the driver's-side window. Alfie sits happily on his lap. "Did you have a good visit with your mum?"

"I did." I go around to the passenger door of the van and get in. Alfie immediately leaps across the seat and lays his head on my lap. "So, tell me more about your pr*eee*sentation. Who did you pr*eee*sent to?"

"A group of investors. They're the same guys who gave us the money to start up Shout!"

"What is this idea? Another app?"

He nods. "It's a social prompter called FollowUp."

I scratch behind Alfie's ears. "What is a *social prompter*?"

"Basically, you enter all your invitations and engagements into the app, and it spits out communications that you can send via text, email, WhatsApp, or whatever platform you use. For example, if you receive an invitation to lunch that you want to decline, you can click on 'lunch' and 'regular' or 'one-off' and 'business' or 'pleasure' then press 'Go.' And the app will give you an appropriate response. Like . . ." He fiddles with his phone, then begins to read the screen. "*No can do, I'm afraid. I don't do Mondays.* Or *Ah, would love to, but I'm slammed next weekend. Sounds like it will be a ripper!* or *Have a great birthday. Wish I could be there but I'm going underground till I get through this busy period at work.*"

I look at the responses in wonderment.

"I still have a lot more coding to do. Eventually we'll be able to personalize it with the person's name, the event, follow-up excuses if they change the date, auto phone calls to give you an excuse to leave midway through an event, and also phrases to use if you are confronted by the person in real time. You'll be able to give it instructions to accept an invitation now but decline on the day saying you have an illness. It will also remind you what your excuse was for future communications with that person, so you don't go making any gaffes."

"Wow," I say. To have these turns of phrase at my fingertips—to not have to ask Rose or agonize over a response for hours—that would indeed be an app I would be willing to pay for. "It's genius."

"I think it will have a market. And now that we have investors, I've got work to do."

"So no more freelancing?"

"Not for the moment, no."

I consider this. "Is this cause for celebration?"

"I think it might be." A small smile comes to his lips. "But how should we celebrate?"

"Usually I celebrate by reading. But that's not really very sociable."

Wally frowns. "I often reward myself after a day of work with a few games of *Fortnite*. But, like reading, it's kind of a solitary endeavor."

We drift into silence as I ponder alternatives for celebration. After a short time, I notice Wally is staring at me. *Right* at me.

"Staring competition?" I ask eagerly.

"Actually, I was wondering if I could kiss you."

I giggle. Again. This time I can't even blame the orgasm.

That night, as we make love, I don't think about getting pregnant at all. Not once.

I see him, under the surface of the water. His hair fans around him like a halo. He's struggling. I hold tighter. Just a little bit longer, I think. It's almost over.

When I do let go, he is slow to rise to the surface. He's bloated and unnaturally white. Limp. His eyes and mouth are open.

I jolt awake.

"Fern. Fern! Wake up. You're having a nightmare."

I'm in my room. It's quiet, as usual, but something is different.

Wally shakes me. "Fern?"

"I'm awake," I say.

"Are you all right?"

Wally hovers over me. It's hard to make out his features in the dark room. I nod.

"Are you sure? It sounded like you were having a nightmare."

"Yes," I say. "Just I have them sometimes."

Wally lies back down. He scooches up close behind me so we are a pair of crescent moons. He throws an arm over me. The weight and warmth of it is a surprising comfort. I focus on enjoying it, while I steady my breath.

On this night, sleep comes surprisingly fast.

In the morning, when I open my eyes, I am looking at Wally. His eyes are closed and his long, black eyelashes lightly touch his cheeks. My eyes drift down to his shoulders, his chest. He has a hairy chest, with a freckle just above his left nipple. His body is definitely on the slender slide, particularly his legs, which are dangerously close to skinny. But his arms and chest are shapely and muscular, and I admire them curiously.

Until I lurch upright. "Shoot!"

Wally jolts awake. "What?" He scrambles around the bed, looking for his glasses. "What's wrong?"

"I slept in!"

He pushes his glasses onto his nose. "What time is it?"

"Seven oh seven A.M.," I say, scrambling out of bed. I haven't slept in for years. My body is my alarm clock and it wakes me every morning without fail between 6:10 A.M. and 6:30 A.M. Without fail *until now.* The fact that my body has failed me is unsettling enough, without the other unsettling things I'm starting to register. Like the fact that I'm dressed in last night's clothes. Partly dressed. I'm not wearing a top or bra, but my skirt is bunched up around my waist and I am still wearing socks. My skin and teeth feel grimy. It takes me a few moments to realize that not only did I not undress properly before bed, I didn't brush my teeth or wash my face or apply lotion to my shins or anything. I did none of it! And now it's after 7:00 A.M.! By now, I should be in downward dog on my yoga mat in the living room.

"You have to go, Wally," I say.

"Why?" he says, at the same time as there is a knock at the door. His eyebrows rise. "Are you expecting someone?"

"It's probably my neighbor. She likes to come over and read me the bylaws of our building."

I locate my bathrobe and wrap it around myself, and Wally heads toward the bathroom. Alfie is at my heels as I fling open the front door. I only have a second to register Rose before she catapults herself into my arms.

"Rose!" I choke. "What . . . ?" Normally, I don't mind when Rose hugs me, but today there is something strangling about it. "What are you doing here?"

Rose lets me go and I notice she'd managed the hug while balancing a box in one hand. "I missed you!"

Rose pushes past me, into the flat.

"Why are you home early?" I ask, closing the door.

"Aren't you pleased to see me?" Rose places the box on the table. "Don't answer that. Just sit down. I brought donuts."

Rose sets the box on the table and opens the lid, demonstrating that she has indeed brought donuts. It's odd. Rose doesn't eat donuts very often, because of her diabetes. I, on the other hand, eat a lot of donuts. Often Gayle brings a box of them in to the library and while everyone else stands around deliberating whether or not to have one, I am happily helping myself to thirds.

"Sit!" Rose repeats.

I look at my watch hesitantly. "I have to go to work, Rose! I'm already late."

"What time do you have to be at work?"

"Ten. And I haven't done yoga yet."

I expect Rose to ask me why, but she is obviously distracted. "It's just after seven, Fern. You have time to catch up if I drive you to work."

Reluctantly, I take a seat at the table. The moment I'm seated, the bathroom door opens and Wally comes out.

"Hi there," he says.

Rose looks at me. She looks so baffled I almost laugh.

"Rose, this is Wally," I say instead. "Wally, this is my sister, Rose."

Wally extends his hand. "Good to meet you," he says. "Though I must point out that my name is in fact Rocco." He shoots a reprimanding smile at me.

Rose continues to stare at him. It's strange. Normally Rose is so poised, so polite. She always has the perfect response to everything. Today, she seems like the sister who doesn't know how to behave.

"Pleased to meet you too, Rocco," she says finally, taking his outstretched hand. She holds it for longer than appropriate (maximum of three seconds, she'd always told me) and stares at him in a manner I would have considered rude. "You look familiar. Have we met before?"

Wally picks up his shoes from beside the door where he'd lined them up neatly the night before. "Not that I recall, but you never know. This world is a small place. Anyway, I'll leave you two to catch up. Fern, I'll talk to you later?"

It is a statement, but he poses it like a question, rising in intonation at the end. In light of this, I decide to go out on a limb and answer it as one. "Sure. Talk to you later."

Wally gives me a little salute and lets himself out with his shoes still in his hand. It's so peculiar I find I can't stop smiling.

I look back at Rose, who is gaping at me.

"He *slept* here? Fern! You can't just invite a strange man into your home!"

"He's not *that* strange." I wonder if she is referring to the salute.

"He's a stranger, Fern. We don't know him. Is he the one who drove you home the other night after bowling?"

I nod. "In his van."

"That's another thing," Rose says. "I saw Mrs. Hazelbury on the way in and she's not happy about that caravan outside."

"It's not a caravan," I say. "It's a kombi van—"

But Rose isn't listening. "What did you say his name was again? Rocco?"

"Yes. But I call him Wally."

"What's his last name?"

"Ryan."

"Rocco Ryan." Rose frowns frustratedly off into the distance, contemplating that.

"You still didn't tell me why you came back from your holiday early! Is everything all right with Owen?"

A tiny smile comes to her lips. "Everything is perfect with Owen. We're back together!"

Rose is beaming. I get the feeling that I should be excited. But I'm confused.

"Back together? But . . . did you break up?"

"Well . . . no." Rose's smile fades. "It's complicated. Suffice to say, I have been worried about the state of our relationship these last few months. But not anymore." Her smile returns. "Now, I'm more confident about it than ever."

I smile, still not totally understanding.

"So, where is Owen?" I ask. "Back at your place?"

She shakes her head. "He's got to finish the project he's working on. But he'll be back as soon as he can. In the meantime, we need some serious sister time. Just you and me, and these donuts. What do you say?"

She dives into the box and pulls out a chocolate-iced donut for me. She has one too, after checking her blood sugar on her glucometer. When we are done, I shower and get ready, and then Rose drives me to the library. It's not until much later that day that I realize that Rose never actually explained why she was home early.

• • •

JOURNAL OF ROSE INGRID CASTLE

It wasn't easy leaving Owen. But if there was even a chance that Fern was in danger, it was worth it. It sounds dramatic, I realize that. Just because she'd met a guy didn't mean she was in danger. But the statistics in this area are grim. Ninety percent of all people with intellectual disabilities will be sexually assaulted in their life. Ninety percent!!! Call me overprotective, but I'm going to make damn sure that my sister is going to be among the ten percent.

I have to admit, it's helpful, journaling all of this. And my therapist is right, the subconscious has a funny way of connecting things. Joy connects to fear. Good connects to bad. And so, on a day when I'm feeling good about my decision to come home, guess who I find myself thinking about?

Gary.

Gary was Mum's boyfriend when we were eleven. Mum's first boyfriend, or at least the first we knew about, after Dad left. Gary was a welcome addition to our lives at first. A novelty, you might say. He was a PE teacher. He wore shorts and trainers every single day, even on the weekends. I remember wondering if he even owned other clothes. The best thing about Gary was that when he was around, Mum was nicer.

Gary was affectionate–which was also a novelty. He used to give us bear hugs and shoulder rubs. It was strange, being touched in this way by an adult. Sometimes I liked it, but most of the time it confused me. One time, as we all sat in front of the television, he picked up my legs and began to massage them. I wanted to ask him to stop, but Mum was there and she didn't say anything, so I didn't either. He tried it with Fern next, but she told him to stop. Fern could always get away with those things better than I could.

One day, Gary took us swimming while Mum was getting her hair done. Fern and I were excited. I don't know if it was the swimming or just the idea of doing something so normal that intoxicated me. Fern loved the water. When we arrived at the local council pool, she dived into the open section away from the lanes and paddled away immediately. I wasn't as good a swimmer as Fern, and I got into the pool slowly and stayed close to the shallow end. Gary sat on the side the whole time, watching. When I ventured toward the deep end, he called me back.

"I promised your mum I wouldn't let you drown," he said, sliding off the edge and into the pool. I still remember his arms circling my waist under the water and pulling me against him. I remember his bare thighs pressing against mine. And I remember the distinct feeling that something wasn't right about it.

"Relax," he whispered. "Just relax."

It was the strangest thing. There were people everywhere, all around us. And yet I was entirely alone.

FERN

Rose gets me to work on time (just). After all the excitement of her surprise return, it is a relief that my morning at the library is uneventful. The afternoon, however, is another story.

I am in the children's corner reading to a child who has refused to take part in the school holiday singing and dancing group (*Too loud,* she'd said, and I quite agreed) when I hear a shout from the other side of the library.

"Get. Out. Of. My. Face."

The little girl looks up at me worriedly. I share her concern. The voice is deep and guttural and doesn't sound friendly. It's most unusual to hear a voice like this in the library.

"Stand back! Get the fuck away from me!"

I get to my feet to try and locate its owner. I see a large man towering over Carmel. Carmel looks uncharacteristically unsure of herself. She holds out both palms toward him in a surrender gesture, but he doesn't appear to be backing off.

I scan the area around them. A few people quietly vacate their computers, gathering in small groups closer to the door. Gayle watches from the front desk, her ear pressed to the phone. I cross the floor quickly to stand beside Carmel. Up close, I can see the man is shaking and sweating. He appears to be in quite the state.

"Excuse me," I say. "Are you requiring some assistance?"

He looks at me. "Who the fuck are you?"

"I'm a librarian," I say. The children, I notice, have stopped singing and dancing. The whole library is silent, which is unusual for this time of the day.

"A *librarian*?"

He seems surprised by this; I take it as evidence that he's found himself in the wrong place. "Yes. You're in the Bayside Public Library. Where were you hoping to be?"

"I need my money!" His eyes look bizarre, large and black like a cartoon character's. He grinds his jaw and picks at his fingers. He is clearly agitated. In his right hand, he holds a pocketknife, the small sharp blade pointing outward.

"I'm sorry, but weapons aren't permitted in the library," I say. "I'm going to have to take that." At first, he doesn't protest, but at the last moment he shifts, extending his arm with the blade. It narrowly misses my shoulder.

"Fern," Carmel says quietly.

"Hey!" I cry. "You almost got me."

"Where's my money?" he says. "Do you have it?"

"We don't keep money on the premises," Carmel tells him. Her tone is sharp and authoritative, but he mustn't take well to it, because he lunges forward, jabbing the knife at her. I pull her backward by her shirt and frown at the man.

"Careful! You could hurt someone with that."

The man looks right at me for the first time. "Where's. My. Money."

The man is sweating, panicky. He must be really worried about his money.

"It must be frustrating, not knowing where your money is," I say. "It ruins my entire day if I lose something, believe me. Most likely, it will turn up. In the meantime, why don't you sit down on this beanbag and I'll read you a book?"

He doesn't sit, but I walk to the nearby cart anyway. A copy of Michelle Obama's new book is waiting to be reshelved. "How about this one? You're lucky it's here, this one has a lot of reserves on it."

He doesn't appear to be listening, but it's amazing what people pick up, even while distracted. People with ADHD, for example, retain information better if they read while walking or engaging in simple play. I open the book. "'When I was a kid, my aspirations were simple,'" I read. "'I wanted a dog. I wanted a house that had stairs in it, two floors for one family.'"

The library has cleared out, I notice, as I read. Carmel is still beside me, a little too close if I'm honest. The man continues to pick at his fingers. I notice they are red raw and make a mental note to recommend aloe vera once I finish reading.

After five minutes, he finally slides into the beanbag. He rests the pocketknife on the floor beside him. I pull up a second beanbag. We are sitting like that when the police arrive. As they handcuff him, he says loudly, "But we were reading a book!"

I shove it between his handcuffed hands. "Keep it."

When I turn around, Carmel is standing there.

"I'll pay for the book—" I start, but before I have finished talking Carmel has enveloped me in a suffocating hug.

"That was very brave," Carmel says later, as we sit side by side in the stationary ambulance. Both of us are unharmed, but the ambulance officers have wrapped blankets around us in case of shock. I'd feel far more comfortable if I could get back to work in the library, but the ambulance officers—and Carmel—have been quite insistent.

"Do you think that man was on drugs?" I ask Carmel.

"Yes, I do. The police think it was methamphetamines."

Janet once told me that, in her previous job, due to the location of the library, she had come across a lot of drug addicts. The library, being free and cool in summer and warm in winter, became a sort of refuge for them. People complained about it, apparently, but Janet was their biggest supporter. *The library is for everyone,* she used to say, *but some people need it more than others.* She told me about a young woman—barely a teenager—who died of an overdose inside that library. The girl was a regular, apparently. Janet said she was sad that the girl was gone, but happy that the library had been a safe place for her for so many months. She had attended the girl's funeral and erected a little statue in the garden for her. That was the kind of person Janet was.

"I wish you'd had a chance to meet Janet," I say to Carmel.

Carmel smiles. "I heard you and Janet were close."

"I learned so much from her," I say. "Not just about books. She taught me about people. How to help them, respect them, and how to enrich their lives through books."

Carmel looks at me. Her eyes, I notice, are a marbled blue with yellow edges. "Perhaps you can share some of Janet's wisdom with me sometime? And your own, for that matter. It's clear that you are very good at what you do. Not to mention beloved in this library."

Beloved. I've never thought of myself as beloved before.

"Maybe I could even shadow you as you work, to see what I can learn?"

I frown. "Shadow me?"

"Follow you."

"Oh," I say. "With your cart?"

She smiles. "No. No cart."

I think about this for a moment. And then, it might be because of the kindly way Carmel is looking at me, I nod.

Carmel looks pleased. "Wonderful. And then, maybe you could shadow me? I could even show you how to use the printers and the photocopiers?"

I sigh. "I understand that you are making an effort, Carmel. And you have shown interest in Janet, which I appreciate. But I cannot and will not learn the printers and the photocopiers."

Carmel laughs. "All right, I accept that," she says. "For now."

After work, I stand at my living room window waving at Wally. He is sitting in the driver's seat of the van, reading a novel, and it takes him a moment to notice me. When he does, he waves back. He doesn't come up and I'm glad. I'm already overwhelmed by the day and I know further interaction would push me over the proverbial edge. But I enjoy him being within sight, where I can wave to him whenever I want. It makes me feel content, this little interaction.

My phone rings and I look away from the window. Rose's name is on the screen.

"I *knew* the name Rocco Ryan sounded familiar." Her voice is high-pitched and excited. "I googled him. He is the Rocco Ryan who founded Shout!"

"I know," I say.

"Fern, it is a *huge* app. *Huge!*"

"I know," I repeat.

"You *know*?" Rose sounds disbelieving. This irritates me. To think she would know more about my friend than I do.

"Of course I know. Wally told me."

A pause. "Fern, do you know what Shout! is?"

I roll my eyes. "An app," I say. "Something to do with ordering drinks."

"According to the article I read, Rocco and his partner sold it in 2016 for a hundred million dollars. A hundred million dollars, Fern! The article also said that Rocco is one of the most promising computer programmers the world has ever seen. He was in Silicon Valley before he came to Australia. He's been compared to Linus Torvalds and Steve Wozniak! Apparently, people were lining up to work with him when they sold Shout!, but then he just went off the grid. It was quite mysterious. People assumed he was living it up on a private island or something. . . ."

I glance around the room, noticing a spiderweb in the corner that I really must take care of.

"Fern, your friend is a gazillionaire. Does that interest you even a little bit?"

I sigh, considering her question. Does that interest me? I suppose it does. At the same time, of all the things I know about Wally, the fact that he is a gazillionaire (not technically an actual word) is the very least interesting.

"Not especially," I say, waving again at Wally through the window. As Rose starts to reiterate all the reasons I should *be* interested, Wally waves back.

On Monday morning, Wally comes to my door to ask if I'd like to have dinner with him.

"It's Monday," I explain. "I have dinner with Rose on Mondays."

Wally leans against the doorframe, his gaze resting lazily over my shoulder. "Tomorrow, then?"

"I have dinner with Rose Tuesday nights too."

Wally narrows his gaze. "Do you dine with Rose on any other evenings?"

"Thursdays."

He laughs. Then he stops. "Seriously?"

"Yes."

"Every week?"

"Mmm-hmm."

"Wow."

I frown. "Why *wow*?"

"I don't know. That's just a lot of dinners with one person."

"Is it?" Given the fact that married couples presumably have dinner together seven nights a week, it doesn't seem like such a lot. Then again, Rose and I aren't married.

"I guess I could cancel," I say on a whim. But even as I say it, I get a funny feeling. I don't think Rose would like to be canceled on. "It's just one night. She's probably jet-lagged after her long flight, anyway."

I expect Wally to smile at this, but instead he gives me a funny look. "Who are you trying to convince, Fern?"

Wally leaves and I text Rose. Bizarrely, I feel nervous as I thumb the words onto the screen.

Do you mind if I cancel dinner tonight?

In a matter of seconds, my phone begins to ring.

"Why are you canceling?" Rose demands the instant I answer.

"Well . . . it's just . . . Wally asked if I wanted to have dinner with him."

"Oh." Rose is silent for a few seconds. "It's just that I'd already defrosted the chicken."

"Couldn't we have it tomorrow?"

A sigh. "But I've been looking forward to it all day."

Rose's voice has a different sound to it, slightly juvenile and whiny. A gnawing sense of unease tugs at me. At the same time, the idea of canceling on Wally, and having to explain this to him, is enough to make me dig my heels in. "I'm sorry, Rose. I need to cancel."

This time the silence on the other end lasts so long, I wonder if Rose has hung up.

"Rose?"

“Have dinner with Wally,” she says abruptly. Her voice sounds funny. I open my mouth to ask if everything is all right but before I can, she has ended the call.

I forget about the Rose situation the moment Wally walks into my flat (fifteen minutes early) that night. I’m anxious about the fact that all I have in the fridge is sausages, yogurt, and puff pastry, but Wally quickly puts me at ease by ordering pizza, which we eat at my round table. It is most strange, seeing my second chair hosting a guest. Normally, it is simply a storage space for my unread books.

“Rose googled you,” I say as we settle onto the couch afterward. “She read an article that said you sold your app for a hundred million dollars.”

Wally cocks his head thoughtfully. “The article was accurate. That isn’t always the case.”

“Wow,” I say. “You live economically for someone with a hundred million dollars.”

He laughs. “I don’t *have* a hundred million dollars. I got my share of it. But I had a business partner and we had a number of investors who all got their cut. And a good chunk went to tax and our charitable organization for underprivileged children . . . But you’re right, I do live frugally, considering my means.”

“Why do you work at all?”

He appears to consider this. After a moment, he shrugs. “What else would I do? Sit around counting my gold? Besides, working is important to a person’s mental health.”

I agree wholeheartedly with this. I can’t think of anything more important to my mental health than my work at the library. “How *is* your mental health?” I ask. “I mean . . . the last time you were working on an app, things didn’t go so well for you—”

"This time it's better," he says, smiling. His gaze is still over my shoulder, but closer these days, almost touching my face.

We remain like that for a moment, Wally smiling at me; then, Wally sits up straight. "Oh, I almost forgot. I've been meaning to ask you . . ." He reaches into his pocket and retrieves a folded-up piece of paper, which he unfolds onto his lap. It appears to be for a private health fund.

"What's this?" I ask.

"Changing health insurance," he says, rolling his eyes. "I've had to do a mountain of paperwork. And it appears I need an emergency contact person in the country."

He holds out the page to me, and I know what he's going to say before he says it. It's rare that this happens to me. Under the circumstances, I should feel pleased.

"Would you consider . . . being my person?" Wally asks, holding out a pen.

I clear my throat. "I would be delighted to be your person, Wally. Truly delighted. But I feel there's something you should know first. Something important."

Wally looks surprised. But he nods and sits back in his chair. "All right. What is it?"

I close my eyes, take a breath.

"When I was a kid," I say, "I did something terrible."

• • •

JOURNAL OF ROSE INGRID CASTLE

After that first time at the swimming pool, Gary touched me all the time. He said if I told Mum, she'd be blame me, which I'd already figured out. Mum was mad enough with me already, I wasn't going to provide her with new reasons to hate me. It was frightening how many opportunities Gary found. Officially, Gary didn't live with us, but you'd never know it with the amount of time he spent at our house. He was often there even when Mum wasn't.

And so, I stuck to Fern like glue. Safety in numbers, I figured. It worked to some extent. But if Fern took a shower, if she went to the bathroom, if she just wasn't paying attention, Gary would come and sit next to me. He was discreet. His hand could slide into my shorts or up my skirt without making a sound. I didn't make a sound either. No matter how much I wanted to, every time I clammed up, became mute.

Sometimes, he even did it when Mum was there. We might be in the kitchen or sitting around, watching television, and he'd suggest we start a massage train. He'd be at the back, of course. I was always next, then Fern and then Mum. Since Fern and Mum were in front, they couldn't see when he fondled my breasts and groped me. I think he enjoyed the danger of it. I couldn't figure out if I wanted Mum to turn around . . . or if I didn't.

But even that was nothing compared to what Gary did when no one was around. The first time it happened was on a weeknight. We'd been watching television and I'd decided to take a shower. I locked the door and put a chair in front of it to be safe.

When I emerged twenty minutes later, the house was quiet. As I tried to walk quietly to my room, I passed Gary, sitting on the couch.

"Your mum and Fern have gone to the supermarket," he said.

My blood ran cold.

Mum often had to do a late-night dash; she wasn't organized when it came to food. Fern often went along to make sure Mum didn't just come home with wine and cigarettes.

And so, there were Gary and I, alone in the house for god knew how long. I was wearing just a towel.

"How about I give you a proper massage?" he said. "Not just the shoulders?"

That time, I did try to protest. I said I was tired and wanted to go to bed. "Good," he said. "Let's do it in the bedroom. It will be more comfortable."

"No," I said. "I really think–"

"You need to stop thinking," he said. "This will help you relax."

He laid me down on my bed for the "massage" and did things to me that I didn't completely understand until I was much older. But I knew what he was doing to me was bad. And I figured, for him to do those things to me, I must have been bad too.

FERN

"It happened when I was twelve."

Wally is still smiling, but it's fading. His eyes are showing the first hints of confusion. "What happened?"

"We were camping. Billy and I were playing a game—"

"Wait." Wally holds up a hand. "Who is Billy?"

"Mum had a couple of boyfriends while we were growing up. She had one named Gary, but he didn't last long, which was good because I didn't like him. Then she had one named Daniel. Billy was Daniel's son. We all went on a camping trip together. It was supposed to be a time for us to get to know each other better and bond."

Wally sits forward, his elbows resting on his knees.

"We *did* bond, on that trip. It was fun having another person to play with. Billy was really competitive. He spent most of that camping trip trying to hold his breath under water longer than me. I'd read a book about free diving, so I knew how to fill up my lungs completely, how not to panic under water. Billy couldn't get close to holding his breath for as long as I could."

"What happened, Fern?"

I wrap my arms around myself and start to rock. "On the night he died, he was so frustrated. He wanted to stay under the longest, but he just couldn't do it. Every attempt was worse than the last." I looked up at Wally. "And so . . . I helped him."

"Helped him . . . what?"

My voice is the barest whisper. "Helped him stay under the longest. I held him down."

Wally's face remains still. Too still. "No," he says. "No, you didn't."

I feel the first tears hit my cheeks. "I thought . . . I thought he would pop up and grin at me and say how happy he was that he'd beaten my time! But he didn't. When I let him go, it was too late."

Wally is staring at me in horror. "But . . . you must have known that if you held someone under the water for long enough, they would drown?"

"I did know that!" I wring my hands and then press my eyes into them. "I *did* know that. An adult can drown in sixty seconds, that's what all the literature says. I held him under for forty. It was timed! I don't know how it happened. I would never, never . . ."

"What happened when you realized what you'd done?" he asks.

"Rose . . . told me I couldn't . . . tell anyone. She was worried I'd go to jail. She said we had to say that Billy got tangled in the reeds and drowned, or I'd get into big trouble."

"This is why you're always worried about what you might do?" Wally takes a deep breath, then drops his head into his hands. "It's . . . awful," he says. "Unimaginably awful."

I nod. My face is wet with tears. "I told you I can't be trusted, Wally. I'm dangerous."

He looks up, shakes his head. "It was a terrible accident. But . . . it was clearly an accident, Fern. You would never intentionally hurt anyone." Wally slides closer to me and pulls me against his chest. "You'd never hurt anyone," he repeats, and for some reason, maybe because it comes from Wally, I almost believe it.

To my great surprise, Wally doesn't cut me out of his life. I wait for it to happen, either immediately or perhaps in a phasing-out-type arrangement, but day after day, week after week, he shows up—at the library or my doorstep, with suggestions of dinner or an evening walk. It is unfathomable. It's the kind of loyalty you might expect of a lifelong friend or family member. It doesn't make sense that Wally has elevated me to such a rank when we've only known each other a few weeks. And yet, he has.

And so, over the next month or so, I amend my routine to create space for Wally. Early evenings are spent together, apart from the evenings I spend at Rose's place. At the end of the night, Wally returns to his van and I go to sleep alone. We both prefer it this way, as it keeps our morning routines intact. And I make up for the late nights by taking naps in the secret cupboard at work every time I get the chance.

For a few weeks, I am lucky enough to sometimes get to see Wally during the day, too, when he pops into the library here and there. Unfortunately, it's not long before he moves into a coworking space in the city and can no longer visit me at work. I miss him when he's gone. It's a curious feeling, missing someone. I feel it in my chest—a blend of butterflies and indigestion.

I start to loathe dinners with Rose. And it's not just my recent preference for Wally's company. Since returning from London, she's become unbearably interested in every mundane facet of my life—from what I had for lunch, to who I sat with, to what I dreamed about. So when Rose phones and cancels dinner one night—terrible food poisoning, apparently—I feel only minimal guilt at my elation.

Wally is in my doorway when Rose calls, and he appears equally delighted. “That’s the best news I’ve heard all day. And I’ve had a pretty good day.”

“Why have you had a good day?”

“The video I made for FollowUp has gone viral.”

He leans against the doorjamb. Wally and I spend a lot of time in my doorway. There’s something about the no-man’s-land of it that I like—if he doesn’t cross the threshold, it doesn’t count as a “visit” and as such isn’t a disruption to my routine.

“Gone viral . . . ,” I repeat.

“ ‘Viral’ means lots of people have seen it,” Wally explains. “The connotation is that it has spread, like a virus would.”

“Clever.” It’s so rare that newfangled slang makes sense to me, but this is the kind of slang I could easily get on board with. Having decoded this part of the conversation, I take another moment to process it in reference to his previous comment. “And . . . the fact that Rose has canceled is better than that?”

He smiles, but it is almost as though there is a frown behind it. I have recently learned that this face means I have failed to understand something that he finds perfectly obvious (I know this because I asked him what the face meant, and he confirmed my interpretation). “Seeing you is always the best part of my day, Fern.”

I smile.

“Let’s skip dinner,” Wally says, crossing the threshold. And just like always, we are entirely on the same wavelength.

In the morning, Wally is gone but the side of the bed that he sleeps on has been disturbed in that way that says he’s been there recently.

Watching his side of the bed for a few moments before I start my day has become a part of my routine too. Then I move on to the usual routine: breakfast, coffee, yoga. I have just settled myself in lotus position when I notice the date on the calendar on my wall and a thought comes to me, so clear and fast it is as though it's been tucked just out of sight, just waiting to be retrieved.

My period is two days late.

According to Google, a period that is up to five days late is normal and a typical part of a healthy cycle. What's more, cycles can be influenced by a great many things—changes to routine, excessive exercise, and travel. This information is a great comfort to me. While I haven't traveled in recent weeks, I've certainly had my fair share of exercise (yoga, karate, sex) and changes to my routine (Wally), so those things combined would certainly explain my late period. And so, I spend the next few days carrying out my daily routine with almost painful precision, hoping this will rectify things.

Before I know it, my period is six days late.

"Fern? Come and look at this," Rose says. Rose is in the corner of IKEA, hovering by a white BILLY bookcase, inspecting it with what feels like an inordinate level of scrutiny. "This will work, don't you think?"

Rose continues to say something, but I can't hear very well, because I have my earplugs in. I still am not quite sure how Rose managed to convince me to come to IKEA. She knows I don't like shopping—and IKEA, let's face it, is the mother of all shops. I do almost all of my own shopping online and, frankly, I don't understand why anyone would do anything else. Virtually everything, including IKEA, is available online and pretty much all of the larger department stores offer free delivery and returns. And if there is an item I desperately want but can only get in a big shopping center, I ask Rose to get it for me.

Ironically, it is exactly this logic that Rose used when convincing me to come.

"I don't like shopping!" I had whined when she asked me.

"Fern." She put her hands on her hips. "You know when sometimes you ask me to go to the store to get you something?"

"Yes."

"Do I go?"

I roll my eyes.

"Do I go?" Rose repeats.

"Yes."

"I'm not asking you to understand why this is important to me. I'm only asking if you can do it."

And, so, here I am, at IKEA. It smells like cinnamon rolls and meatballs, an eye-wateringly disgusting combination, and it's as bright as a summer's day. I'd wanted to wear my swimming goggles, but that would have meant a detour to my flat, so I'd settled for sunglasses.

"What do you think?" Rose asks and I lip-read, gesturing to the generic-looking bookcase.

I think I'd like to get out of here before I get a migraine. But I give the bookcase a cursory glance. "It's not very big," I say.

Rose frowns. "I'm sure they sell bigger ones—"

I curse silently. If I'd only said "I love it," we could be writing the number down and heading to the warehouse area (the one area of IKEA that I, if not *enjoy,* appreciate for its resourceful organization). Instead, Rose is wandering distractedly to another section of the store, looking for someone to point her in the direction of bigger bookcases.

"Fern?" she calls. "Come and look at this!"

The store is uncomfortably full, and I have to push past several people to follow Rose. Everyone is saying *excuse me* and *sorry* and smiling at each other, but my head is starting to spin. How can so many people be buying bookshelves?

"Let's just choose one and go home," I call after her. She says something in reply, and I have to remove my earplugs to hear her. "What did you say?"

"I want to make sure I find the right one," she says. "I don't want to rush into it."

We emerge from the crowd of people and I make a beeline for a little wedge of space I spot next to a toddler bed and wrap my arms around myself. Even with my sunglasses on, the lights are making me woozy.

"I *was* thinking white, but what do you think of this natural timber?" Rose says, gesturing at the wooden frame of another set of shelves. "And look, it comes with a matching lamp!" She lifts the timber lamp and it flashes directly into my eyes. If I didn't know better, I'd think my sister was deliberately trying to set off a sensory attack.

"Rose," I say. "I have to go outside."

"Just one more minute! I want to look at the bedside tables. Then we'll go."

She takes my hand and pulls me back through the crowd. We

pass several young couples, arguing. A pair of twin toddlers bounce on a bed in frenzied joy as their heavily pregnant mother screams at her husband to control them. Rose continues to pull me but when we come to a clear space, I plant my feet.

Rose looks back over her shoulder. "Fern? What are you doing?"

Nausea overwhelms me. I sink into an armchair and drop my head into my hands. Rose's nude ballet flats appear in my small field of vision.

"Fern!" I hear her exclaim. "For goodness' sake. I just want to show you one more—"

I vomit on her shoes.

"Here," Rose says, holding out a plastic cup of water. "Drink this."

We are in the parents' room, on a chair designated for nursing mothers, which strikes me as ironic, all things considered. Rose is rubbing my back in rhythmic circles, saying "Shhh" and "Everything is going to be all right." From the moment I vomited, she'd taken care of everything, collecting a roll of paper towels from a sales assistant, cleaning everything up, waving away offers of help. She'd found me water, and told everyone it was fine, her sister just wasn't feeling well. She seemed so serene, so in control. It reminds me why I need her so much.

"Are you feeling better?" she asks, after I have finished my water.

I nod. "A little."

"What happened in there?" she asks. "Did it all get a little too much? Or was it something you ate? Maybe—"

"My period is six days late, Rose."

Rose stops rubbing my back. After several beats, she says, "*What?*"

I repeat myself. Rose takes a couple of steps away from me, then lowers herself into another chair.

"Have you and Rocco been having sex?"

I wonder why else she would think I'd be worried about my period. "Yes."

"And you think you might be—"

"Yes," I say. "I think I'm pregnant."

Back home, Rose and I cram into my little bathroom. The pregnancy test sits flat on the bathroom vanity before us. One line is clearly visible, and a second fainter line is starting to appear beside it.

"Well," Rose says, holding her temples. "You're definitely pregnant." She takes a deep breath and sits on the toilet.

I remain standing, leaning against the wall.

"I wonder what Wally will say," I say.

Rose looks up. "You're going to tell him?"

"Of course."

Rose looks startled, which is puzzling. I have a rudimentary understanding of common courtesy, after all, and the only times I have heard of people *not* telling the father of their baby that they are pregnant are in daytime television shows when the pregnancy is the result of an affair or a one-night stand. When the two parties are exclusively seeing each other, the custom appears to be some kind of excited announcement.

"Surely that is the expected thing to do under the circumstances?" I say. "Inform the father of the baby that he is going to be a dad?"

"Yes," Rose says slowly. "*If* you're going to keep it." She is quiet for a long time. "Is that what you are suggesting?"

I'm not sure what I'm suggesting. The fact that I'd originally decided to have the baby for Rose feels like a million years ago. Back then, there was no Wally. The baby was nameless, faceless. Now, the baby is inside me. It is ours. And everything feels, all at once, completely different.

"What if I were suggesting that?" I ask.

Rose closes her eyes for a short moment. "Do you really want to know what I think?" She opens her eyes.

I nod.

"All right. Honestly, the idea worries me. We both know you've had your . . . difficulties in the past." She doesn't say it explicitly. She doesn't have to. "What if something happened when you were with the baby? Babies are vulnerable, Fern. Bad things can happen, even by accident. . . ." Rose sighs. She looks like she might cry. "The only *possible* way this could work is if you had a stable, levelheaded partner. And . . . Rocco *isn't,* is he?"

I regret telling Rose about Wally's nervous breakdown. I'm not entirely sure how it happened. One minute we were eating chicken satay for dinner and talking about how the library was abolishing fines for overdue books, and the next, Rose knew everything. Her gift for getting information out of people is truly astonishing. Owen used to say she'd make a great interrogator.

"Think about it, Fern. Rocco couldn't cope with some basic business pressure. He found it so stressful that he had to leave his country, abandon his whole life and start a rudderless existence, living out of his van! What would happen if he were presented with real difficulty like disease or death? Or a baby that just wouldn't stop crying?"

I open my mouth to answer the question, then realize I have no idea. She's right, of course. I couldn't be trusted with a baby. Neither could Wally. How foolish to even consider it.

Rose stands and takes both my hands in her own. "I wish it were different, Fern. I really do."

I nod.

"I'm here for you," she says, wrapping her arms around me. "Now, don't worry. We're going to figure this whole thing out. I promise."

I hold still, waiting for the hug to end. But Rose just continues to hold me, pinning my arms to my sides. I feel like I'm imprisoned, stuck. Wearing a straitjacket.

• • •

JOURNAL OF ROSE INGRID CASTLE

Fern is pregnant. The crazy thing is this is an eventuality I've never considered. Sadistically, I can't help but think how different it would be if it were me who was pregnant. If I were suddenly carrying the baby I'd yearned for. Instead of being in damage control, we'd be celebrating. It's like the universe is playing a game with me, pushing me as hard as it can, seeing when I will break.

I should be used to these kinds of curveballs in my life. Growing up, whenever I got used to one set of circumstances, something happened to throw me off. Like after Mum broke up with Gary. For a while, things were normal again. Better than normal. Living with Mum's moods seemed a small price to pay to be free of Gary's abuse. But things didn't remain normal for long.

I'll never forget that morning when I was twelve and I woke up and heard Mum singing. *Singing!* It was too bizarre. Mornings were *always* quiet at our place. In our normal routine, Fern always woke first–her body clock was very reliable–and then she would wake me. From there, we'd creep around the house, careful not to wake Mum. Mum was bad enough after a good night's sleep, we certainly didn't want to poke the bear by waking her up.

But that morning she was *singing*!

As Fern and I slunk out of bed, even Fern was worried. My sister has always been a creature of habit, and this change to the routine didn't sit well with her. When we arrived in the kitchen, Mum beamed at us.

"Good morning, beautiful girls! Who feels like eggs?"

At twelve, I was old enough to know about alcohol and my first thought was that Mum must be drunk. Drinking didn't usually make her nicer, admittedly, but there had been a couple of times when she and one of her new friends shared a bottle of something and she'd been something resembling warm toward me (until the next morning). But "beautiful girls"? Mum never said anything like that. She occasionally made comments about our looks, but only insofar as they referenced her own. ("You take after me, Fern, tall and skinny as you are." And then, of course, "Rosie Round.") But that day, we were beautiful!

She served us eggs and we ate them in silence as she prattled on about the weather ("Lovely!"), the day ahead ("What are you girls doing at school?"), and the things we were looking forward to. Fern answered all of Mum's direct questions, agreeing that the weather looked nice. I remained suspicious.

That afternoon, when Fern and I got out of school, Mum was waiting for us. That enough was cause for alarm. Mum didn't pick us up from school—she hadn't since we were seven. Her smile did nothing to comfort me; Mum always smiled in public.

"Surprise!"

Both Fern and I walked toward her slowly. She went for Fern first, picking her up and swinging her around in a way that parents did with much younger children. Fern went so stiff it was as though Mum we spinning a metal rod. Finally, Mum let her go and took a deep, excited breath. "Girls, I have someone I'd like you to meet."

She turned and gestured toward a smiling man in jeans and a rugby jumper, leaning against a shiny silver car.

"This," she said, "is Daniel."

My blood ran cold. I knew that Mum wanted to find someone else. After she'd broken up with Gary, she got a computer and was always having Fern or me take her picture for one of those dating websites. Now, it appeared, she had found someone.

"Daniel is a friend of mine," Mum said. "We've known each other since we were babies–"

"So a long, long time," Daniel interrupted, grinning.

I glanced at Mum–if there was one thing she hated, it was people telling her she was old. But to my surprise, she laughed, a strangely pitched laugh that landed wrong somehow.

"I have been asking your mum if I could meet you for weeks, and finally she agreed," Daniel said. "You have a very protective mother!"

To look at, Daniel did not seem intimidating. He was a few years older than Mum, I guessed, with the face of a soccer coach or trusted schoolteacher. He had no mustache, which was comforting, but only slightly. He gave an impression of being . . . unpretentious. Nice. A . . . dad. The ones you saw on the telly.

"I told him I don't introduce just anyone to my girls, but as he is such an old friend–"

"Enough of the old!"

They both laughed. It was so strange. Mum even *looked* different. Her eyes danced. She looked . . . beautiful. Her hair was in a ponytail and it looked thick and shiny and she was wearing a white-spotted sundress that swished about her ankles.

"So . . . I was thinking maybe Daniel could accompany us to the playground this afternoon. What do you say, girls? It's completely up to you."

Another bizarre thing. Mum never asked our permission. About *anything.*

As for the playground, I had a handful of memories of going to the playground when we were five or six, but it had been years since Mum had taken us. She said that perverts loitered in public parks and that we must never go there.

Fern and I were silent for so long that Mum laughed. "My girls like to think these things over. They don't make rash decisions."

"You've taught them well," Daniel said.

"It's okay with me," Fern said eventually, and Daniel whooped and tried to give her a high five, but Fern just stared at his hand silently. I simply nodded, because what else was I supposed to do? I'm not sure if it was because Mum noticed my hesitation, or maybe because she didn't notice it, but as I made my way to the car, she intercepted me and started swinging me around like she'd done to Fern a few minutes earlier. I may have even drawn some comfort from the interaction had I not noticed Mum glancing over my shoulder in Daniel's direction as she swung me, making sure he was watching.

FERN

On Monday morning, I go to work as usual. After the weekend of high drama with Rose, I derive some comfort from the normalcy of it, thinking a typical day is exactly what I need. However, I am sorely let down when I arrive in the staff room to find Carmel sitting at my desk.

"It's shadow day," she says brightly. "I'm going to follow you as you work today."

I had completely forgotten about "shadow day." And though I'm not opposed to it *per se,* I fear it will present an issue when it comes to ducking off to the secret cupboard intermittently for a nap. Which is a shame, because I'm tired today.

"You don't have to perform for me, Fern," she says when I don't say anything. "You should act as you would if I weren't in the library at all. Imagine I'm out of the office and you are in charge," she says with a little laugh.

"All right," I say, when I see no viable way to protest. I place my backpack in the filing cabinet's empty bottom drawer and lock it, then quickly scan my schedule and emails. After that, I head for the floor, Carmel hurrying after me.

Out in the main library, I make my way to the children's section.

"I thought you were on the front desk this—" Carmel starts, but instead of finishing her sentence, she gives herself a little shake. "Sorry," she says. "Carry on."

I nod. My eye has already been drawn to a group of mothers in yoga pants sitting cross-legged on the floor, drinking coffee and chatting. A few meters away, their toddlers happily pull books off the shelves and drop them in piles. I make a beeline for the kids.

"Would you like me to read you a story?" I ask a little boy with red hair and pale blue eyes.

He nods eagerly as a couple of the mothers glance over and start to apologize halfheartedly for the mess. I ignore them, pick up a copy of *Incy Wincy Spider*, and sit in a small wooden chair I've grabbed from a nearby aisle, and begin reading. One by one, the other kids plant themselves at my feet. When I finish, a small girl hands me another book, and I read it. I read two more books before an elderly lady on a walking frame approaches.

"Excuse me, Fern, I'm sorry to interrupt while you're reading but I wanted to tell you how much I enjoyed *Cat's Eye.* I was utterly transported from start to finish."

The yoga mums have finished their coffee now and they begin to load their kids back into their strollers. Amid a flurry of bleary-eyed thank-yous from the mothers, I take the opportunity to stand, and Carmel, who has been sitting quietly nearby, does the same.

"I thought you'd like it, Mrs. Stevens," I say. "Now that I have earned your trust, would you consider reading Margaret Atwood's

2000 novel, *The Blind Assassin*? Follow me, I'll see if we have a copy in."

Mrs. Stevens had been turned off by the title *The Blind Assassin,* and refused to read it, so I'd had to lure her into the delights of Margaret Atwood the back way. I was still hopeful that she might enjoy *Alias Grace* or even *The Handmaid's Tale* if she was introduced slowly. "Ah, here it is. Why don't I borrow this for you right now?"

The day goes quickly and most of the time I don't even notice Carmel hovering. It's rather nice, not even having to check my schedule for where I need to be. I simply roam the floor and go where I'm needed. To my surprise, Carmel doesn't stop me, not even once. She is a true shadow.

At the end of the day, she sits on the edge of my desk and lets out a long sigh.

"Wow. I never realized what a gift we had in the library."

I replay the sentence in my head, trying to make sense of what she is saying. Still, I come up blank.

"You, Fern," she explains. "*You* are the gift."

Unlike the shadow analogy, which I had come to respect, the gift analogy bears little logic. I find myself with questions—if I am the gift, who is the giver? And who is the receiver? And what is the occasion? But rather than help Carmel understand the failing in her logic, I decide to let it go. After all, Carmel has been a faithful shadow and hasn't once brought up the photocopiers, which as far as I am concerned is a win.

At the dot of five o'clock, I place my backpack on my shoulders and start the walk home. It's my practice to walk home in silence, preferring my quiet thoughts to an audiobook as I wind down for the day. The evening is mild and there are people about, jogging, walking in groups of two or three, or pushing bulky strollers all over the pavement. I even pass a pregnant woman, carrying hand weights and walking briskly. It strikes me as ironic that it is at exactly the moment I pass her that my phone beeps with a text from Rose.

I have made an appointment for you at the family-planning clinic tomorrow morning.

I still haven't told Rose she is the reason this baby exists, despite plenty of opportunities. It's not that I think I can keep the baby myself—I understand now that that wouldn't be what's best for the baby. But as for deciding to hand him or her over to Rose? That might take a little more time. After hours of discussing my options over the weekend, Rose and I had decided it would be prudent to visit a family-planning clinic. I am aware, of course, that the family-planning clinic is not a place to go to plan one's family, but rather, a place most people go for the opposite reason—to *undo* an unplanned family.

"Just a visit," Rose had said, "we don't need to decide anything right away."

And so, as I turn onto my street, I text a reply to Rose: *Okay.*

When I reach my block of flats, Wally's van is parked outside, and the back doors are wide open. Wally is sitting in his folding chair with his computer on his lap and, despite the sunshine, his bobble hat is perched high on his head. He grins when he sees me coming.

"Welcome home," he says, reaching for his second fold-up chair, which is tucked into a compartment in the back of the van. He unfolds it and I sink into the canvas seat and, for a glorious moment, close my eyes. I am usually on my feet most of the day but today I feel more tired than usual.

After a deep breath, I say, "Do you want children, Wally?"

I open my eyes.

Wally doesn't seem surprised by the question, but over the course of our short relationship, I have asked him a number of investigative questions as part of (I assume) the normal exploratory process of getting to know someone. Off the top of my head, I can remember asking: "At what age did you start walking?," "Do you recall ever believing that you could jump off a roof and fly?," and "Why do you think so many people believe in religion?" On no occasion has he ever expressed any concern or issue with my questions. Nor does he now. As always, he treats my question with the utmost respect, taking the time to sift through his innermost thoughts before delivering his answer, verdict, or opinion.

"No."

I feel it in my stomach first, a slight tension, like a gentle punch or squeeze.

"A number of reasons have led me to this conclusion," Wally continues, leaning farther back in his seat and winging his elbows behind his head. "For one thing, mental illness. Studies have shown there is a strong genetic link, and anxiety is likely handed down through generations. I would feel awful for inflicting that on a helpless kid." He frowns off into the distance. "Population growth is another of my concerns. People don't understand how bad an issue overpopulation is. Fishless oceans are predicted by 2048! Our planet just does not have the capacity to provide food, water, and adequate shelter for the population numbers we are expecting in the future."

He shakes his head sadly. "Finally, the world is not always a kind place, especially if you don't fit the stereotypical mold of what it is to be normal. As you know, it's hard to be a person on the fringes of society. It's hard for me, even as an arguable success. Imagine how hard it would be for a child, particularly a child who doesn't go on to enjoy a level of success in his or her given field. I've already gone through the hardship of being an outlier. I'm not sure I could do it again as a parent."

As usual, I am impressed by Wally's response. It is a good argument, well made. So often in life, people speak in riddles, weighing in on both sides of an argument with pros and cons rather than picking a side. Wally doesn't do this. It's one of the reasons I like him so much.

So, that's it, I think. We agree. A baby is a bad idea.

"Any other questions?" he asks cheerfully.

"That's it, I think."

"Well, I'm just finishing up my work," he says. "Do you want to sit and read for a bit?"

I shake my head. "I have some household administration to attend to."

I think I say it too loudly and brightly, because Wally gives me a puzzled expression. He keeps watching me all the way to my door. I know, because I watch him back. I'm very pleased with myself because I manage to make it all the way into my flat before the tears start to fall.

The next day, I trudge to the bus stop. Rose was supposed to drive me to the family-planning clinic, but she'd texted a few minutes ago to say she has been held up and could I make my own way there? I don't mind getting the bus, though I would have appreciated a little warning. Looking up the schedule, walking to the bus stop—these are all things I like to plan for in my schedule, and Rose knows this. It makes me feel an illogical irritation with her. Illogical, because Rose had no need to be taking me to the clinic *in the first place.* Still, the illogical irritation is there. But illogical irritation is something one is allowed to have with one's sister. I have read enough books about sisters to know that is true.

On the bus, perhaps as a subconscious act of rebellion, I sit in the seat reserved for people with mobility issues and pregnant women. It will be the one time, I figure, that I'll qualify for this seat. It is peak hour and raining, so it's not long before the seats fill up around me. After a few stops, another pregnant woman gets on, this one at least seven or eight months along. I find myself staring at the woman's round belly.

"Excuse me," the woman says, holding her belly. "Do you mind?"

I look at her. "Do I mind what?"

She gestures to her belly. "Um . . . it's just . . . could I . . . ?"

"She wants to sit down," a man calls from a few rows back.

I turn to look at the man, who I notice is making no move to leave his own seat.

"Get up, for Christ's sake," he barks. "That seat is for pregnant ladies!"

"I'm pregnant too," I say when I turn back to the girl, but so quietly I can barely hear myself.

"Get up!" someone else calls. "What is the matter with you?"

The driver pulls over and turns around to see what the commotion is all about. "This woman won't get up for the pregnant lady," the man from the back of the bus says.

The driver looks at me, then at the visibly pregnant woman. "Those seats are reserved for pregnant or disabled passengers, love," he says gently.

"I'm pregnant too," I say louder, standing. My voice sounds funny, as if something has caught in my throat. To my horror, I realize I am crying. I lower my chin and press the button for the next stop.

I alight from the bus, even though we are several stops before my destination, and walk the rest of the way to the clinic in the rain.

I am soaking wet when I arrive at the clinic. The clinic is behind an innocuous shop front alongside an optometrist and a barber. I've walked fourteen blocks, during which time the rain has not relented for a single second. Still, despite the unexpected bus trip and the walk, I still arrive five minutes early for the appointment.

Rose does not. When I fail to see her standing out the front, I feel a distinct note of disappointment. Subconsciously, I'd already handed over the responsibility of announcing my arrival at the desk and filling out any forms to Rose. Instead, I let myself inside, into a small waiting room.

"May I help you?" the receptionist says to me. She's a grandmotherly sort, probably in her midsixties, with graying brown hair and lime-green eyeglasses on a chain. I ignore her and take a seat. The woman's eyes follow me, but she leaves me be, her eyes returning to her computer after a second or two.

The room is about half full. I notice a pair of teenage girls, seemingly without a guardian; a girl of around eighteen years of age with her mother; and a couple who look to be in their midthirties, both weepy-eyed and silent. All of them leaf through magazines, perhaps to distract themselves or to blend in. I don't reach for a magazine. It's never seemed wise to touch communal property at a doctor's office, given the fact that they are little more than conduits for germs. Then again, this doctor's office is a little different from most, and the patients are no more likely to be carrying germs than anyone in an office building. They, like me, are here for a different reason. It's funny how awareness of this slides in and out of focus. One minute, I'm fine, and the next, it hits like a sudden, somber surprise.

As the clock ticks over to 10:01 A.M., Rose comes bursting through the door, wearing a plum-colored mohair jumper that makes me itchy just to look at. Though she is carrying an umbrella, her hair is soaking wet. She looks like a different person. "Fern! There you are!"

She is surprisingly loud, and everyone in the waiting room looks up from their magazines. The woman behind the desk peers at us over the top of her glasses. "Fern Castle?" she says.

Rose looks at me. "You haven't told them your name yet?"

"No," I say, much quieter. It's not like Rose to make a spectacle.

Rose kneels on the floor in front of me. Everyone else in the waiting room looks back at their magazines, pretending not to pay attention to us.

"Good," she says. "Because . . . I had a thought this morning. It might sound crazy. Okay, it *is* crazy."

"What is crazy?" I ask. I look at the pieces of hair stuck to her face and wonder if it is Rose herself.

"It's just . . . this morning I realized I'd never forgive myself if I didn't ask . . ."

One of the teenage girls isn't even pretending to read her magazine anymore. Instead, she outright stares at us. I stare right back at her, and I am rewarded when she finally looks away.

"Ask me what?"

Rose looks around, as if only now noticing the other people in our immediate proximity. "Uh . . . maybe we should talk somewhere more private?"

"But what about—" I start to say, but it's too late. Rose is already on her feet on the way to the reception desk to tell the receptionist that we won't be requiring our appointment today.

Rose takes me to a café not far away from the clinic and orders two cups of tea and a scone with jam and cream without even consulting me. It's still raining, the kind of rain that fills up the gutters and makes awnings bulge. It hadn't been forecast, this rain. Everything about today has been a surprise.

When the scone arrives, Rose pushes it in front of me.

"So . . . this morning, I had an epiphany."

I pick up the scone and examine it. There doesn't seem to be an efficient way to eat it without causing a spillage of jam and cream. In the end, I just lean forward so the spillage will land directly on the plate.

"I thought to myself, here I am desperate to have a baby . . . while you are pregnant with an unwanted baby. Then it came to me! What if *I* kept your baby?"

My mouth is full of scone. I contemplate spitting it out but decide there is no graceful way of doing that, so instead I hold a napkin to my mouth and chew quickly.

"Just think about it, Fern. I know it's a lot to take in, so please don't answer me yet. I just thought . . . maybe this is a way your baby could have the loving family it deserves. I spoke to Owen this morning, and—"

I swallow. "Owen knows?"

Rose looks guilty. "I hope you don't mind. But when I suggested that he and I might raise the baby, he was over the moon. I shouldn't have done that without speaking to you first."

I sit back in my chair. I like Owen a lot. The idea that the baby could be raised by two loving parents, two *neurotypical* loving parents . . . it's the start to life that every child deserved.

"I know that two parents isn't everything," Rose says. "But . . . I often think about what would have happened to us if we had two parents in the picture. When Mum overdosed, we would have had a backup. I would love to give the baby that."

"I'd love that too," I say.

Rose looks like she is holding her breath, waiting for me to make a decision. But there isn't really a decision to make. It is, after all, what I'd intended in the first place.

"Okay," I say.

Rose's eyes fill up with tears. Then she throws her arms around me in another of those straitjacket hugs, only this time the wet mohair jumper gets up my nose, so I feel like I'm choking.

• • •

JOURNAL OF ROSE INGRID CASTLE

Daniel, we found out, was a commercial pilot. He had been married to Billy's mother, a woman named Trish, for ten years before they divorced, and they were still on friendly terms. I knew this because Fern asked Daniel about it. Fern had an amazing way of being able to ask these kinds of questions without upsetting people. Even Mum didn't seem to mind when Fern asked why they broke up.

Daniel smiled, like this wasn't rude—like it was, in fact, a very good question. "I travel a lot for work, being a pilot. I think Trish got sick of being alone all the time. And I, well, I wasn't always the best husband, let's put it that way. We're much better as co-parents than we were as husband and wife."

It was funny the way he spoke about Trish. With fondness! He never used the kinds of words Mum used to talk about our dad. *Deadbeat. Loser. Dickhead.* I wondered how Mum felt about Daniel talking about Trish fondly. Outwardly, she didn't seem bothered by it, but I knew Mum better than that. It would be driving her crazy. But she was on her best behavior around Daniel. She was her same old self when he wasn't around, though, and as strange as it sounds, I preferred it this way. The new, uber-nice Mum was unsettling for sure, but the constant back-and-forth from nice to horrible gave me whiplash.

I was on guard around Daniel at first, naturally. Reassuringly, he was much less interested in Fern and me than Gary had been. He was polite enough—asking about our day at school and appearing genuinely interested in the answer—but he seemed to be far more interested in conversation with Mum than he was with us. He never tickled us or massaged us, or even touched us at all, beyond the offer of a high five every now and again. He did, however, talk a lot about Billy. Billy, Daniel's son, was fourteen, and it was clear how much Daniel adored him. Fern and I wanted to meet Billy, and Daniel kept saying we would "soon." I got the feeling he was waiting for something—but I never knew what.

It took six months before the meeting finally happened. By that time, we were planning a camping trip, at Daniel's suggestion. "Three or four days together," he said, "so the kids can bond." Mum seemed overjoyed about this, though she'd never showed any interest in camping previously. Fern also seemed happy and immediately started reading a book about camping. I was the only one who seemed to be bracing for something bad. Why was it that I was always the only one bracing?

The fact that we didn't have any camping gear didn't seem to be an obstacle; Daniel simply suggested we go to the shops. I'll admit, I was excited about that. Mum never had money to buy much other than food at the shops, and when we needed something else essential, like clothes or crockery, we got it secondhand at an op shop. But even more exciting than buying something new was the fact that Billy was coming with us to buy the tent. Daniel had told us a lot about him by then, and Billy had built up an almost mythical status in my mind. Not to mention the fact that I was twelve at the time and boys were fast becoming something that interested me.

When we pulled up outside Billy's mum's very nice house, Billy was waiting on the manicured nature strip. He wore jeans, a hoodie, and a baseball cap. His head was down and he was chewing a fingernail aggressively. His mum was by his side with her hand on his shoulder and she waved at the approaching car.

"Hello!" she said to us when Billy opened the door to get in. She looked both Fern and me in the eye. "I'm Trish, Billy's mum. You must be the twins! Let me guess–you're Fern and you're Rose?"

Fern and I stared at her as if she was an alien. We had never met a woman like Trish before. She was different from Mum–fatter and frecklier, with a round face and a gummy smile. Another difference was her obvious adoration of Billy–before he got into the car, she planted several kisses on his cheek, which he wiped off as Fern leaned over and touched her bracelet against mine. I frowned at her. *What is it?*

But she kept her gaze on Billy.

"Be good for your dad," Billy's mum said as he slid into the back seat, taking his place beside me.

Billy had a round face, green eyes, and hair that was swept over his face. He grinned at me. "Hey."

"Hey," I replied.

"What kind of tent are we going to get, kids?" Daniel said as we began driving.

"I've taken the liberty of doing some research," Fern said. She had her camping book in her lap, as well as a handful of flyers from camping stores. "For a family of five, hands down the best option is the Montana 12. It features near-vertical sides and a very spacious three-room interior with zippered dividers and a third removable wall so you can further divide one of the end rooms into two smaller compartments. It also features a large front awning with built-in sidewalls that allows you to create a big verandah at the front of your tent. Or, if we want separate tents, I have recommendations for those too."

"Someone has done her research," Daniel said.

"Glad someone around here does," Billy said. Daniel laughed good-naturedly. It was hard not to be buoyed by the sense of camaraderie in the car. It looked like Billy and Daniel were going to stick around, at least for a little while. That had to be a good thing. Still, as I heard Mum's tinkling laugh I felt that familiar sense of dread. *Something is going to ruin this,* I thought. If there's one thing I knew about Mum, it was that she had a gift for destroying everything good.

FERN

For the next week, Rose is around constantly. She shows up in the morning to offer me a ride to work. She appears in the evening with a homemade meal. She drops off flyers about prenatal yoga and hypnobirthing. She phones and texts on an hourly basis simply "to check in." In the past, Rose always respected my desire for forewarning—always having a scheduled plan, never showing up without announcing it first. Not anymore. But, as it turns out, her visits are fortuitous, because just about every time Rose shows up, she averts a crisis—confiscating soft cheese and deli meat from the fridge (which apparently was liable to give me listeria and kill the baby) or dropping in when I was at work and finding I had left my oil burner on (which was strange as I rarely use my oil burner anymore). "It's a good thing I was here," she always says. The one time I can count on Rose to leave me alone is when I go to visit Mum. So I feel a strange sense of relief that Thursday as I stride through the automatic doors of Sun Meadows.

I take the stairs up to Mum's room. Teresa, Mum's speech therapist, is there again, and Mum is in her usual chair, her tray table beside her, a chocolate iced donut sitting on it alongside a cup of water. I watch from the door for a minute.

Teresa is holding open what looks like a children's picture storybook.

"The . . . cow . . . jumps . . . over . . . the . . . moon," Mum says.

"Very good!" Teresa says.

"Thank . . . you."

"Very, very good," I say, from the door.

Mum looks at me and beams. "Pop-pet."

"Great timing, as usual," Teresa says. "We're finishing up. She's doing a great job. Just before you arrived, she told me she was thirsty! I brought her a drink of water, and she asked for ice! By next week, she'll be reading novels aloud!"

"That seems a stretch," I say.

Teresa chuckles as I sit down on a chair beside Mum. Mum has a bit of chocolate on her lip and I lean forward to wipe it off. "It's . . . good . . . to see . . . you," Mum says.

Teresa gives me the thumbs-up gesture. She waits for a moment, as if expecting something in response, so I mimic her gesture. She grins, and I focus my attention back on Mum.

"It's good to see you too," I say.

It's true, it is good to see her—especially today when I'm feeling all twisted up inside. When you feel like that, there really is nothing quite like seeing your mum.

Mum has always been a good listener, even before the accident. On the odd occasion, she could even be wise. I have a memory of talking to her once after being excluded from a birthday party in grade three. I didn't want to go, obviously. Parties were always loud with music and bright colors and squealing. Worst of all, there were almost always balloons (balloons ranked high on my list of terrors, given their tendency to pop at unpredictable times and elicit a loud bang). But every other girl in the class had been invited, including Rose, so I was upset.

"I understand why you're upset," Mum had said. "It's one thing deciding not to go, but it's quite another being told you can't."

It had been indescribably gratifying to be understood like that. I yearn for the same sort of wisdom from her today.

"I'm pregnant, Mum," I say.

I look at her to see if she registers this. And I see, from the way her forehead wrinkles, that she does.

"Remember the boy I told you about?" I say, and she nods. "Well, one thing led to another and . . . I'm pregnant. Anyway, obviously I can't look after a baby myself. So . . . I'm going to give the baby to Rose."

I say it fast, perhaps too fast, as it comes out a little wobbly. But I know Mum understands, because her eyes widen.

"Rose can't have a baby," I explain. "She has bad ovaries. Premature ovarian aging, it's called. And I'm pregnant. So it makes sense that I should give my baby to her. Right?"

"Why can't . . . you . . ."

I lower my voice. "You know why I can't keep it, Mum. It would be . . . dangerous."

Mum still doesn't speak, but after a minute or two I notice her becoming red in the face. For a second, I think she's choking. I hand her the cup of water, but she waves it away. She opens her mouth and chokes something out, and though I'm straining to listen, I can't make it out. "What? What did you say, Mum?"

She stares at me very intently, even though she knows I prefer less eye contact, to make sure I'm listening and says, "Your baby. Don't . . . give it . . . to Rose."

The next afternoon I am reshelving books at the library and thinking about what Mum said.

"Don't give my baby to Rose?" I'd repeated, looking for confirmation.

But Mum just shook her head, which might have meant I was right . . . or wrong. She'd said a few things after that, but nothing that made much sense. It was like she regressed in front of my eyes. As such, I suspect it would be silly to give much credence to what she said.

"Can I get some help over here?"

I glance up. The man who is speaking, an elderly chap with an extraordinarily large head covered in liver spots, doesn't bother to get up from the computer where he is stationed.

"What is the problem?" I call, from several meters away.

"My granddaughter set me up with an email address," he bellows. "But I don't know how to check if I have any mail!"

I glance around for Gayle or Linda or Trevor . . . even Carmel.

They've all disappeared. Traitors. The man crosses his hairy, meaty forearms in front of his chest, and glares at me. I wonder if it's too late to make up an excuse and walk off.

I sigh. "What's your email address?"

"I don't know!" He throws one hairy arm in the air. "Something 'at' something dot com. Sounds ridiculous to me, quite frankly."

"Right. Well . . . we do run introductory computer courses on Tuesday evenings . . ."

"I play bridge on Tuesday evenings."

"Or you can schedule a private lesson? For a time of your choosing."

"Perfect," he says. "I choose now."

He stares me down. I stare right back. This old guy doesn't know who he's dealing with.

"Fern?"

I turn, sagging in relief. Carmel has turned up at the eleventh hour.

"Ah, Carmel. This gentleman is having some trouble with his email."

"Someone is here to see you," Carmel says, her eyes flicking to the entrance of the library. I glance over and see Wally standing there, carrying a large bunch of sunflowers.

My heart skips a beat.

"Are you going to help with the email or not?" the old man barks. "I don't have all day!"

Wally lifts his hand in a wave. He is wearing a navy suit. It must be new. I've seen him in a charcoal-colored suit before which was also very nice, but not as tight in the trousers. His hair is also combed with a side part, which looks very dapper, very old-Hollywood.

"Fern, you've overstayed your shift," Carmel says. "Why don't you get going and I'll help this gentleman with the computer?"

I look at the clock. "I haven't overstayed my shift. I'm closing. And there's twenty minutes until—"

"Fern," she says firmly. "You. Have. Overstayed. Your. Shift."

Carmel sounds most bizarre, like a kind of serial-killer robot. Her stare is also uncomfortably intense. My instinct is to ask if she's all right, and also to correct her again as I most certainly haven't overstayed my shift, but I have grave fears this may send her into some sort of episode. And so, I acquiesce.

"Oh. Kay," I reply. "Thank. You. Carmel."

Wally's van is in the parking lot and once we reach it, he opens the passenger door for me, a gallant gesture which makes me feel rather good. I climb inside and place the sunflowers beside me on the bench seat. They are wrapped in brown paper with a small water-filled plastic bag tied around the stems to keep them hydrated, which is a rather innovative design. No one has ever given me flowers before. To be honest, I've always felt they were a little indulgent, and I've always been fearful that the smell would be cloying. I am surprised to find that, on this occasion, I couldn't be more pleased with them and, even in the restricted space of the van, the smell is reasonably inoffensive.

"Thank you for the flowers," I say when Wally gets into the driver's side of the van.

"You're welcome," Wally says, smiling at a spot over my shoulder. "Sunflowers haven't got a strong scent. In fact, the florist said unscented, but I detected a faint odor."

I conjure an image of Wally in the florist pointing at posies, sniffing each bunch and shaking his head until he declared the sunflowers the perfect bunch. It's a happy image. It makes me smile.

"Now, if you'll allow it, I'd like to take you to dinner," he says.

Instantly, my florist fantasy dissipates, replaced by another, less appealing one. Wally and me in a crowded restaurant, shouting to be heard over the music. Pungent dishes and intoxicated diners. I open my mouth to explain to Wally that I can't possibly go out for dinner, that restaurants are among the worst places for overstimulation, but he holds up a hand, silencing me.

"Hear me out! A guy that I know runs a Greek restaurant in Windsor. They are hosting a private function tonight in their upstairs room, so the main dining room is closed. He's agreed to open it, just for us."

I frown. "What do you mean?"

"We will be the *only* ones in the restaurant. We can choose the lighting, the music, the food—everything."

Slowly, it starts to sink in, what Wally has done. Not just the flowers, but all of it. An entire evening—all coordinated to be perfect for *me.* It is an entirely unprecedented level of thoughtful.

"Why are you crying?" he asks.

I reach up and touch my face, which is indeed wet. "I . . . I'm just a little overwhelmed, I think. This is so lovely. A restaurant. I didn't think I'd ever be able to go to a restaurant."

In my peripheral vision, I see Wally smile softly.

"What does one even wear to a restaurant?" I ask. I gesture to my denim overalls. "Can I go like this?"

"You could," he says. "But I brought you something that I thought you might like to wear instead. . . ." He reaches into the back seat and brings back a white plastic bag.

"There's more?"

I reach into the bag and retrieve a long halter-neck dress with diagonal stripes. Each stripe is a unique color—not one is doubled up. It must include every single color and shade on earth.

"I saw this in a shop and it . . . it made me think of you," Wally says.

"It is the most beautiful dress I have ever seen."

I change in the back of the van. The dress fits, though the fabric is a little scratchy. It matches perfectly with the rainbows on my sneakers.

"Beautiful," Wally says when I appear in the front seat. On a whim, I swish the skirt a little bit to show off, but I immediately feel silly and stop.

Wally drives to the restaurant carefully adhering to the road signs and speed limits, which I appreciate. As we drive, I take a minute to reflect on the fact that I'm going on a proper date! To a restaurant! It is like a dream, except I've never had dreams like this. It's like the books I've read, the happy ones, where things work out.

We pull up in front of the restaurant, but before I can open the car door, Wally places a hand on my arm. "There's one more thing." He leans over and opens the glove compartment. "These are noise canceling and Bluetooth connected, so we can hear each other," he says, handing me a pair of giant headphones that look like earmuffs. "And these . . ." He hands me a pair of swimming goggles in pink and purple and aqua and pulls out another pair of bright green goggles for himself. "I think are fairly self-explanatory." He pulls the green ones over his face. "What do you think?"

"You look like an aviator frog," I say. I pull on my own goggles. "What about me?"

"A rainbow aviator frog."

I smile.

As promised, the restaurant is quiet and the lighting is low. We are greeted by a waitress with a nose ring, purple hair, and a tattoo of a dragon creeping out of the chest area of her white button-down shirt . . . and yet she stares at *us* when we arrive.

"Reservation for Wally," Wally says.

I snort.

The waitress leads us to a table set with a white tablecloth and bright blue chairs. As we sit down, the waitress hands each of us a laminated menu and fills our water glasses from a porcelain jug. The restaurant smells of garlic and meat.

"Are you okay?" Wally says.

I nod. "It's lovely."

Wally looks so funny in his goggles, I let out another snort.

"What?" Wally says.

"Nothing."

The waitress brings over pita bread and tzatziki and tells us she'll be back in a minute to take our order. I dive into the bread before it's even hit the table. This pregnancy hunger is no joke. I feel like I could eat every carbohydrate in the place.

"Did you miss lunch?" Wally asks as I dip my second piece of pita.

I am grateful to have a mouthful, so I can just smile and shrug. I can't tell him, of course, that I missed neither lunch nor afternoon tea. I can't tell him, because then he might ask more questions and find out that I'm pregnant.

As I swallow my next mouthful, I become aware of sounds drifting down the stairs—soft music, chairs scraping, intermittent laughter. It's not overwhelming, but I can hear it even with my earphones on. I'm about to ask Wally if he knows what is happening up there, when the waitress appears to take our order.

Wally and I remove our headphones long enough to order a lamb souvlaki (for Wally) and baked Greek fries with meatballs (for me). We also order bread and hummus, olives and water. Music starts up above, slightly louder than before. I replace my headphones.

"So . . . ," I say to Wally. "Was there a particular purpose to this evening or was it just . . ." I stumble on the juvenile-sounding word. ". . . a date?"

"As a matter of fact, there was a purpose. A celebration. I've created an ad hoc version of FollowUp."

Ad hoc version. I fear I ought to understand this reference. Over the past few weeks, Wally has explained the process of creating and launching an app, but each time, despite the clarity and simplicity of his explanations, I invariably found myself tuning out after a minute or two. And the constant nausea has done nothing to assist my concentration.

"It means the app is ready for testing," Wally explains. "I've spent the last few weeks coding and I think it's going to work! With Shout!, it took us five times as long to get to this point, but I've been so motivated and a lot of that is to do with you being in my life. And, so, I wanted to do something special for you."

Wally smiles at me and it becomes entirely undeniably clear that I cannot break up with Wally. The fact that I thought I could feels like mere madness.

"Fern," Wally says. "What is it?"

"I have to tell you something," I say.

"Damn," Wally says, removing his headphones. "I can't hear you. I think my battery ran out."

I take off my own headphones and place them on the table. The music upstairs is louder now, and I can hear stomping on the ceiling above.

"I said . . . I have to tell you something."

Wally leans forward, his face a mask of concern. "What is it?"

I open my mouth. And a bomb goes off, right there in the restaurant.

I drop to the floor. The noise is earsplitting. I clamber under the table, covering my head with my hands. I've barely recovered from the first explosion before there is another. And another. Bizarrely, music continues to play. I search for Wally under the table, gripping his hands as I hear another explosion. I wrap my arms around myself and rock back and forth, waiting for it to end.

"I'm sorry," Wally says, once he's bundled me outside. "I had no idea it was a wedding upstairs."

I am still shaking so much I can't stand up straight. The terrifying, smashing noise reverberates in my head.

"They were smashing plates. It's customary at Greek weddings. I didn't think of it."

Plates. That's what that deafening noise was? People smashing plates?

"I'm so sorry." Wally looks like he might cry. "I thought I'd thought of everything."

The waitress comes out of the restaurant with paper napkins and a glass of water.

"Is she all right?" she says to Wally. "Should I call a doctor?"

Wally brushes a strand of hair behind my ear. "Do you need a doctor?"

"No," I say.

The waitress nods, and after a minute goes back inside. Wally remains by my side. "What can I get you?" he says. "How can I help?"

I take a deep breath and look at him.

"Can you please call Rose?"

Rose screeches to the curb so fast that Wally and I have to lift our feet from the gutter to avoid getting run over. She gets out and slams the car door, shooting a dark glare at Wally.

"What the hell happened?"

Wally and I stagger to our feet. I had finally stopped shaking, but I suddenly start again. Rose looks so angry.

"We went out for dinner," I say.

"In a *restaurant*? You know you can't handle that environment." She looks at Wally. "You know she has sensory-processing issues, don't you? She's hypersensitive to sound and light and touch."

"And smell," I add.

She looks back at me, as if seeing me for the first time. "What on earth are you wearing?"

"Goggles. There was no one else at the restaurant—"

"Well, evidently there was! Jesus. Fern, let's just get out of here." Rose looks into the restaurant, at the waitress who is having a good gawk at us through the window. "Have you paid the bill?"

I look at Wally.

"Not yet," he says. "I was . . . distracted. I'll do it now."

"For god's sake, I'll do it." Rose stalks into the restaurant, unzipping her purse. "The last thing we need is for you to be arrested."

Wally stands up, but by the time he is on his feet she is already gone. He looks at me. "I'm so sorry, Fern."

"No, I'm sorry."

He shakes his head. "I . . . I had no idea it would be so . . ."

"Difficult."

"Yeah. Difficult."

There is a brief silence when no cars drive past.

"Why can't I just be normal?" I whisper.

"You are. It's everyone else who are weirdos."

We smile at each other sadly. After a moment, Rose comes out of the restaurant. "Say your good-byes," she says, taking me by the arm and putting me into the passenger seat of her car. It feels so different from Wally opening the door for me earlier. Then, I felt like a woman. Now I feel like a child.

As we pull away, Wally gives me a weak smile. I can't help but smile back. He is still wearing his goggles.

• • •

JOURNAL OF ROSE INGRID CASTLE

We drove to the campsite in Daniel's car, listening to the Traveling Wilburys. Fern and I didn't know the band, but we picked up the words quickly and it was actually kind of fun, all of us singing along like that. Daniel had sweets in the console that he passed back at intervals to Fern and Billy, who ate them eagerly. He also had cans of Coca-Cola. I still remember him holding out the red can for one of us to grab and Fern and me staring at it. We'd never drunk Coke. It wasn't just because of my diabetes. Mum said it was full of chemicals that would rot our teeth and give us cancer. But there was Daniel, offering us a can, waggling it impatiently, waiting for one of us to take it.

I could have blamed my blood sugar, but something told me that would be the wrong thing to do. I saw Fern open her mouth to say something—probably that Mum didn't like us drinking Coke—so I quickly beat her to it.

"Thank you, Daniel," I jumped in, taking the can.

Mum caught my eye and I knew I did good. Different rules for different situations, that was her mantra.

Still, neither of us drank the Coke.

We arrived at the campsite before dark and unpacked in a flurry "before we lose the light." Like the drive, I quite enjoyed it–the feeling of being part of something, working together as a team. Us against the light.

Fern and I set up our own tent with impressive speed, mostly because Fern had memorized the instructions. We finished so quickly that we were also able to help Mum and Daniel pitch their tent (which was much more complex) and then collect a huge pile of kindling before dark. (Billy set up his own tent, then sat on a log while the rest of us worked.) Daniel commented that Fern and I were "born for camping" while Billy was "born for laziness," and Mum smiled a lot–even when Daniel wasn't looking.

Once the tents were set up, Daniel cooked some sausages and corn on the cob over a little camping stove and we ate them with bread sitting around the campfire. Afterward, Mum and Daniel disappeared into their tent, so Fern and I went to ours. We had just got settled when we heard the rustling of twigs outside the tent. We didn't even have time to exchange a glance before the zip lowered and Billy's face appeared in the gap. "Anyone for poker?"

Fern and I broke into a chorus of gasps and shushes. "We'll get in trouble!" I cried, horrified and, if I'm honest, a bit exhilarated. Mum and Daniel's tent was just meters away and Mum's hearing was ridiculous. At home, Fern and I had learned how to have entirely soundless conversations by mouthing words for this exact reason. But if Billy was afraid of being reprimanded, he hid it well. He crawled into our tent, a torch in one hand, a deck of cards in the other.

"They won't hear us. They've already sunk a bottle and a half of wine." He reached outside the tent and retrieved a can of beer. "But they didn't drink this."

"What are you doing?" I whispered. "Put that back!"

He opened the can and took a swig. Fern and I were scandalized.

"They'll know," I cried. "You'll get into trouble."

He shrugged. "So, are we playing?"

I looked at Fern, whose eyes were cautious.

"How do you play?" I asked.

Fern knew, of course, but I didn't have the slightest idea.

"I'll teach you," Billy said, taking another swig from the can. "We can be on the same team. Scooch up."

Billy crawled over to sit beside me and gave me a conspiratorial wink. His sense of fun was infectious. As we played, his wrist rested on my knee so we could both see the cards. I'd never been so close to a boy in all my life. Periodically, he leaned closer and whispered something to me–the rules, or whether or not he thought Fern was bluffing–and I smelled his scent, a mix of spearmint chewing gum, beer, and smoke from the campfire. He couldn't convince either of us to try the beer, so he polished off the can on his own. He didn't even slur his words.

Billy and I lost the game of poker that night, but I didn't care one bit. For a couple of hours, it felt like I'd tripped and fallen into someone else's life–someone with loving parents, family holidays, and poker games. Someone who knew what it was like to feel happy. And, sometimes, when your world has been filled with fear and anguish, that feeling, even if fleeting, is all you need to carry on.

FERN

Mercifully, Rose doesn't say much on the way home. I don't either. Even if I wanted to, I couldn't have, because that incredible sense of fatigue that always follows a sensory meltdown overcomes me. I feel like my eyelids have weights on them. I let them close and lean my head against the cool window. I'm starting to drift off when the car comes to a stop.

"We're home," Rose says softly.

I open my eyes. "No, we're not."

"Okay," she says. "We're at *my* home."

"I'm exhausted, Rose," I say, although it must be no later than eight o'clock. "I want to go home."

Rose opens her door. "You can sleep here tonight."

"No, thanks."

"Fern," she snaps. "After everything that has gone on tonight, please do me a favor and don't argue."

I cross my arms. I don't like sleeping at other people's houses as a rule, not even Rose's. I never sleep well. Admittedly, I don't exactly sleep well anywhere, and it's worse than usual lately as I have to get up multiple times a night to pee. But tonight, especially after everything that's happened, I just want my own bed.

"Fern. I don't have time for this. I had back-to-back meetings today and was only just on my way home when I get the call that you've had a spectacular meltdown and I have to come and rescue you. Don't get me wrong, I'm happy to do it, but I'm tired and the least you can do is come inside." She gets out of the car.

"If you're too tired to drive me," I say, also getting out, "I'll walk home—"

"Fern Elizabeth Castle!" Her tone is sharp, like a schoolteacher's. "You're staying here, and that's final."

"It's not final. I'm an adult, Rose. I can choose where I sleep."

Rose raises her eyebrows. "If you're an adult, why do I need to be your round-the-clock carer?"

Rose and I face off for several moments. That's when I notice what she is wearing. "If you were on your way home from work, why are you wearing leggings?"

"Really, Fern?" Rose stares at me. "After I've driven across town to rescue you in the middle of the night, you want to talk about what I'm wearing?"

I want to tell her that yes, I do want to talk about that, but I can't because Rose turns and stalks into the house before I have the chance. I remain where I am for several moments, huffing and sighing, before finally following her into the house.

As suspected, I sleep badly. Among other things, the sheets on Rose's spare bed are some sort of polyester blend that makes my skin crawl (I make a note to talk to her about it tomorrow). But the sheets aren't the main reason for my insomnia. The main reason is that I can't stop replaying last night, reliving the horror over and over again. Me crawling under the table, covering my head with my hands. Cowering like a child. Having to be rescued by my sister while on a date. It's little wonder Rose treats me like a child. That's exactly how I'm behaving. What on earth must Wally think?

Around 6:00 A.M., I give up on sleep, pull on my rainbow dress, and head to the living room. Rose is already up, sipping a cup of tea on the couch in her dressing gown.

"You're awake early," she says.

"I don't sleep well at other people's places," I say, stretching my neck. Even though I told her this last night, I feel it bears repeating.

"That dress looks itchy," Rose says. "Polyester?"

"Yes. Like your sheets."

"I can give you a T-shirt and shorts if you like?"

"No, thanks," I say. Unlike the sheets, the dress is worth the itch.

Rose sits forward on the couch and places her mug on the coffee table. "Tea?"

I'm about to decline but then I realize I won't get out of here without at least having a warm drink with Rose, so I ask for a coffee. I intend to drink it quickly so I can go home to do my yoga and get the rest of my day back on track.

While Rose is making my coffee, I notice Alfie scratching at the door, so I walk over and let him inside. I am closing the back door when I notice the base of a structure in the far corner of the garden. It looks like a cubby house in the process of construction. "What's that?"

Rose walks out of the kitchen carrying a pink mug. "What's what? Oh." She gets a sheepish look about her. "Actually, I want to talk to you about that." She hands me my coffee and points at the couch. "Sit."

I remain standing. "What is it?"

Rose sits and crosses her legs. "I know you don't like staying at other people's houses, Fern. I know how important your routine is. And that's why . . . I was thinking . . . well, what if this *was* your place?"

I put my coffee down. "I don't understand. Where are *you* going?"

She frowns. "Nowhere. I will stay in the main house. And you . . . would move in there." She points outside at the structure. "It's a granny flat. It could be your own little place . . . at my place."

"You've already started building it?"

"I was going to surprise you. But . . . now you're here and . . ." She gives a little shrug and a guilty smile. I look again at the structure. It looks like a children's playhouse. An oversize dollhouse. Not a place for an adult to live.

"It will be bigger than it looks now," Rose says, reading my thoughts. "Once it's finished, obviously. It will have a bathroom and a kitchenette. It will even have air-conditioning!"

"My flat already has air-conditioning."

"But your place is blocks away! This way, you'd be right here."

Rose smiles, but she sounds impatient. Even a little annoyed. So I do my best to disguise my horror at the idea of moving into her backyard doll's house.

"Fern . . . don't *you want* to be here? After the baby's born, don't you want to be a part of his or her life? See him or her every single day?"

I think about this. "Yes."

"Well, while you're pregnant, I want to see *you* every single day. You get that, right? I want to be here for you in case you need anything." Now she smiles cajolingly. "Ice cream, perhaps? A foot rub?"

Rose stands, picks up my coffee from the coffee table, and hands it to me. I don't have a problem with living with Rose, per se. I've lived with Rose for over half of my life. It isn't even the fact that I am reluctant to upset my routine—I suspected my pregnancy was going to do its fair share of that anyway. It's the fact that, in saying yes to moving in, I'd be saying no to another life. A life where I'm not entirely dependent on Rose. A life that I've been enjoying recently.

"But I like my place," I say carefully. "I like . . . my independence."

But it feels ridiculous, just saying it aloud. I still have dinner with Rose three times a week, I still call her whenever there is the slightest drama in my life. How independent am I really? Rose doesn't respond, so I guess she's wondering the same thing.

I look down at my coffee.

"Is this about Rocco?" Rose asks, after a short time.

"No," I say. "And yes."

"I know you like him, Fern. But there is no happy ending to this, you know that, right?" Rose's voice is softer now. "You saw how it went last night. Rocco is doing well right now. Getting himself started in a new business, traveling. The last thing he needs is to get himself into a complicated relationship. Fern, you're going to be showing soon. What will you tell him then?" She doesn't give me time to answer. "I really think it's better for everyone if you end it with him sooner rather than later."

I hate it, but I know she's right. Last night proved it. Wally and I can't have a normal relationship. We can't even go out for dinner without it turning into a disaster. She's also right that I'll be showing soon. How would I explain that to Wally? Yes, I'm pregnant, but don't worry—my sister is going to raise our baby?

"All right," I say. "I'll move in."

Rose nods, but looks at me expectantly.

"And I'll break up with Wally."

Rose nods again. She doesn't smile, but I can tell that she's happy with my decision. She leans in for a hug, but this time I'm too fast. I dodge her and head to the kitchen. I can move in and break up with Wally. But a hug on top of that is more than I can take. At least for today.

• • •

JOURNAL OF ROSE INGRID CASTLE

After the first night, Billy always came to our tent after Mum and Daniel went to bed. Every night as we played cards, we chatted in cycles about nothing of significance—jokes and stories, comparing notes about teachers, asking each other questions about school or sport or favorite foods. Mum knew what we were up to (we weren't *that* quiet), but she and Daniel seemed happy enough to turn a blind eye. I wasn't stupid enough to think this would last. I knew she would be storing it up, along with a list of grievances that she would use against us when we got home, but, like her, I was having so much fun I found it difficult to care.

On the second night, I took a sip of beer when Billy offered. On the third night, I had a few sips. Mum and Billy never seemed to notice that there was beer missing, and I loved the way it made me feel close to Billy. We played a different card game each night—Billy's aim was to find a card game that Fern wasn't good at (spoiler: he never found one). Every time Fern won, Billy complained and rolled his eyes while I shushed him through giggles.

"Give us a chance, would you?" he'd say, smiling.

I had to admit, I was enjoying being the one who was less proficient with games, purely because it meant I got more of Billy's attention. Sitting by his side, sharing his can of beer and listening to him whisper the rules to the games in my ear . . . it felt like something I could do forever. I guess it was around this time I realized I had feelings for Billy. I couldn't help it. I felt it each time his knee brushed against mine. I may have been imagining it, but sometimes it felt like he pressed his thigh against mine on purpose. The idea that he was seeking me out, actively wanting me . . . it was intoxicating. I wanted to be around Billy as much as I could. I became his shadow, from the moment he woke up until the moment he went to bed. Where Billy was, I was too.

"Like a puppy dog," Mum said under her breath one day. "Don't go making a fool of yourself, Rosie Round."

She said it out of earshot of anyone else (classic Mum), but the comment ate away at me. If Mum had noticed my feelings for Billy, did that mean Billy had noticed too? I made my mind up to keep my distance. So later that day, when Billy suggested we all go down to the river for a swim, I offered to stay back and help Daniel repair a hole in the tent.

"Aw, come on," Billy said, looking genuinely disappointed. "It will be more fun if we all go."

I managed to shake my head. "I'll meet you there, later, okay?"

He didn't protest again, but he looked sad as he and Fern trudged off. When I snuck a look at Mum, she looked victorious. Once again, I realized, I'd let her manipulate me.

I repaired that hole just about as quickly as I could. When it was done, I all but ran down to the river. Mum and Daniel came too, walking just a short distance behind me. I reached the river a minute or so before them and noticed Billy and Fern were nowhere to be seen.

I scanned the trees, the water, the rope swing. Downstream a couple of inflatable boats held half a dozen people who were shouting to each other and laughing. But no Fern or Billy.

"That's odd," Daniel said, when he and Mum joined me. "They said they were coming here, didn't they?"

"I'm sure they're about somewhere," Mum said, even though there weren't a lot of other places to go down there. Daniel had just suggested I run back to camp when we were startled by the disturbance of water, followed by a sharp, deep intake of air.

"Billy!" Daniel exclaimed. "There you are!"

Billy stood waist deep in the water, gasping for breath. He didn't appear to be harmed. He was grinning. His torso, which was long and pleasantly defined, shimmered with water.

"Where *were* you?" Daniel exclaimed.

"Where is Fern?" I said.

Billy's grin slipped. "She's not here?"

I felt a flutter of panic. There were lots of reeds in this part of the water. What if Fern had got tangled in them? What if she was stuck? I was about to launch myself into the water to look for her when there was another splash, another gasp for air. And then, Fern was there, wet from head to toe. Unlike Billy, she was barely panting.

Billy groaned. "No way!"

"We were seeing who could hold their breath the longest," Fern explained. "I won, again."

"She must have an oxygen tank under there," Billy muttered.

"I read a book about free diving," Fern explained.

Billy rolled his eyes.

"It's called lung packing, Billy," Fern said. "It's a very simple technique."

Billy shoved her playfully and Fern frowned. I knew she would see this kind of gesture as confusing after she had provided him with such useful information. After a moment, she shoved him back. Fern had been doing karate for a few years by then and was stronger than she looked. Billy fell backward into the water.

"Feisty," he said, laughing as he got back on his feet. "Best out of three?"

Fern looked confused but she nodded and they both inhaled deeply and then dived under the water again. As they disappeared, I noticed Mum was watching the interaction closely.

"I think someone's got a crush," she said to Daniel, waggling her eyebrows.

"Who?" Daniel said, oblivious. He was bent over, digging through stones, most likely looking for a smooth one for skimming. But hearing Mum's comment, he stood. "Billy? On Fern."

Mum's smile grew. "I think it might be mutual."

Daniel frowned. "Do you want me to talk to him?"

"No!" Mum said, waving her hand. "You'll only embarrass him. Besides, it's a little crush, it's not hurting anyone."

Daniel shrugged and, after a moment, went back to looking for stones. Once she was sure he was distracted, Mum looked me dead in the eye, and smiled.

FERN

Wally knocks at my front door at 6:45 P.M., exactly fifteen minutes earlier than the suggested time of 7:00 P.M. This little detail alone is enough to make me second-guess myself. It's been a week since I decided to end my relationship with Wally, but this has been the first time I've had the opportunity and inclination to do it. Wally always seems to be working late, or traveling, or in meetings. He hasn't been to the library once. Rose has used this as reinforcement that I am doing the right thing.

"You see? He doesn't have time to even see you. When would he have time to raise a baby?"

She has a point. As usual.

Wally knocks again, and I open the door.

"Hey," he says. For the first time in ages, Wally isn't wearing a suit. He is wearing that lumberjack shirt he had on the first time I saw him at the library, with jeans and sneakers. He is even wearing his stripy hat. He gives me a smile that, somehow, makes me feel sad.

"Hello." The pitch of my voice is a little higher than usual. I'd had a flutter in my chest all day thinking about what I was going to do tonight, but suddenly the flutter is more of a flapping. I wrap my arms around myself and take a deep slow breath.

"Are you okay?" Wally asks, still in the doorway.

Over the past week as Wally and I have communicated via text message, he has asked me this many times. He has also asked me to forgive him. Each time, I have informed him that there is no need to ask forgiveness; to the contrary, *I* am the one who should apologize. Still, Wally has obviously sensed something is up, perhaps due to the absence of *x*'s in our text messages these past few days (a tip from Rose so as not to give him "mixed messages").

"I'm perfectly okay," I tell him. "Please, come in."

Upon entering, Wally turns quickly right and left. I'd forgotten the state of the flat would come as a surprise to him. The last time he was here the place was, of course, furnished. But over the past few days Rose and I have more or less cleared the place out, moving my belongings to Rose's (the spare room, until the doll's house is finished). Tomorrow, I will be returning the key to the landlord.

"I've moved into Rose's house," I explain.

Oddly, this doesn't appear to be news to Wally, even though I hadn't mentioned anything about moving out of my flat. He looks at me sadly. "Are you breaking up with me?"

The words catch me off guard. *Breaking up.* All of a sudden, it sounds like something teenagers do in the hallway at high school, between classes. (Not teenagers like me. I read books in the hallway at high school, between classes.) It also indicated that he had indeed noticed the lack of *x*'s in our text messages.

"I'd like to end our relationship, yes," I said.

"Because of dinner last week?"

"No."

"Then why?"

I look at his too-loose jeans, his black lace-up sneakers, and have a sudden recollection of thinking he was homeless. It's funny, remembering the time you didn't know someone once you *do* know them. The first time I had met Janet, I'd thought she was going to be brash and loud. She wore brightly colored resin jewelry that I had always found went hand in hand with brash, loud people. I'd got that wrong. And I'd got Wally wrong too.

"Is it because of your sister?"

I tell him it's not, but his jaw tightens anyway.

"Can I say something?" he says. "I know you love your sister, but . . ." He shakes his head, sighs. "Something isn't right about her. It's like she doesn't know where she ends and you begin. It's like she thinks . . . you *belong* to her or something."

I frown.

"And you don't have great boundaries with her either. You blindly believe things that she tells you. You don't question anything she says."

I think about that for a moment.

"Was it Rose's idea that we break up?" he asks.

I cross my arms. Wally raises his eyebrows.

"Why isn't that a surprise?" he says. "Fern, if you can tell me one reason you want to break up, then I'll—"

"I've met someone else," I say.

This silences Wally, as it was intended to. For now, I try not to think about the fact that it was Rose's idea to say this. ("You can't let him talk you out of it. As soon as he starts arguing with you, you need to say you've met someone else. He can't argue with that. It will make it clean and fast.")

"When?"

"A few weeks back. You haven't been around a lot, lately." I avoid his gaze.

"Wow. So . . . it's serious? You really like the guy?"

("It has to sting," Rose had said. "But it's a kindness in disguise.")

"Yes," I say.

Wally's face looks heartbreakingly sad. "I'm sorry. I . . . was caught up in the business. I didn't make you a priority."

("It will be hard, Fern. You will want to let him talk you out of it. But you can't. When he gets upset, you need to say nothing at all.")

This part, at least, is easy, because I can't speak. All my thoughts and feelings have settled in my throat, forming a seal. I wrap my arms around my middle. He takes a step toward me, but then at the last minute changes his mind. "Well," he says. "I guess I'd better go then."

I nod. The seal in my throat tightens.

He heads for the door. The flap in my chest becomes something else, something heavier. More like a heavy, sinking pain. When his hand is on the door, he turns back.

"Can you do something for me?" he says.

I nod.

"Remember what I said about your sister."

He doesn't wait for me to respond, just turns and lets himself out.

Living with Rose isn't so bad. She buys new sheets for my bed (100 percent bamboo) and makes space in the living room for me to do my yoga. And in the evenings, we spend quiet time together watching movies or reading books on the couch. I have heard that pregnancy makes you tired, and as it turns out, it is no joke. Luckily, I find plenty of opportunities to nap—on my yoga mat, in the children's section of the library on the beanbag, in Gayle's car when I go out to fetch a lemon. I sneak these little kips as often as I can, and when I do, I have dreams. Unusual dreams in vivid color. Usually about Wally.

I'm unprepared for the relentless way I miss Wally. All day, every day, I miss him. It is a gnawing pain in my chest, a pain that makes me want to crawl out of my skin. It reminds me of the way I missed Mum after her overdose—enough to make me howl. I'd learned somewhere along the way that you were supposed to miss people silently. Missing people aloud upset people. It made them feel like they weren't enough, that you didn't care about them. Rose, in particular, felt like this.

You only care about Mum! I'm the one who has looked after you all your damn life!

I don't want anyone to feel like I don't care about them. So I grieve silently, invisibly. It's worked for me so far, in this life. But there's another loss coming my way, very soon. My baby. And that one, I fear, might be the one that topples me.

The morning sickness reaches its peak at around eight weeks. I feel constantly nauseated and the smell of food is often enough to make me weak. When borrowers approach me at the library, I don't even bother pretending someone is calling me, I simply keep my eyes forward and keep walking. One lunchtime, Trevor reheats some leftover Chinese food in the microwave and the smell is so overpowering I have to remove the food, put it into a plastic bag and take it immediately to the outside rubbish bin, ignoring his cries of protest. When Trevor tries to question me about it, I'm still feeling too sick to talk, so I merely hold up a palm and head for the secret cupboard.

I become acutely aware of every change to my body. The tenderness of my breasts, the patterns of my hunger, the length of time between visits to the bathroom. It's a nonsensical puzzle for which there are few answers. In fact, the more I read about having babies, the more I realize that the process is primitive and dated. It is astonishing to me that with all the medical advancements of recent times, they haven't come up with a better way to do it. For goodness' sake, not only does a woman have to house the fetus in her uterus for nine months and then push it out of an inadequately sized orifice (or, even worse, have it cut out of her if it won't come by itself), she is then expected to care for the baby on an hourly basis, feeding it fluids from her still-healing body! Lunacy! There has to be a better way. But no matter how much I research it, I have yet to find an alternative.

At twelve weeks, Rose and I go to the baby's first scan. Rose introduces herself to the sonographer as the "mother," and I find myself with the title "surrogate." I'm taken aback by the emotion I feel when I see movement on the black-and-white screen. I imagine the hormones are to blame. The sonographer shows us the baby's head, the baby's spine, the four chambers of the baby's heart. She even flicks a button so the picture becomes three-dimensional—turning the baby a reddish pink color and giving it a look of ET. That's how I know it must be the hormones that are behind my feelings. No one but a mother could love something that strange looking.

But then again, I'm not the mother. I'm the surrogate.

"Is there a dad in the picture?" the sonographer asks, as we are finishing up. "I can print out a photo for him, if so."

"Dad would love a photo," Rose says. "He's out of town on business at the moment."

According to Rose, Owen will be coming home as soon as he finishes up his work assignment. Last week, he even sent a little Paddington Bear from London in the post along with a printed card saying he'd also bought a Paddington book which he couldn't wait to read to him or her. That had made me smile. Owen was going to be a great dad, and my baby—Rose's baby—would be lucky to have him. Still, as I watch the picture of the baby on the screen—as the surrogate—I feel an ache in my chest that makes me finally understand that feeling people call "a broken heart."

What are you up to over there?" Rose asks me. She's in her jogging clothing, on the way out the door, and I'm sitting at the kitchen table with my book, and the library's *What's On* catalog, which details upcoming events in the library. I also have my hospital admission paperwork.

I was impressed by the promptness with which the hospital admissions paperwork arrived, following my twelve-week ultrasound. It arrived the very next day. Apart from appreciating the efficiency of their system, I was pleased to find that it had come the old-fashioned way, five high-stock pages of A4 paper, folded in three. Most paperwork is emailed these days—a shame, I think, as I've always enjoyed filling out paperwork the traditional way, with pen and paper. I like the precise little boxes—one for each letter. I enjoy the gentle scratch of my ballpoint pen against the page, the pop of blue against the black-and-white page.

"Fern? What are you doing?"

Lately it feels like Rose has an insatiable interest in what I'm doing. It doesn't matter if she's rushing out to a meeting or in the middle of watching a gripping television program, her interest in my goings-on is as relentless as it is complete.

I sigh. "I'm reading and doing some paperwork."

She appears behind me, peering down at the page, which is terrifically irritating. I've completed most of it. The only boxes that remain empty are under the "Emergency Contacts" heading.

"Put me down as your emergency," she says immediately. After a short pause, she adds, "Unless there's someone else you want to list?"

I might be imagining it, but I hear the faintest hint of a laugh in her voice. I wonder what is so funny.

"There's no one else," I say, filling in four little boxes with the letters of her name. Because Rose, once again, is my person. Other people may come and go, but she will always be here. I know I'm lucky for that. It's just that today it makes me feel sad.

When I am four months pregnant, Rose says she wants to talk to me about something important. More and more, it feels like everything is important to Rose. What I eat. How much I sleep. Not sleeping flat on my back. But today her expression is more somber than usual. It piques my interest.

We sit at the kitchen table and she sets a stack of documents on the table before me.

"What is this?" I ask.

"This is an adoption order, which legally transfers all parental rights and responsibilities from you to me."

I frown at the documentation, pages long and full of legalese. The words "*Relinquish parental rights*" jump out at me.

"It's just a formality," Rose says. "We don't need to make anything official until after the baby is born. But I did want to talk to you . . . about Rocco."

I look at her. "What about him?"

Rose frowns and chews her bottom lip gently. "I've been doing some reading about the adoption process, and when the baby is born, I think it would be better if you didn't name him on the birth certificate."

"Why?"

"Well," Rose says carefully, "if you do name him, he will be required to consent to the adoption, which will be a little bit awkward as he doesn't know the baby exists."

She makes a good point. One I hadn't thought of. "So . . . who would I name as the father? Just make someone up?"

"Well, no, because then you'd be required to have *him* consent to the adoption."

"Oh."

"Therefore, I think it would be easiest to simply say you don't know who the father is."

I laugh. "I don't know? That's ridiculous. How could a person not know who the father of their baby is?"

Rose doesn't laugh. "It's not as ridiculous as you think. If you had more than one sexual partner at the time of conception, or if you had a one-night stand with someone you never saw again, it's possible that you wouldn't know who the father is."

I stop laughing. "And that's what you want me to say? That I had multiple sexual partners at once, or a one-night stand with a stranger?"

"I know you wouldn't do that, Fern, of course you wouldn't. But it doesn't matter. It's just about doing what's right for the baby."

I stare at the table in front of me. I suspect she's right. Still, it bothers me. I understand that the baby will be better off with Rose and Owen. But erasing Wally from the document? It's almost like he never existed. Some days, that's how it feels, actually. Like he was a character in a book I read, rather than an actual person in my life. If it wasn't for the baby I was carrying, I'd suspect that was *exactly* what he was.

"Okay?" Rose asks, and I nod, because my throat chooses that moment to swell up and I can't reply.

It gets hotter, and I become more pregnant. I'd always found the heat irritating, but pregnancy adds another suffocating layer. The library, at least, is air-conditioned, but each day the walk home becomes harder to enjoy. By the end of the fourth month, my elastic-waist skirts are tight even around my hips, digging in and cutting me in half and driving me crazy. The moment I get home I tear them off and wear one of Rose's loose nighties instead.

Rose has also added another suffocating layer to my life. She's around constantly, and not just in the morning and evening—some days she even pops into the library, just to say "hi," wanting to feel the baby kick. The timing of these visits is invariably poor—when I've just finished my break or when I'm about to head into a staff meeting—and, perhaps it's the pregnancy, but I find myself getting annoyed with her.

As she arrives today—third unannounced visit this week—I think of what Wally said to me. *It's like she doesn't know where she ends and you begin. It's like she thinks . . . you* belong *to her or something.*

"What are you doing here again, Rose?" I ask.

She looks surprised, and a little wounded, by the question. "Visiting you, of course."

"Don't you have to work?" I ask.

"I was in the area," Rose says, and I wonder what interior design business would have brought her to this area. She takes my arm and leads me over to the couches in the children's area. It reminds me of what Wally said about me. *You don't have great boundaries with her either.* After Wally had said this, I'd taken the opportunity to google "great boundaries" and I'd come across an article entitled "How to Set Healthy Boundaries," which suggested three helpful tips when saying no.

Be polite but firm.

Explain why, but do not overexplain.

Stay calm and on message.

I decide it might be a good moment to employ these strategies.

"Thank you for the visit, Rose," I say, which I think meets the *polite* tip, "but, I need to work." *Firm without overexplaining.*

Rose frowns. "But I've come all the way to see you."

"I thought you were in the area," I say. "But in any case, perhaps calling ahead next time would be a good idea."

Rose blinks. "You want me to go?" Her face is blank now but there is a challenge in her voice. Maybe even a dare. The hairs on the back of my neck stand up.

"Yes," I say.

I stand and turn away from her, but not before I see her jaw drop. As I walk into the staff room, I force myself not to look back. Setting boundaries isn't easy. I walk straight to my desk and google "great boundaries" again. Seems like I'm going to need a little more help with this.

When we were little, Rose was a pro at giving someone the silent treatment. It was, Mum and I used to say behind her back, her area of expertise. The slightest infraction could result in several days of steely silence. Now that we are adults, it's improved a lot, but she still occasionally does it. So, when I get home from the library that night, I'm prepared for the worst.

Instead, the minute I walk in the door, I receive a smile and a large flat cardboard box, tied with a bow.

"Sit down!" Rose's face is clear and shiny, and her eyes are bright. "I bought you a present."

She pushes me onto the couch and sits on the coffee table, right in front of me. "I've been a bit preoccupied with the baby lately, and I think I might have been a bit pushy and overzealous at times." She smiles. "Guilty as charged! So this"—she touches the box—"is my way of saying that I really do appreciate you."

I glance nervously at the box.

Rose puts it into my lap. "Open it."

After I fumble trying to undo the bow, Rose takes over, untying it quickly and pulling out a dress. She stands and lets it unravel against her. It's a long dress, striped with every color of the rainbow. It has elbow-length sleeves and an empire waistline, with light flowy fabric that runs to the floor. I rub the fabric between my fingers. It's as soft as butter. "Do you love it?" Rose says.

I open my mouth.

"I know you loved the rainbow dress that Rocco bought you," Rose explains. "And this is so similar. I bought it from Ripe Maternity then took it to the alterations place to get French seams, so they wouldn't irritate you." Her smile becomes wider. "And it's one hundred percent organic bamboo!"

Before I know it, Rose is pulling my T-shirt over my head and instructing me to stand up and take my skirt off. I do as she says, and then stand there in my bra and underwear. She puts the dress on me and makes me twirl. It's kind of bizarre, but I go along with it. Rose can be quite convincing when she's in this kind of mood. It's something I'd forgotten about her. She has a gift for knowing when she is at risk of getting on my nerves and managing to sneak back into my good graces at the eleventh hour.

Sisterly relationships are so strange in this way. The way I can be mad at Rose but still want to please her. Be terrified of her and also want to run to her. Hate her and love her, both at the same time. Maybe when it comes to sisters, boundaries are always a little bit blurry. Blurred boundaries, I think, are what sisters do best.

• • •

JOURNAL OF ROSE INGRID CASTLE

On the second-to-last night of our camping trip, Mum and Daniel went to bed right after dinner. "Don't stay up too late," they said, as they disappeared into their tent. It had been a long day of swimming, hiking, and collecting firewood, and everyone was a little worn out.

"Are we playing cards?" Billy asked the moment they were gone. He'd been getting bolder with the beer drinking and that night he'd even had one under the camp table during dinner, while Mum and Daniel were right there.

"I'm just going to rest my eyes for a minute," Fern said. She had been the most active of everyone that day—always diving the deepest, climbing the highest, collecting the most firewood. She looked absolutely exhausted.

"I don't think we can play cards without her," I said.

"You're right," Billy agreed.

I assumed that was going to be the end of it, so I was surprised when Billy said, "We could go to the river to skim stones if you like?"

I hesitated. We weren't supposed to leave the camp without telling Mum and Daniel. Daniel had been so adamant about it that Mum had joined in. "Did you hear that, girls? No leaving the camp without telling one of us where you are." But if Billy was worried about getting in trouble, he hid it well.

"Rose?" Billy prompted. "Do you want to?"

Of course I wanted to. I wanted to only slightly more than I feared getting caught. And, as it turned out, that was enough.

"Sure," I said. "Why not?"

It was pitch black as we followed the foot-worn path through the trees toward the river with only Billy's torch to light the way. We didn't talk for fear of being heard, and that was fine by me. Every stick and leaf we stepped on crackled unbelievably loud. My heart was in my throat the entire way to the river, I was so worried that Mum would wake and find us missing.

"You're shaking," Billy said, laughing. "What is the matter?"

"Remember what Mum and Daniel said about not leaving the camp?" I whispered.

"Ah." Billy waved his hand. "They don't care as long as we leave them alone."

I thought about that. On this trip, at least, that did appear to be the case. "I guess you're right."

He laughed again. "Usually am."

We stopped in front of the river and started picking up stones.

"I'm glad we did this," Billy said.

"Me too."

"I think you're awesome, Rose."

I felt my cheeks turning crimson. I continued to collect stones. "Thanks. I think you're pretty cool too."

I snuck a look at him. He was grinning. I found myself grinning too.

"Right," he said, standing. "Shall we skim?"

I nodded.

Billy picked a stone and lined up the arc. He shifted on the rocks so his legs were hip distance apart, and practiced the skimming motion. Then it was time for the real thing: one, two . . . but on three, instead of releasing the stone, he turned suddenly and kissed me full on the mouth.

The air vanished from my lungs.

It wasn't a kiss out of the movies. Our teeth knocked. He said, "Ow." We laughed. Billy pulled back. "Smooth, right?"

"The teeth knocking especially," I agreed. "Did you practice that?"

"Only in my head."

We smiled at each other. The next time he kissed me, our teeth didn't touch. It was slower. Better.

"Rose?"

Billy and I leaped apart, blinking into the darkness. It took me a moment to recognize the voice.

"What are you doing?" Fern said.

"Just skimming stones," Billy said, withholding a smile.

"Yeah," I said. "Billy is hopeless."

Fern looked at us. There was something about her expression. Fern always saw more than people thought. I had a feeling she knew exactly what we were doing. She didn't look happy about it.

"Let's go back to camp," I said.

Fern waited until Billy disappeared up the track and then fell into step beside me. I waited for her to inundate me with questions, but she didn't. She didn't say a word. Back at the camp, Fern went straight to bed without a word and I lay awake, thinking about Billy. It wasn't until later that I thought about the way Fern had looked at Billy down at the lake. Like she was angry. Like she hated him. It actually looked like she wanted to kill him.

FERN

At eighteen weeks, while setting up chairs for the Toastmasters group, I feel the baby move for the first time. It doesn't feel like much—barely anything at all. Like someone is tapping me from the inside. A small, rather benign, experience and yet, at the same time, the very definition of pleasure. It is, I suspect, what happiness feels like.

After that, I am aware of the baby every second. I spend hours reading books and googling. Is it cold when I am cold? Hot when I am hot? Does it hear my heart beating loudly from the inside? I pay attention to its movements to try to intuit its likes and dislikes. Judging from its movements, he or she is a little like me, because the one time I can guarantee movement is at night when it's quiet, and I am lying in bed. I find myself looking forward to that time all day, when I pull up my nightie and watch the little elbows or feet or shoulders bumping around under my skin. I love that time because Rose isn't around to see it. It's our time. Just the baby and me.

I've always enjoyed my job at the library, but as the months of my pregnancy pass, work becomes even more of an oasis. Carmel is part of it. Since our shadow day, she's given me a lot more freedom, but she's also asked for a few things in exchange. Greeting people as they enter the library with eye contact is one of them, so I've devised a system where I look at the patch of skin between people's eyebrows instead. Delightfully, everyone is none the wiser, and the results of this pseudo eye contact are surprisingly good. Now, people smile and wave to me as they enter the library. Some pause to tell me how much they enjoyed a book I recommended; others compliment me on my fashion choice of the day. Once, I even became engaged in an impromptu discussion with a group of women who'd all read *The Secret Life of Shirley Sullivan* by Lisa Ireland. I'd suggested they start a proper book club at the library, and Carmel gave me permission to host it in the training room and order fruit and cheese (not as good as cake, but not bad). All in all, with my new eye contact trick, I find the front desk is no longer the fearsome place it once was, and I have Carmel to thank.

One day, as I am taking my place at the front desk, I become aware of Gayle hovering nearby. Her eyes flicker here and there. She looks quite bizarre.

"Is everything all right, Gayle?" I ask her as I lower myself into the ergonomic chair at my desk.

"Fine," she says. "It's just . . . may I ask you something?"

I wince as my lower back hits the seat. "You may."

"I just wondered . . . if you had anything to tell us." She glances demonstrably at my burgeoning belly. "An announcement, perhaps?"

I notice Linda, a few meters away, listening. When she sees me looking, she glances quickly at the bookshelves.

I am perplexed by the question. I am six months pregnant now, and it is, quite frankly, obvious to anyone without vision impairment that I am pregnant.

"If you're asking if I am pregnant, I can confirm that I am. Nearly six months along," I add, as people (including the nurses at Sun Meadows, the lady I'd passed at the bus stop yesterday, and the sales assistant at the pharmacy where I buy my prenatal vitamins) seem interested in these sorts of details.

Gayle and Linda gasp in unison. "Six months!" Gayle says. "My goodness. Why didn't you tell us?"

I wonder if this was a social faux pas. Am I expected to tell every person that I work with that I am pregnant? I assumed they would notice my growing belly and consider themselves informed, but I am well aware of the offense it can cause if I fail to adhere to certain social graces.

"Well, you don't like to announce these things too early," I say, as this does appear to be the case. "In case, heaven forbid, something goes wrong."

Gayle nods, apparently satisfied with this explanation.

"So who is the father?" Linda asks. "It isn't that handsome American, is it? From the bowling?"

I busy myself by scanning my desk calendar. As I haven't been seen with any men other than Wally, it's natural that this is what people will assume . . . but I don't like to confirm it since I haven't told Wally himself. I'd hoped this would be one of those social situations where people felt it was impolite to ask. As this clearly isn't the case, I ignore the question and start shuffling books around my desk instead. After a moment or two, Gayle and Linda take the hint and scuttle away. The downside of this is that Carmel chooses this moment to approach.

"Just the woman I was looking for!" she says. "Gayle is giving a how-to class on IT troubleshooting this morning, which covers the printers and photocopiers. I thought you might like to join."

I open my mouth to protest, but Carmel gets in first. "It's a two-hour class, and you can sit down the whole time."

We lock eyes. Carmel hasn't commented on my pregnancy yet, but it's obvious she knows. . . . Last week, for example, when she caught me coming out of the secret cupboard after a two-hour nap, she simply looked the other way. And the week before last, she asked me to cover some new books in contact paper, which allowed me to sit down for nearly half my shift. Then there are all the other times she's brought me a glass of water or suggested I pop outside for some fresh air.

"It's pretty straightforward and if you pick it up, you could even teach the class in the future," Carmel says. "It would mean you could sit down for a few hours each week while teaching. And there are free cakes and cups of tea!"

It's the cakes that get me across the line. I still bring my sandwich to the library, but these last few weeks I've found myself ravenous between meals—and the idea of cake is simply too much to resist. I head to the training room fifteen minutes early (naturally) and take a seat at the front of the class. As others arrive, I'm encouraged by the fact that they—all older than me by at least a good thirty years—share my distaste for IT troubleshooting. I also understand that, like me, they are in a bit of an if-you-can't-beat-them-join-them situation. As such I feel a certain camaraderie with the old folks. Like me, they grumble into their seats, glancing suspiciously at the handbooks laid out at each station before giving Gayle their reluctant attention. Like me, they are hopeful to learn, but even more hopeful that the whole process will be easy to discount as too complex, too difficult, beyond their abilities.

So we are all disappointed to find Gayle's voice soothing and simple, her teaching manner easy to digest. At the end of the two hours, I believe I could guide one of my classmates through a number of troubleshooting situations quite easily.

Carmel is waiting for me as I exit the class, and I am forced to report that the class was more straightforward than expected. When pushed, I also tell her I might consider running the class after another session or two under Gayle's guidance.

From the coy smile on Carmel's face, she takes it as a win.

That afternoon, when I go to see Mum, Teresa is there as usual, with her machine. Mum has been getting better each time I see her. She strings two or three words together without a pause now. "How are you?" "Aren't you cold?" "Can I have . . . more water?" She's not reading novels as Teresa had suggested, but she's definitely making improvements.

"Hello," I say from the doorway.

Teresa looks up. "Fern!"

Mum doesn't look like she's having a good day. Her hair isn't done. She's wearing pajama pants and a T-shirt and has just socks on her feet. And her face is tearstained.

"I think Nina's had enough for one day," Teresa says to me as I walk in.

"What's wrong, Mum?"

Mum shakes her head and dabs at her cheek with a tissue. Teresa makes a motion with her head that I have learned means that I should move out into the hallway so we can have a little chat, which I do.

When Teresa joins me, she lowers her voice. "I need to warn you about something."

Teresa pauses, as if expecting me to say something. She hasn't asked a question, but I give her a nod as a compromise.

"Your mother has been saying things, these past few weeks," she says.

"Yes, I know."

"Yes. But she's been saying some strange things. And I don't want you to worry. Confabulation is common with patients with an acquired brain injury."

"Confab—"

"Confabulation is the spontaneous production of false memories which never occurred. Sometimes it's memories of actual events that are displaced in space or time."

I am intrigued. "You mean she's making up stories?"

"In a sense. Except she doesn't know it. Confabulation isn't lying. Your mother believes she's telling the truth. With many patients there is some truth, mixed with fantasy. It's like her brain is playing tricks on her."

"What is she saying?"

"Different things. She talks about your sister a lot. She says loving things and then . . . other things."

"What kind of things?"

"It's quite ridiculous. Sometimes she says she is trying to kill her."

"But Rose hasn't seen Mum for more than ten years."

Teresa laughs. "It sounds stupid, but in the moment, she believes it. The best thing is to not make a fuss and just try to keep her calm."

"What else does she say?"

"Lately she's been talking about a little boy called Billy."

I feel myself stiffen. "What did she say about him?"

"She's brought it up a number of times. She says that Billy drowned. Or apparently drowned. But it was actually murder."

She laughs sadly before I have the chance to react. I glance back through the door at Mum.

"She was getting herself quite upset," Teresa says, needlessly.

"What should I do?"

"The best way to handle it, in my experience, is to act as though what she is saying is true and you are taking it seriously. Most likely, she will then forget about it and move on."

"Okay."

Teresa smiles. "Don't worry, Fern. I know it sounds strange, but honestly, confabulation is very common. In a few minutes, she'll have forgotten the lot."

I look back at Mum, still dabbing her eyes. *But what if it's not confabulation?* I wonder. *What do we do then?*

That night, Rose and I make spaghetti Bolognese. I wear the goggles Wally gave me while I chop the onion, and I don't cry a single tear. Rose rolls her eyes at me, but I don't care. I like wearing them.

"I saw Mum today," I say to Rose as I dice.

"Hmm?" Rose pauses from grating a carrot and fiddles with her rose bracelet.

"Mum. She was talking in sentences," I say. "*Actual* sentences. She's been having electromagnetic therapy. It's the new speech therapist she's been seeing."

Rose stops fiddling with the bracelet and looks up. "What is she saying?"

"She can repeat things that Teresa says—"

"Who?"

"Her speech therapist." I feel a whisper of irritation. "You would know if you'd visited her."

Rose blinks. For a moment I think she's going to argue with me but instead she says, "So she's repeating things?"

"Yes and she can ask for a drink, say she's hot, that kind of thing."

"Oh." Rose turns her back to me, slicing the top of a zucchini.

"Teresa also said she mentioned Billy, Rose. And murder."

Rose keeps her back to me, but she becomes still.

"I'm worried, Rose. What if someone suspects something?"

Now Rose turns. "Well, what did Teresa say? Did she seem concerned?"

I shrug. "She says confabulation is common among patients with acquired brain injuries."

"Confabulation?" Rose's bracelet falls off her wrist and clatters against the floor. She swears under her breath.

"She thinks Mum's brain created a story. She says it's common for people with acquired brain injuries."

"And what did you say?"

"I didn't say anything."

Rose exhales. "Of all the things Mum could talk about with her newfound speech. She really does have a gift for ruining our lives." Rose bends over and picks up the bracelet.

I hesitate. "Rose?"

"Mmm?"

"Was she *really* a bad mum?"

Rose looks at me. "You *know* she was."

When I don't respond, she looks aghast.

"Fern, she neglected us terribly. She dragged awful boyfriends in and out of our lives. For god's sake, she overdosed on pills, leaving us without even one parent who could care for us!"

"You're right."

"Hallelujah."

"But—"

"But nothing." Rose groans. "I get the sense that she's sorry for what she did. I think she loves us, Rose."

Rose throws up her hands. "Agree to disagree, then. I know that you want to have a relationship with her, Fern, but trust me, she's not a good person. There are things you don't understand."

Rose waits for a response from me, so after a few seconds, I nod. After all, there *must* be things I don't understand. Because as I look back over my memories of Mum, at least 90 percent of them are good.

• • •

JOURNAL OF ROSE INGRID CASTLE

Fern didn't talk to me the day after she saw Billy and me kissing.... She made basic conversation ("Pass the tomato sauce," "No thanks, I don't want to go to the river"), but things were frosty enough that even Mum and Daniel noticed something was up.

"What's going on with you kids?" Daniel asked over lunch.

"Nothing," the three of us said in unison.

"Are you sure?" Mum asked.

"Yep."

That was our line and we were sticking to it, at least where Mum was concerned. But even in private, Fern wasn't talking. It was strange. I was starting to get the feeling that I was right when I suspected Fern liked Billy. And now she was mad at us.

"Come on, kids, snap out of it," Daniel said, finally. "it's your last night. Go swim. Go on. Off with you."

We tried to protest, saying we were tired, but Mum and Daniel were adamant. I think they wanted some privacy.

We walked to the river in single file. Billy got straight into the water, keen to get away from the obvious tension. I sat on the riverbank beside Fern and waited. One thing I knew about Fern was that she wouldn't talk until she was ready.

After an hour had passed and she still hadn't talked, I felt nature call. Billy was showing no signs of getting out of the water—splashing and swimming and swinging from the rope—so I headed deep into the trees. After everything that had happened, I didn't want Billy seeing me pee. It was slow going; it was dark and I was barefoot—I had to watch every step I took.

When I returned to the river, Fern was gone.

"Fern.," I called. "Fern! Where are you?"

It was strange for her not to be in the spot I left her. It might have been that, combined with the fact that I was a worrier, that put me instantly on guard. "Fern?"

"Here," came a small voice.

And then I saw her, illuminated by a patch of moonlight in the shallows of the river. She was standing eerily still.

"What are you doing?" I asked. There was something about her facial expression . . . it gave me a bad feeling even before I saw what she'd done.

I took a step toward her and she lifted her hands. Something rose to the surface of the water beside her. A sliver of pale, unmoving flesh.

"Fern," I whispered. "What have you done?"

FERN

Time passes. It's one of the few things in life that I can rely on. The library is my solace. Once my colleagues recover from their initial shock at my pregnancy, their questions about the paternity of my baby cease and they are extremely supportive. Gayle knits me a pair of baby booties and Linda gifts me a bunny rug. Carmel purchases me a book of 10,001 baby names. I haven't told anyone yet that I'm not going to be the one naming the baby, or putting booties on it or wrapping it in a bunny rug. It feels like the sort of thing that I'd be better off waiting to tell them. If I tell them at all.

At home, Rose vacillates between pestering me—about what I am eating, how much I am working, whether I am exercising—and pampering me. Last night, for example, I came home and found Rose on her knees setting up a foot spa for me—"to relax, after being on your feet all day."

Owen, Rose tells me, is finishing up his contract and will be back in time for the baby's birth. I'm looking forward to having him back, and it's clear Rose is too. She thanks me, profusely and often, *for giving her her life back*. It occurs to me that this is exactly what I wanted to do for her in the first place—give her a baby and restore her relationship with Owen. I don't understand why it doesn't feel as good as I expected.

Every day, I think about Wally. I don't pause to think about him or "allow" myself to think about him, he's merely in the periphery of my every thought, like the smoky edges of an old photo. He's there every time I stare at someone, every time I arrive somewhere fifteen minutes early, every time I put in my earplugs or put on my goggles. Every time I feel a movement in my belly. He's part of everything.

Every now and again, after Rose has gone to bed, I hop on the iPad and search his name. I usually only ever get hits for old articles about Shout! But one day, when I'm about seven months along, a new article about him pops up, along with a photo. He's wearing his navy suit with the tapered pants. His hair is combed with a side part again and his glasses are new and he looks positively terrified. The article is announcing FollowUp, his new app, the headline declaring that he has "smashed back onto the scene with an app that makes Shout! look amateur." I don't read the article, I'm too taken by the photograph. I touch the screen, half expecting to feel the stubbly skin of his cheek under my hand. Then, after checking that Rose is nowhere to be seen, I lean forward and kiss the screen, right where his lips are.

I survive the next couple of weeks mostly thanks to Rose—who feeds me, cares for me, even ties my shoes when I can't reach. When I become too pregnant, Rose offers to shave my legs. It is hard to describe the intimacy of this. I can't imagine having anyone in the world but Rose do this for me. Nor can I imagine the alternative—leaving them unshaven. In this way, as well as many others, my sister holds the key to my sanity (even though I never gave it to her).

Owen's return is delayed, and then delayed again. In the meantime, Rose and I busy ourselves with what she'd previously deemed to be "Owen" tasks—such as assembling the crib and the changing table and painting the nursery. I relish the opportunity to be busy to take my mind off the baby, Billy, Mum, Wally—all of the things I've lost or am losing.

In the ninth month, I'm still working at the library. With all the excitement of my impending delivery, Rose seems to have abandoned her quest for me to give up work and rest around the clock, which is great, even if I do spend more time than usual in the secret cupboard. It's tiring, the third trimester. Aside from the Braxton-Hicks contractions I get periodically, my legs have become quite swollen and I get terrible pelvis pain if I'm on my feet for more than an hour or two. Carmel doesn't seem to mind it when I disappear; she doesn't even ask where I am anymore. It's funny how at first I'd thought Carmel was so different from Janet, but now, as it turns out, I think they would have liked each other quite a lot.

One morning at the library, I find myself making small talk with Gayle. It starts out normal, with her asking me how I've been—a question that I've always found difficult to answer. Usually I ignore this kind of question, pretend I didn't hear, but today, on a whim, I decide to indulge her.

"Are you inquiring after my physical health, Gayle?"

She appears to think about this, as if she herself isn't entirely sure. After contemplating for a few moments, she says, "I suppose I'm asking if anything of interest has happened to you lately."

"But how am I supposed to know what is of interest to you?"

Gayle thinks again. "You know, that's a good question. Perhaps you can tell me if anything of interest *to you* has happened lately."

I think about this. "Well, let's see. I read Kelly Rimmer's new novel, *The Things We Cannot Say,* over the weekend. I thoroughly enjoyed it."

Gayle beams. "I read her last one and loved it. It must have been out last summer because I remember sitting outside on my garden swing with a gin and tonic while I read it."

Before I know it, Gayle and I have discussed gin, garden swings, and her new herb garden, as well as Kelly Rimmer's other books, and none of it has felt like a chore in the least. The fact that we are focused on our work as we talk assists with this, I believe. We are still chatting comfortably when the automatic doors slide open.

"Isn't that your sister, Fern?"

I glance up, instantly annoyed. Rose hasn't been back since the last time I told her it wasn't convenient, and I'd thought she'd got the message.

"Rose," I say, before she can speak. "I'm sorry, but I'm working."

Rose shoots a look at Gayle. "I know. But this is important. Is there somewhere we can speak in private?"

"At home," I suggest. "Tonight?"

She shakes her head. "Now, Fern."

Rose and I appear to have come to something of a stalemate. I let out a long sigh.

"Go into the courtyard," Gayle whispers. "I'll cover for you."

Carmel has been so lenient with me lately that I'm not sure I would need anyone to "cover" for me, but I appreciate the sentiment, so I don't point this out. Instead, I thank Gayle and head outside to the courtyard with Rose. As we walk, Rose peppers me with inane questions about my day, the weather, if Gayle has recently changed her hair, and by the time we reach the courtyard, I'm feeling a little uneasy. Rose doesn't typically make small talk with me. She knows I dislike chatter for chatter's sake and the rapid fire of today makes me wonder if something is wrong.

"What is it, Rose?" I say.

Thankfully, Rose doesn't draw it out. "It's Mum."

It is perhaps the very last thing I expect her to say. Rose doesn't impart information about Mum to me, it's the other way around. Rose hasn't seen Mum for years.

"What . . . *about* Mum?" I ask.

I notice Rose's face is unusually somber. "I just had a call from Sun Meadows."

This is odd. Why would Sun Meadows call Rose?

"Why would they call *you*?"

Rose looks a little sheepish. "I'm Mum's emergency contact."

I stare at her. I have been visiting Mum every week for sixteen years and *Rose* is Mum's emergency contact?

She takes a long deep breath. "It's not good news, Fern. Mum . . . she died."

I hear the words. I *understand* them. And yet, I feel . . . nothing. I become oddly aware of all the sounds around me. The birds in the nearby tree. My breath whooshing past my ears. My heart beating.

"There aren't many details yet," Rose says. "They will probably have to do an autopsy. They think it must have been a stroke."

"But . . . she couldn't have had a stroke. She was in good health. Better than ever."

Rose shrugs. "Unfortunately, even healthy people have strokes sometimes."

A tear slips from my eye and I wipe it away quickly with my shirtsleeve. Another immediately takes its place.

"I know this is hard for you, Fern. I know you loved her."

"Can I see her?" I ask.

Rose shakes her head. "They've already taken her . . . for the autopsy."

I stare at her. "Already?"

"Yes."

"But . . . when did she die?"

"The hospital called me yesterday. Apparently, she didn't wake up in the morning."

"Yesterday? Mum's been dead for a whole day and you didn't tell me?"

Rose looks surprised. "Please don't get upset, Fern."

I try to fathom how I could not be upset. It is, after all, exquisitely upsetting.

"I'll take you home," Rose says, placing a hand on my arm. "Why don't you wait here a minute and I'll explain what has—"

"No," I say, pulling my arm free and wrapping it around myself. "I'm staying here."

But Rose is already walking back toward the door to the library. "I'm sure they'll understand, Fern."

"*NO!*" It comes out louder than I intend, but at least Rose stops walking. "I don't want to go home. I have work to do. . . ."

Rose stares at me. "Really? You want to stay here?"

"Yes."

"You're *sure*?"

"I am."

Rose looks confused. I'm not sure why. The library has been my home for as long as I can remember. After a lifetime together, you'd think she would have known that. But more and more lately, I get the feeling that Rose doesn't know me at all.

I feel agitated as I walk back into the library. I don't pause as I pass Gayle and Carmel, I just continue straight into the secret cupboard. Inside, I pull my phone from my pocket and dial Sun Meadows.

A receptionist named Jessica answers the phone. "Good morning, Sun Meadows, how many I assist you?"

"My name is Fern Castle. My mother, Nina Castle, was a patient there and I have just been informed that she has passed away. Can I speak to someone about this please?"

The receptionist tells me she's sorry for my loss and then asks if I can hold the line. I've always thought that was a stupid saying—after all, what line do they want me to hold?—but today I am too upset to worry about it. After a minute, she patches me through.

"Hello?" says the voice.

"Hello," I say. "My mother, Nina, was a patient and—"

"Fern?" she says. "It's Onnab. I was one of your mother's nurses. I'm so sorry for your loss."

"Oh," I say, realizing that until that very moment I'd been holding on to hope that it had been some kind of terrible mistake. "Thank you, Onnab."

"Your mother was a very nice lady," she says. "I always enjoyed looking after her."

I inhale a wobbly breath. "Thank you, Onnab. I wanted to check if you knew anything about the cause of Mum's death yet.

"I'm sorry," she says. "It will be at least a few days before we get the results of the autopsy."

I sink into the armchair.

"It may be of some comfort that I saw your mother the evening before she died. She seemed happy. To see your sister at last, I think, really lifted her spirits."

I repeat the sentence in my head, making sure I had interpreted correctly. But I couldn't have.

"Mum saw Rose?"

"Yes. At least, I think it was her. Small girl. Brunette?"

I can't believe it. Rose visited Mum. She *visited* her.

I let my head fall back against the armchair. Any anger I'd felt toward Rose dissipates. What that must have meant to Mum.

"Is there anything else I can help you with, Fern?" Onnab asks after a brief silence.

"No," I say, wiping a tear away. "You've already helped enough."

I don't know how long I sit in the secret cupboard. It might be ten minutes. It might be an hour. No one bothers me. Every time I think it's time to leave, I don't even get to a standing position before I change my mind and decide to stay where I am. I am starting to suspect that I might spend the night in this cupboard, when I hear a gentle knock at the door.

"Fern, there's a gentleman here who would like to talk to you."

It's Carmel talking. I think about staying silent, pretending I'm not here. I can't face anyone.

"I told him I wasn't sure if you were here or not. It's . . . Wally? I can send him away, if you don't want to—"

"No!" I say, too quickly and too loudly. "I'll talk to him."

I'm not thinking clearly, obviously. I have no explanation for the fact that I'm visibly pregnant. At the same time, I simply can't be this near and *not* go to him. It is a physical impossibility. For now, I put Mum's death away in the back of my mind, to think about later. Wally and Mum all together is simply too much for me.

I practically run to the reception area. Carmel is at my heels. As Wally comes into view—wearing his suit again—I am so overcome that I can't even manage a smile.

Neither can he. His eyes are fixed on my belly. "So it's true," he says. "You're pregnant."

"How did you know?"

"Rose told me."

"What?" I decide I must have misheard. "*Rose* told you I was pregnant?"

He nods.

"But when did you see Rose?"

Wally's face gets a funny look to it then, like he is sucking the inside of his cheeks. I'm not sure if he's confused or upset or even . . . angry. "Rose has visited me quite a few times over these past few months, Fern."

Now I'm certain I've misheard.

"She phoned me several months ago—she wanted to see me to talk about you, she said. She came to my office."

It doesn't make sense. Rose has spent these past few months telling *me* not to contact Wally. She couldn't have contacted Wally herself.

"She's been back several times since," he says.

"To talk about *me*? Why?"

"Good question, since she's barely mentioned you—not that first day or any other time."

I struggle to take it in. "Well . . . what did she want then?"

He shrugs. "First, she wanted to have coffee. Then she suggested lunch. Each time I agreed because I wanted to know how you were doing. But she never told me much about you, other than that you were happy with your new boyfriend. Then . . . yesterday, she told me you were pregnant."

I don't understand. Why would Rose say that after making me promise I wouldn't tell him?

"She said she's been on the fence about whether to say anything, because you'd made her swear to keep it a secret. But now that you're in financial trouble, she said she had to reach out."

I open my eyes. Financial trouble?

My head is spinning. Wally watches me closely, his eyes on my *face,* as if he'd expected my surprise. But I still don't understand. It feels like everyone is in on a secret, except me.

"Wally, I'm not in financial trouble."

"Rose said you'd say that. She said you're too proud to admit it."

"Well, I'm not."

He takes a few deep breaths. "How far along are you?"

"Nearly eight months." It's a miracle that I'm able to fudge the date, given the amount of noise in my head. Wally is here, standing *right in front of me.* It feels like a dream.

He sneaks a look at me. "And . . . you and . . . the new guy . . . are okay?"

I almost say, "What new guy?" Then I remember. He's talking about the father. The fictional father of my baby.

I manage a nod. But I'm thinking of that phone conversation Rose and I had, after she found out Wally had founded Shout! I remember the excitement in her voice. *A hundred million dollars,* she'd said.

"I'm sorry." Wally reaches out and touches my shoulder. "I've upset you."

"I'm just confused. I don't know why Rose came to you."

"She came to me," he says, "because she knows I care about you. She knows that I'd give you the money in a heartbeat if you needed it." Wally clears his throat. "And she used that information to try and get money for herself, Fern, not for you."

I shake my head. "No. That can't be right."

"Look, Fern, I know you've met someone else. But Rose is right, I do still care about you. And as someone who cares about you, I feel a responsibility to tell you that I think something is very wrong with your sister. Very, very wrong."

I shake my head. I don't want to believe it, but deep down I have a horrible feeling that he is right.

I think something is very wrong with your sister.

An hour after Wally leaves the library, I'm still ruminating on that. Is he right? And if he is, why am I the last to know about it? Is it one of those things I don't notice? Like people communicating with their facial expressions? Is it possible that, because of the way I see things, I've been missing an entire side of Rose? I think, suddenly, of Mum. She'd always worried so much about Rose. Was that because something was wrong with her?

I slide my phone out of my pocket and stare at it a moment, thinking. After hearing about Rose contacting Wally—asking him for money—I'm questioning everything. Finally, I redial the number for Sun Meadows. The same receptionist answers and I ask to speak to Onnab.

"Hello again, Fern," Onnab says. "Is there something else I can help you with?"

"Yes. I'd like to know who the last person was to see Mum alive."

A pause. "Well, let's see . . . it would have been whichever nurse was on night duty. I can check the schedule. She would have checked on everyone during night rounds."

"Would that have been before or after Rose visited Mum?"

"Hmm," she says. "Actually, I'm not sure."

"Rose hadn't seen Mum for a long time. It was her first visit in ten years," I say, suddenly. I'm not sure why. Perhaps I want assurance that this, combined with Mum's unexpected death, doesn't mean anything.

Onnab is quiet for a long time but I can hear her breathing, so I know she's still there. "Fern, as far as I know, the death isn't being treated as suspicious. Is there any reason you think it should be?"

I repeat the question in my head.

"Fern?" she says again.

I want to respond, as she has asked a question. It's just that I don't know the answer.

The afternoon passes in a blur. I serve people, restack books, do all the things I'm supposed to do, but my mind is anywhere but the library.

The Braxton-Hicks kick in around 2:00 P.M. I time them on a notepad as I go about my business at the library. Some people get all panicky about Braxton-Hicks, but I've read the books, I know they are only real when contractions are increasing in frequency and intensity. I get some relief from my thoughts and my pains by getting lost in my work—helping an elderly man find a selection of reading material about the *Titanic* to prepare for a talk he is giving at his Rotary Club. ("No romances," he'd said, pointing a finger at me accusingly. "Nothing with Leo DiCaprio or people getting steamy as the ship begins to sink.") I provide toiletries to a young homeless woman (and even give her my own sandwich for lunch, as after my interaction with Wally I'm not feeling especially hungry). Then I go to tidy the children's section, which is looking a bit worse for wear after the toddler drawing class that morning.

By 3:30 P.M., my Braxton-Hicks are getting more consistent in timing—around ten minutes apart for almost an hour. And while the pain is not debilitating, I'm starting to find it difficult to concentrate on my work. . . .

"Are you all right, Fern?" Carmel says when she finds me in the archive area, breathing quietly through a cramp.

"Fine," I say. "I'm fine."

She watches me closely. "Why don't you go home early today? You look a little tired."

I am taken aback at the suggestion. I've only taken two sick days in my entire working career and have only left early once for an emergency dental appointment. But with Carmel offering, and after the day I've had, I find myself nodding. "All right," I say. "Thanks, Carmel."

"Would you like me to order a taxi to take you home?" Carmel says.

"A taxi would be great," I tell Carmel. I don't tell her that I'm not going home.

By the time I arrive at the hospital, my contractions are four minutes apart.

Inside, everything is orderly and signposted, and I find the maternity ward promptly and report my arrival at the desk. The nurses are impressed with the documentation I provide, detailing the steady increase in the frequency of my contractions over the past few hours. Upon seeing me double over to breathe through a contraction, they unanimously agree that I should be taken straight through to the delivery room.

A nurse with gray hair and a navy-blue cardigan is the one to take me through. I follow her into a bustling hive of activity—people in scrubs and masks, requesting assistance or giving it; the phone ringing; people chatting. From an adjacent room, I hear a low moan reminiscent of a cow's. At the same time a nurse walks by, carrying an icy pole that smells like grapes and bubblegum. I pause as a particularly strong contraction takes hold. My nurse pauses with me, administers a firm rub to my lower back, and tells me, "You're doing great, love."

When it has passed, I follow her into a bright room—delivery room 4. A gown lies on the vinyl bed. In one corner, a tray of instruments sits beside a medical-looking crib, complete with overhead warmer.

"Your baby will be in there soon," the nurse says, flicking a switch. The crib lights up, emitting a low hum that travels through me like a mild electrical current. From somewhere outside the room, I hear someone whimper. It makes me jump.

"Pop that on, love," the nurse says, gesturing to the gown. "Everything off underneath, including bra and undies, then take a seat on the bed, and the doctor will soon be in to examine you. Is someone on their way to be with you?"

"What? Oh . . . um, no."

The nurse is headed for the door to give me some privacy, but then she pauses. "Oh. Is there someone I can call for you?"

I shake my head. But suddenly I'm not so sure. The lights. The sounds. The strange people.

"Oh, love," she says kindly. "Labor can be hard work—you'll want someone here to support you. A friendly face. Someone you trust."

Someone I trust.

How complicated that statement has become. *What if the person I trust most in the world is entirely untrustworthy?* I want to ask. And then, another thought occurs to me: *And what if she is the one person I can't get through this thing without?*

"Fine," I say finally. "There is someone."

Rose arrives at the hospital fifteen minutes after the nurse, Beverly, calls. In that short time, my pain level has gone from manageable to torturous.

"Why didn't you call me earlier?" Rose snaps as she bustles in. "We had a plan, remember?"

"Enough of that," Beverly says firmly, glancing up from her notes. "I don't want anyone upsetting our mother-to-be."

I glance at Rose. Rose has never taken well to people ticking her off. So I'm surprised when she gives Beverly a tight smile, removes her handbag, and places it on the window ledge. "You're right," she says. "I'm sorry. Are you all right?"

This is one for the books. I can't remember Rose ever saying sorry to me . . . ever.

"I'm fine," I say, before realizing this is far from the truth. My body is tensed up, my arms are wrapped around myself, and I'm rocking gently.

Rose looks at me knowingly. "Busy in here, right?" she says softly. "It's all right. I'll take care of everything."

To her credit, take care of things she does. In a matter of minutes, Rose has dimmed the lights, closed the door, opened the window, and explained to every nurse that I don't like people crowding me. Then she helps me down off the bed, explaining that I need to move around. Within a few minutes, I can breathe again.

That's the funny thing. Whatever else Rose has done, I realize, she is the only person on earth who can do this for me.

Rose is outside talking to the doctor when Beverly comes back to check my progress. I am sitting on the chair, the only place I feel comfortable. I tell Beverly I don't want to get on the bed, and she replies, "Of course, love. I can check you right where you are."

I am starting to warm to Beverly. I'm even becoming fond of her saying "love."

While she's checking me, she says casually, "Your sister tells me you are being a surrogate for her? What an amazing gift."

I manage a nod.

"I would have loved to have a child. They didn't use surrogates in my day, though. Even if they did, I only had a brother. I had friends, but it really seems like a sister thing, being a surrogate. I imagine, being twins, the bond is even more unique. If you get along, that is." She laughs.

Beverly doesn't seem to be expecting an answer, and I am glad. If she had, I might have told her the truth. That people without sisters think it's all sunshine and lollipops or all blood and guts. But actually it's always both. Sunshine and guts. Lollipops and blood. Good and bad. The bad is as essential to the relationship as the good.

Maybe the bad is even more important, because that's what ties you together.

The pain of labor is blinding. At first there is a rhythm to it, but after a while it's just pain. Breathtaking, magnificent pain. People I don't know are constantly touching me, assessing me, talking about me. When they talk *to* me, Rose answers on my behalf. I am grateful. It allows me to close my eyes and retreat into myself, remaining silent apart from the low animalistic grunts that emanate from me every minute or so as I struggle through a contraction. It makes sense to me, this noise, because in a way, I have become nothing more than an animal.

At some point I am offered pain relief, which I decline. For this, I am lauded by Rose and the nurses and told I am strong, when, in fact, I have refused it because I simply cannot bear the idea of anyone else touching me, even to administer pain relief. For now, I'll take the physical pain over the mental. But I am not strong. I think I might die. If not from the pain, then from the sensory overload. It comes at me from every angle. I am certain I *would* die, if not for Rose. She anticipates my needs—a cold drink, ice chips, space—and takes care of them quietly and without fuss. She never touches me without asking, and questions those who insist on touching me, confirming that it is absolutely necessary. She talks to the nurses and then reports back to me periodically: "It won't be long," "Things are going well," and, finally, "The baby will be born within the hour."

Twenty minutes later, when my water breaks, the room fills with people and the lights are turned up. It's too loud. Too bright. I can't breathe.

"You're ten centimeters," Beverly says. "It's time to push."

I shake my head. I can't. I need to get out of here. I try to stand but faces and hands rush in, trying to stop me. It makes it worse.

Then I hear Rose. "Just give her some space."

They step back slightly, but it's not enough. I'm too hot. It's too much.

"Fern, you can do this," Rose says. "You *have* to do this. For the baby."

I shake my head again. Rose looks around at the people crowding around me. I see the powerlessness on her face. She can't make these people go away. They are here to deliver the baby. They won't go anywhere.

She looks back at me. Her eyes are filled with tears. "Close your eyes. Imagine you are somewhere safe. The library. You have all the space you need. And you are with someone that you trust."

I do as she says. And it's Wally's face that I picture as I give birth to our daughter.

• • •

JOURNAL OF ROSE INGRID CASTLE

I tried to save Billy. I ran into the water, hooked my arms around his shoulders, and tried to lift him out of the water. But he was heavier than I expected. A dead weight.

"Billy?" I gently slapped his face. "Come on, Billy."

Billy didn't come on. He didn't turn his head to suck in a breath or cough and splutter or gasp for air. He didn't do anything.

I dragged him to the shore and started trying to administer CPR. I had no idea what I was doing, but I'd seen it done on television. As I tried to breathe life back into Billy, Fern stood beside me silently. When it was clear Billy wasn't coming back, I fell onto the shore beside him, and dropped my head into my hands.

All I could think was . . . Fern couldn't go to jail. She couldn't. It was misguided, the wrong thing to do, but she'd clearly done it to protect me. She didn't understand the consequences, not really. I needed to protect her.

"Billy was desperate to stay underwater longer than you, right?" I said, after several silent seconds. "To beat your time?"

Fern blinked in confusion.

"He dived into the water, Fern. He got tangled in the reeds. We thought he was holding his breath. By the time we realized he was in trouble, it was too late. That's what you need to say when anyone asks you questions about this. Billy got tangled in the reeds and he drowned. Okay?"

Fern listened intently and agreed. Luckily this time she followed instructions . . . to the letter.

FERN

When I rouse from sleep, I keep my eyes closed for a few seconds, steeling myself for an onslaught to the senses. It's been an arduous twenty-four hours. Every time I open my eyes, there's someone different in my room, checking on the baby, or me, or bringing me food or medicine. The last time I awoke from a nap, for example, it was to quite the kerfuffle. Rose was here. She was over by the baby's crib, speaking to one of the nurses.

"Has she been breast-fed?" Rose had said. The kind soothing voice Rose had used during my labor had gone. She sounded angry.

"Yes. Last night and early this morning. What is the—"

"The problem is *I* am the baby's mother, and I did *not* want the surrogate breast-feeding!"

"I do apologize," the nurse (not Beverly) had said. "It wasn't written in the notes. Let me look into this for you."

Rose and I had discussed breast-feeding on occasion during the pregnancy, of course. Each time, Rose said how awful it was, the pressure that "breast-feeding Nazis" put on new mothers, and assured me that formula was perfectly adequate in this day and age. But she'd never explicitly said she didn't want me to breast-feed. And so, during the night, when Rose had gone home and the nurse put the baby to my breast, I hadn't seen any reason not to give it a go.

The breast-feeding had brought on some afterbirth pains, and the nurse had been kind enough to administer some medication, which was fantastically effective. Possibly too effective, bringing on a temporary euphoria and then putting me to sleep within minutes of taking it. I've never been a big taker of painkillers, but after a few of these pills, I have to admit, I'm wondering why.

Now, when I open my eyes, Rose is at my bedside again, this time reading a John Grisham novel. I don't know how long I stare at her before she turns to look at me and frowns. She looks like she's going to speak, but she is interrupted by a young blond nurse with a high ponytail who appears in the doorway.

"Time for a feed," the nurse says brightly, and Rose immediately puts down her book and starts rummaging in her tote.

"Come on in," she says to the nurse. "Ah, here they are! I brought these bottles from home. We're going to be formula feeding."

Something about the way Rose says it sounds funny. *Formula feeding.* I laugh out loud. It is, perhaps, the medication. Rose and the nurse both frown at me for a moment before turning their attention to the baby.

"How is the little one doing?" the nurse asks. "Does she have a name yet?"

"Not yet," I call, but they ignore me.

"I was thinking about Alice," Rose says.

"Very pretty," the nurse says. "And how's Mum doing?"

"Fine," Rose says. "She's good."

Neither of them even *look* at me. It's as if, having now birthed the baby, I've been absorbed into the environment, disappeared. . . . The idea makes me laugh again. This time they look at each other, but not at me.

"I'll go make up the formula, shall I?" the nurse says, and Rose nods. When the nurse has left, Rose comes to my side.

"Did you ask Wally for money?"

She blinks. "How do you know about that?"

I laugh. "Wally told me."

"You've seen Wally?"

"Yes. Yesterday afternoon. At the library."

In her crib, the baby begins to fuss. The sound of it causes my breasts to leak through my nightie. But I've barely had a chance to look at her before Rose picks her up and puts her to her shoulder.

"I'm sorry I didn't tell you," she says carefully. "But . . . it makes sense, doesn't it? He is the baby's father. And he has plenty of money. Why shouldn't he support her?"

"Why would he?" I ask. "He doesn't know she is his daughter. Besides, do you really need the money? Surely Owen makes enough money to support her?"

The baby's fuss becomes a cry. I want to take her from Rose, but she walks away from me, to the window.

"What is it?" I ask when she remains silent. "Rose?"

"I wasn't going to tell you until after I took Alice home." Rose's back is still to me as she looks out the window. "But . . . as it turns out, Owen wasn't coping so well with the idea of raising another man's child. After giving it a lot of thought, he's decided he can't do it. He's staying in London indefinitely."

I stare at her back.

Rose turns around. "I know how important it is to you that this baby is raised in a two-parent family. But it wasn't meant to be."

She comes to the side of my bed and puts a hand over mine. "Look, you've had a big twenty-four hours. What you need right now is sleep. I'll get the nurse to get you some more painkillers. Everything will make sense later."

I have my doubts about that. My baby might be raised by a sister I'm not sure I trust. With no husband and no money. At the same time, I can't bear to think about any of this anymore. So when the nurse returns a few minutes later with the formula and some more medication for me, I swallow it down and go back to sleep.

I sleep. Late afternoon, Rose heads home for a shower and to change her clothes and I am left alone with the baby, who is tucked up close next to my bed, wrapped snugly in her pink blanket. It's astonishing how easy it is to while away the time just staring at her, marveling at her tiny eyelashes and squashed-up chin and wisps of black hair falling out the sides of her knitted hat. I must do it for hours before my eye is drawn to a woman standing just outside my door, talking to one of my nurses.

"Her sister has advised that now would be a good time," the woman is saying. She appears to be in her late thirties or early forties, and she smiles when she catches my eye. "Ah, Fern," she says, taking a few steps into my room. "You're awake."

"Who are you?"

"My name is Naomi Davison. I'm an adoption counselor. I've been speaking with your sister, Rose, and I wondered if now would be an okay time to have a chat with you? I promise I won't take long."

The nurse remains beside the woman. I get the feeling that if I give some indication that I'm not interested, she will be whisked away. But I am curious.

"All right."

She drags a chair up to the bed, and glances briefly into the baby's crib before sitting and pulling some paperwork out of a leather satchel. "As I said, I'm an adoption counselor. As you may or may not know, it's mandatory in Victoria for birth mothers considering adoption to have counseling prior to relinquishing their parental rights."

Naomi places a stack of documents and pamphlets on the tray table in front of me.

"My services are free of charge to both yourself and the intended adoptive parents. My role today is to ensure that you understand all your options, not just adoption. Okay?"

"Okay?" I mimic her tone.

"I understand that you have been considering intra-family adoption," she says.

My blank face must convey confusion, because she goes on. "Intra-family adoption is the adoption of a child by a stepparent or relative."

She looks up. I hesitate, then at a loss, nod.

"Okay. Well, we can talk about that in a moment, but first I want to talk to you about your other options."

It's the first I have heard about other options. But Naomi informs me I have several. Placing the baby in temporary foster care. Shared care. Open adoption—where the child is aware of their adoption and knows who his or her birth parents are (this has been found to be the most beneficial to the child)—and closed adoption, where the child doesn't know his or her true parentage. She talks about the permanence of adoption; how once a child has been adopted, the adoptive parent will continue to be the child's legal guardian even in the event of a marriage breakdown or divorce.

There is also the option of raising the baby myself. It's a lot of information. A lot of options I didn't know I had.

"If you decide to proceed with intra-family adoption, you will be required to sign papers relinquishing your parental rights. After signing these papers, you will have thirty days to submit a signed revocation, should you change your mind. After this time, you will be unable to change your mind. In order to make the adoption official, we require the signature of *both* biological parents except in such circumstance where the father isn't known, which I understand is the case here?"

This time she doesn't wait for a nod, and I'm glad.

"As a registered adoption counselor, I can witness you signing consent documents. Your sister has already signed this one. If you feel ready, you can sign it today. If not, you can take as long as you need, and then give me a call, and I will come back."

I look at the document with Rose's signature at the bottom, and my mind swims.

The problem, I realize, is that there are two Roses. The Rose I rely on, and the other Rose. The Rose who hated Mum. The Rose who goes behind my back to speak to Wally. The Rose who would possibly betray me to get the baby she wants so badly.

I don't know which Rose I'm getting. I don't know which Rose my baby would get.

"If it's all right with you," I say, "I'd like you to come back."

• • •

JOURNAL OF ROSE INGRID CASTLE

Everyone accepted that Billy had accidentally drowned, even Daniel. The river was full of reeds and he had been trying to beat Fern's time for the whole week. The coroner recorded a verdict of "death by misadventure." Which meant, our plan worked.

Fern got away with murder.

But lately I'm wondering if I did the wrong thing, covering for her. Maybe by not allowing her to face the consequences of her actions, I've created a monster. There's no doubt that Fern can be dangerous when she's angry. And now that there is a baby involved, I'm terrified that she will pay the price for my mistake.

FERN

When my three-hourly medications are due, the nurse makes her rounds and I opt to take the full dose. Oblivion is preferable to all the thoughts swirling in my mind. Owen is not going to raise the baby with Rose. Rose wants Wally to give her money. Wally thinks there is something wrong with Rose. Mum is dead, and Rose was the last person to see her. It's too much for my brain to handle. I can see, all at once, the appeal of drugs. Understand the calling of an addict.

By the time Rose returns to the hospital, I am nearly asleep. I keep my eyes closed, but I feel her in the room. I'm not sure if her presence is a comfort or a threat. I am still musing on this when I hear a distinct American accent coming from just outside my doorway.

"I'm here to see Fern."

My eyes spring open. . . . I'd have thought I was having some sort of drug-induced fantasy—if it weren't for the speed at which Rose jumps out of her chair and runs to the door.

"I wish you'd called ahead, Rocco," Rose says. She walks into the hallway, pulling the door to my room nearly all the way closed behind her. "Unfortunately, it's not a good time."

I try to sit up, but I feel dizzy and have to lie back down.

"I don't need you to tell me when an appropriate time to visit Fern is," Wally says. His voice lacks its usual warmth. In fact, he sounds downright angry.

"Actually, you do. Because she's asleep."

"Fine. I'll wait."

There's a short pause. "Look, I'm glad you're here. Why don't you and I go somewhere and we can—"

"I'm not going anywhere with you."

There's a short silence and then Rose closes the door fully. When she speaks again, I have to strain to hear.

"We need to talk, Rocco."

"Fine. Let's talk about how Fern says she doesn't need any money—"

"Of course she won't tell you that. She's ashamed. She's ashamed that she can't even raise her own baby!"

"What do you mean?"

"She's adopting the baby out to me. I'm going to raise it."

"What?"

I hear the wheels of a cart on the linoleum floors and then Rose says, "No, thanks," and the sound recedes.

"Why is Fern giving her baby to you? That's the most ridiculous thing I've ever heard."

"Is it?" I can hear a thread of strain in Rose's voice. "Come on. We both know Fern isn't capable of looking after a child—"

"Of course she is. I think Fern would make a terrific mother."

More silence. I feel the painkillers swirl in my bloodstream, which, while not unpleasant, is quite distracting.

"There are things you don't know, Rocco." Rose sighs. "Fern's dangerous."

Wally scoffs. "If you're talking about what happened by the river when you were twelve, Fern told me about that."

There is a long silence. When Rose finally speaks, she sounds uncertain. "Fern told you?"

"Yes."

"She told you she drowned a boy in the river?"

"Yes. But I don't believe it."

"It *is* hard to believe," Rose agrees. "But it's true. I was there. I am the only person on earth who knows the truth about what happened."

But that isn't true. There was someone else at the river that night, someone other than her, me, and Billy.

The night before he died, Billy and I had wandered down to the river together to skim stones. We were breaking the rules. We weren't supposed to do that. Mum and Daniel told us we weren't allowed to leave the camp at night, but when Billy asked, I threw caution to the wind. There was something about Billy that made me want to do things like that. Something about his company that made him difficult to resist.

He took me by surprise when he kissed me. One minute we were skimming stones and the next our teeth were knocking together. He said "Ow" and I laughed. Then he kissed me again. It was better that time. Still strange, but better.

We were on our third kiss when Rose stepped out of the bushes, startling us both.

"Fern?" she'd said.

She'd been so quiet after that. It was almost as though she was annoyed with me. Her strange mood permeated the camp the next day. That was what happened when Rose got into one of her moods—you could feel it in your bones. By evening, Mum and Daniel were so fed up they sent us down to the river. "Go swim," Mum said to Rose. "Shake it off."

I think Mum wanted to help, but I hated it when Mum told Rose to shake it off. It only ever made her madder.

Billy and I followed Rose down to the river, at a distance. But once she was there, she just stood on the bank, sulking. After a few minutes, Billy strode past her and into the water—he didn't know how Rose could get when she was in one of these moods. I wanted one last swim with Billy, but I felt like I shouldn't, so I stood off to the side, watching them. Billy had spent that whole week trying to hold his breath underwater longer than me and this was his last chance, he said. But it was clear he was never going to do it. It was funny. I could have watched him try all night.

After an hour or so, Rose called me over to her. I was taken aback. She'd been giving me the silent treatment all day. Usually she kept it up for two or three days before she broke it.

"Help him," she whispered.

"Help him what?"

"Help him beat your time."

I'll admit, I wasn't too keen on the idea.

"Go on," Rose urged. "He'll never do it otherwise. And boys love to win!"

Rose was so animated. She looked practically *happy*. There was something appealing about a happy Rose, especially when she'd been in such a bad mood. Letting Billy win would be a small price to pay, I supposed. So I agreed.

The next time Billy broke through the surface of the water, I told him my tricks. "Breathe slowly and calmly for at least two minutes. Then exhale everything in your lungs and take the deepest breath you possibly can. Then once you're underwater, relax and let your thoughts drift away."

Billy listened carefully before attempting it. And he did quite well, for a first timer. He was still no match for me, though. And when oxygen bubbled to the surface, I felt pleased. Until Rose said, "Help him."

I frowned. "What do you mean?"

"Help. Him. Win."

"You mean . . . ?"

She nodded.

We stared at each other. I was sure I'd misunderstood. "But—"

"It's the only way he'll beat you. Hold him down."

And so, I did. I put a hand on his back, and another on the back of his head. "Only forty seconds," I said to Rose. "Check your watch."

Rose did. Billy started to struggle but in karate I'd learned to grip well. I'd spent months developing forearm and finger strength, so he had no chance of getting free. But he was twisting and kicking. I felt very uncertain. "How long has it been—"

"Nearly there." Rose was looking at her watch.

"Now?" I said.

Rose shook her head.

It didn't take long before he stopped twisting.

Rose kept time on her watch. I felt reassured by that. Rose wouldn't let me do anything bad to Billy. And yet it felt like an eternity before she gave the nod to release him.

As soon as he rose to the surface of the water, I knew something was very wrong. I hooked my arms around his shoulders and lifted his head out of the water. "Billy?" I gently slapped his face. "Come on, Billy. Wake up."

But Billy didn't wake up. He didn't turn his head to suck in a breath or cough and splutter or gasp for air.

I dragged him from the water. He was heavy but I got him to the shore and rolled him onto his side. When he still didn't breathe, I tried to administer CPR. I'd read a book about how to do it, and we'd practiced it at school on plastic mannequins, but it was harder on an actual person. Rose just stood there, in shock. I breathed into Billy, again and again. After several minutes with no response, I sat back on my heels and looked at him. He was the most unnatural color—a slippery, whitish blue. His eyes were open, but lifeless.

That's when we heard Mum.

"Girls?" She was looking around for us, and spotting us on the shore, she appeared relieved. Then she looked past us to where Billy lay. For a moment, she remained completely still. Then she ran. It was a sight to behold. Mum never ran anywhere.

"Billy!" she cried, dropping to her knees beside him. She fumbled at his neck, presumably trying to feel for a pulse. "Billy. Come on. Come on, Billy. What happened?"

Rose and I remained silent, as Mum herself tried to breathe life into Billy. She continued for what felt like hours, only pausing to swear under her breath and, once, to lift her head and say what sounded like a quick prayer, which was odd as I'd never seen Mum pray before. When she finally spun around, her face was streaked with tears and dirt. "What happened? *Someone* tell me."

"I . . . I was trying to help him stay underwater longer than me," I stammered. "I must have held him for too long."

"You held him under?" Mum stared at me. "Why would you do that, Fern?"

I glanced at Rose. Mum followed my gaze. Something funny happened to her eyes. "Did Rose tell you to?"

Somehow, I understood the danger of answering that question. And so I didn't.

"Oh, of course it's my fault," Rose said. "Nothing could be the fault of your precious Fern."

Mum stood up and grabbed Rose so tightly that her feet lifted off the ground. "Billy is *dead,* Rose. Do you understand that?"

"Yes," Rose said evenly. "I understand."

"And now you've implicated your sister!"

"You've always hated me," Rose shouted, crying now. "You've only ever loved Fern. *Everyone* loves Fern!"

Mum let go of Rose and lifted a hand to Rose's face before hesitating and dropping it down.

"I don't hate you, Rose. But it does feel like you've spent your life trying to make me prove I love you. And now, a boy is dead!"

Mum looked down at Billy's lifeless body, then up again, meeting Rose's gaze.

"If you want to prove that you love me," Rose said, "then this is your chance."

Midafternoon, Rose goes to Target to get the baby some smaller clothes. The moment she is gone, I move quickly.

The hospital is quiet, apart from a few mewling, newborn cries. I struggle into my rainbow dress, one of many souvenirs of the bizarre brand of love Rose has for me, and I lift the baby out of her crib. She is warm and feather light. I hook my bag over my shoulder and cradle her against my chest. It's lovely how she seems to fit into the space perfectly, like she was made for this space. Perhaps she was.

It's funny, she doesn't look like an Alice to me, I realize. More like a Daisy or Lily or Poppy. Or Willow? There's something about the strength of it that I like. Yes, Willow. That's her name.

It is so easy to get out of the hospital that I don't feel like I am "breaking out" at all. I skulk past reception and out into the street, covering Willow's face with the blanket as we walk past the smokers. There is a taxi idling there, having just let an elderly man and woman out, which is perfect. I may not be the best mother for my baby. But I am becoming more and more certain with each passing moment that Rose isn't either.

I feed Willow in the taxi and she falls into an openmouthed sleep. I have nothing other than my handbag. No nappies. No clothes. At least I have milk, and judging by how sore my breasts are, more milk is coming in. All in all, it could be worse.

When we pull up, I half expect Rose to be standing there, her faux concern pasted onto her face, ready to launch into a speech about how this kind of behavior is exactly why I can't be a mother to this baby. Maybe she's right. Still, I'm delighted to find that she isn't here. For once, it seems, I'm one step ahead of Rose.

I ask the driver to let us out at the back of the library. My plan is ill thought out at best. I'm not even sure it *is* a plan. All I know is that I have to call Wally. I have to tell him he is the father of my baby. Even if he is upset with me for not telling him, he will surely help me figure out the right thing to do. I know now that the right thing is not to leave my baby in Rose's care.

I let myself into the library through the back door. It's quiet inside, so I manage to make my way down the muted, carpeted hallway without being noticed. Through the opaque glass window, I can see people moving about in the staff room, and I hear Trevor's high-pitched, irritating laugh. I can't chance going across the library to the secret cupboard so instead go through the vestibule and into the bathrooms. Inside, I enter a stall and sit on the closed toilet, resting Willow on my knees while I retrieve my phone. I have fifteen percent battery left, which is astonishing to see—normally, I don't let it get below ninety percent, but I didn't have my phone charger at the hospital. Still, fifteen percent is all I need. I search for Wally's number and that's when I notice. No service.

"*Shit!*" I say. A baby noise bubbles from Willow, a squawk of sorts, as if in solidarity with me.

"Fern? Is that you?"

I freeze, inside the stall. It's Carmel's voice.

"It *is* you!" she says, after a minute. "I recognize your shoes."

I look down at my shoes—sequined silver sneakers that are unlikely to belong to anyone else at the library.

"Are you alone?" I ask.

"Yes. It's just me."

I open the door. Carmel opens her mouth as if to say something but then she sees Willow. She sucks in a breath. "You had your baby!"

"Yes." I smile down at her, wriggling in my arms.

Carmel creeps closer. "A girl?"

I nod.

Carmel's hand goes to her heart. "She's beautiful, just beautiful, Fern." She's smiling, but suddenly her expression becomes concerned. "But why aren't you in the hospital?"

My smile falls away.

"What is it, Fern? Is everything all right?"

"Rose wants to take my baby away from me."

"No," she says. "That's ridiculous. She wouldn't."

"The thing is . . . I agreed to it. I thought the baby would be better off with her. But . . . I've changed my mind."

Carmel listens to me intently, her face full of concern. It's the first time anyone has listened to me intently in a very long time. I feel unexpectedly teary. "Have you told your sister this?"

I shake my head. "Rose has a way of getting what she wants."

"Ah," Carmel says. "I too have a sister."

We look at each other for a moment and I have a strange feeling. Like an understanding traveling between us. It's nice.

"So, what is your plan?" Carmel asks.

"I need to call Wally. I think he can help. But there's no reception in here."

"Then we must find reception," Carmel says determinedly. "The library is quiet right now. Keep your head down and no one will pay you any attention."

Carmel checks that the coast is clear and then we head through the vestibule. Gripping Willow tightly, I push the door onto the library floor open. By the time I see the uniforms, it's too late to turn around. They've already seen me.

"Now," Carmel says, standing between them and us. "I really don't think this is necessary—"

I don't hear the end of Carmel's statement, as I have started to run. I don't get far. A policewoman catches up to me as I reach the side door. She doesn't grab me, perhaps because of the baby in my arms, but she uses her body to block me into a corner. If I were willing to let go of Willow, I could have taken her down with a hip throw. But I'm not.

"We've spoken to your sister," the policewoman says. "You need to give us the baby. We'll take good care of her, I promise. . . ."

She reaches for the baby and I rear back, twisting away from her. It startles Willow and she starts to cry. I'm considering knocking the policewoman down with a leg sweep when I see someone standing at the front desk at the other end of the library.

Rose.

It's Gayle at the desk, and she doesn't appear to be giving Rose a satisfactory answer, because Rose slams her hand against the desk. Then she glances around wildly. When we finally lock eyes, for a moment I think I must have mistaken someone else for her. She looks different. She looks . . . like a madwoman.

"Give her to me!" she cries, running toward me. I hold Willow closer, knitting my fingers together. Breast milk saturates my chest.

"Ma'am, I really need you to give me the baby," the policewoman says again.

I turn away from her, and from Rose. I don't let go of Willow.

I cry. I moan. I sob. I even bite the padded edge of the bed. Once again, like when I was in labor, I am an animal. Willow is gone. Rose was saying I kidnapped her, so they took her from me. The ache of being away from her is nearly overwhelming. My breasts are rock hard, my dress is drenched. My body still aches from giving birth to her. But I don't even have a photograph of her. Even if I did, my phone is out of charge.

"It's all right, miss," the nurse by my hospital bed says to me in a strange, flat sort of voice. It's not Beverly, nor any nurse that I recognize from the maternity ward. I'm in a different part of the hospital. The psych ward. This nurse has a stern face, pinched lips, and nude stockings that don't hide her varicose veins. "The doctor has given you a sedative, so you will feel much better soon."

"Where is my baby?"

The nurse glances at the doorway. Two police officers stand there, talking quietly to one another. I recognize the policewoman as the one who chased me across the library. I never did hand over the baby. Karate had made my finger strength superior to most people's, and they had no chance of getting her off me without a fight. Eventually, they'd held Rose back and allowed me to carry Willow outside, while the police formed a loose circle around me, in case I made a run for it. Outside, there had been four police cars waiting. All of them for me.

"There's just a bit of confusion that needs sorting out," the nurse says. She gives me a look that I can only describe as pity and gives my hand a gentle pat. I pull my hand away.

"I want to see my baby," I say.

The sedative must work, because before I know it, I'm waking from a deep sleep. Nothing has changed except that now, a man is in the corner of the room, talking to the nurse with the varicose veins.

"Where is my baby?" I ask again, quieter than before.

The pair of them startle, then turn to look at me.

"Hello," the man says, grabbing a chair and dragging it swiftly up to the bed. "You must be Fern."

I don't reply. He sits down. "I'm Dr. Aston. I'm a psychiatrist. How are you feeling?"

"Not good. I want to go home."

Dr. Aston nods, looking down at his notes. "Well, hopefully we'll be able to arrange that soon, but first I want to have a chat to you about how you're feeling. I understand you've recently given birth?"

"Yes. Where is my baby?"

"She's in the pediatric wing. I've just spoken with her doctor and she's absolutely fine. I'm told she's being taken care of by your sister."

"I do not want my sister near my baby."

Dr. Aston's eyebrows rise. He glances at the nurse and then back at me. "I understood you intended for your sister to adopt your baby. Is that incorrect?"

"It *was* correct," I say. "But I changed my mind."

"I see. Well, first things first." He looks up as a woman appears in the doorway. "Ah. You want to do this now?"

"If it's convenient," the woman says.

The doctor nods and gathers his notes. "We'll finish this in a bit, Fern. Don't worry, we'll get it all sorted out."

Rose has been saying that for months. Don't worry. Everything is going to be fine. And now, here we are.

The woman comes into the room. She doesn't look like a doctor to me. She is wearing normal clothes. She is in her mid- to late forties, with blue eyes and dark blond hair that she wears in a long braid down her back.

"You don't look like a doctor," I say.

"That's because I'm not." She holds up a lanyard. "Detective Sara Brookes. Is it all right if I ask you some questions?"

I take a moment to process this. A police detective. Then I realize. I kidnapped a baby. She must be here to arrest me.

Detective Brookes sits in the seat that Dr. Aston just vacated and pulls out a small notebook and pen. "I like your bracelet," she says, bizarrely. I can only deduce that making small talk helps perps to "talk." "Is that a bush engraved on there?"

"A fern," I correct. "Because that's my name."

"It's lovely. The name and the bracelet."

We stare at each other for a moment.

"Congratulations, by the way," Detective Brookes says. "I hear you had a baby girl. Where is she?"

"She's in the pediatric wing," I tell her. "With my sister."

Detective Brookes looks surprised. "Why isn't she in here with you?"

I frown. "Because I kidnapped her. Didn't you hear?"

Detective Brookes sits back in her chair. "You kidnapped your own child?"

I nod. "At least that's what my sister is telling people."

"I wonder why she'd say that." She gives me a long assessing stare. "Why don't you tell me a little about your sister?"

The question is too broad. I can't even begin to narrow it, so I just pluck random facts out of my mind, as if from a hat. "She's the same age as me."

"Oh. You're twins?"

"Fraternal twins. And we are very different. She's short, and I'm tall. She has no sensory issues, but I do. She's diabetic, and I'm not."

The detective writes on her notepad. "Are you close?"

"I'm not sure. I don't know where the pediatric wing is."

She smiles. "What I mean is . . . do you spend a lot of time together?"

"I suppose so."

"And she is . . . a good sister?"

"What do you mean?"

"She's . . . kind? Does nice things for you?"

"Sometimes."

"And other times?"

I throw up my hands. "I don't know. She's just Rose, okay?"

I'm frustrated by this conversation. I just want my baby. I'm not sure what Rose being a good sister has to do with anything.

The detective nods. "I understand your mother passed away

very recently," she says, taking the conversation in another strange direction. "I'm sorry to hear that. The hospital staff indicated that you visit weekly."

"You've spoken to Sun Meadows? Why?"

"Just part of our investigation. Your mother's cause of death isn't clear, so we just wanted to check up on a few things. We understand that your sister hadn't visited in a very long time until she went the night before your mother died. Why was that? Didn't she have a good relationship with your mother?"

"Rose?" I laugh. "She didn't have a relationship with Mum at all."

"She never spoke to her?"

"Well, no one *spoke* with Mum. After her overdose, Mum couldn't say two words. She's improved a little over the last year. She was starting to talk in short sentences." I think of what she said to me about my baby. *Don't give Rose the baby.* "Recently she told me not to give Rose my baby."

If only I'd listened.

Detective Brookes writes some more in her notebook. Then she frowns thoughtfully. "That's a pretty bold statement. Why do you think she would say that?"

I look at her. "I don't understand. Why are you asking me about Rose and my mother? Aren't you here to charge me with kidnapping?"

She smiles. "Not at this point." She taps my bracelet with her pen. "Let me guess, your sister has a matching bracelet?"

"Yes," I say. "But with a rose on it."

"Because her name is Rose."

I nod. She rises to her feet. "You've been very helpful. That's all I need for now."

"Wait!" My voice is hoarse. The detective raises her eyebrows. "Will I get my baby back?"

More than anything, I wish I had the ability to read other people's facial expressions. Because when Detective Brookes narrows her eyes and says, "Leave it with me," I have absolutely no idea what it means.

An hour passes. Then two. I'm in hour three when I recognize the person loitering in the doorway.

"Owen?"

"Hey, Fernie."

I blink. It's him. It's really him. "What are you doing here?"

He shrugs. His hands are tucked into his pockets and he seems as close to shy as I've ever seen him. "Can't a guy visit his sister-in-law in the nuthouse?"

He's had a haircut. Which isn't unexpected, I suppose, since he's been away a year. It suits him like this. He appears to have lost weight and gained muscle. Owen had always been well built, but these last few years he'd become a bit softer looking.

London must be treating him well.

"How did you know I was here?" I ask.

"Rose called me. She does that when she gets herself into trouble."

"And you came all the way from London?"

He looks confused. "London? No, I came from Brunswick."

"Oh," I say. "When did you get back from London?"

"I haven't been in London, Fern."

"Of course you have. You've been living there for the past year."

Now he gives me a meaningful look. "I was going to ask what

you're doing in here, but clearly you *are* mad." He chuckles. "Why'd you think I was in London?"

"You haven't been living in London?"

"No. Why would . . . wait. Did Rose tell you this?"

"Yes. She said you have been working on a project over there. She went over to visit you last year."

He laughs, but it is one of those nervous laughs. "Fern, for the last year I've been living on the other side of town. A few months back, I actually came and visited you a couple of times at the library. I didn't want to go to your flat as I thought that might get you in trouble with Rose. When you didn't get back to me, I assumed Rose had turned you against me and I gave up."

"I remember a mystery visitor coming to the library. That was you?"

He nods. It's too strange. Owen glances over his shoulder as if afraid Rose is going to burst in. I also feel afraid of that.

"What did Rose say when she called you?"

"She said you had had a baby," he says, perching on the side of the bed. "And that it was your sincerest wish that she and I raise it together. My instinct was to stay away from her madness, but as it involved you, I had to come and see what was going on."

"But why would Rose say you were in London?"

He sighs. "Why does Rose do anything? Because of how it reflects on her."

"What do you mean?"

He exhales and runs a hand through his new stylish hair. "I left her. Things hadn't been good between us for years, Fern. She was so changeable—happy one minute, enraged the next. I couldn't live like that. I suggested counseling, but she wasn't interested. It was all my fault. Eventually, I couldn't take it anymore."

"So you moved to Brunswick?"

He nods. "I can't believe she told you I moved to London. But, then again, I can. She always has to own the narrative. She could never admit that someone left her."

I take a minute to digest this. "What do you think is wrong with her, Owen?"

"I've spent a lot of this year in therapy trying to work that out. And I have to say, she possesses all the classic traits of a narcissist. Possibly even borderline personality disorder."

"What kind of traits?"

"Her mind games. One minute she was sweet and kind, the next she was ridiculing me in front of our friends. If I became upset with her, she said I was too sensitive, it was all just a joke. If I gave an opinion that differed to hers, she didn't speak to me for days. And her sense of grandiosity! She spent so much money. More than we had. She was forever quitting her job—or getting fired, I honestly don't know which, but it never curbed her spending. I don't think she's held a job for longer than a year the whole time I've known her. At first, I thought she had bad luck, but then it just kept happening. I stopped asking her about it, because she would get furious if I brought it up."

I think of the times she's talked about going to work this past year. And I think about the number of times I've seen her in work clothes. They don't match.

"She's not well, Fernie. You can't give her your baby."

"I know."

We sit for a moment in silence. I realize I have a lump in my throat. Owen's face is more somber than I've ever seen it. He reaches forward and puts his hand on mine. It's warm and strong. It's not just bearable. It actually feels good.

"Thank you for coming to see me," I say.

He shrugs. "I wish I could do more."

I smile, even though I'm sad—and for the first time, I understand why people do that.

"I wish you could too," I say.

Twenty minutes after Owen leaves, Detective Brookes comes to the door.

"May I come in?"

If she's come to arrest me for kidnapping Willow, she won't have to ask any such permissions soon. In jail, I imagine the police can come and go as they please. They won't ask if I feel like stew or spaghetti for dinner, they'll just hand me a meal. It's possible, I realize, that I won't go to jail. I might go to one of those places for the mentally impaired—*One Flew Over the Cuckoo's Nest*–style. Apparently, those places aren't as bad as they once were. I read an article about it recently. Electroshock therapy is only used sparingly, and the facilities are geared toward rehabilitation. Still, I doubt babies are allowed to visit. That's the most frightening part of this—not jail, or a disruption to my routine, not the smells or lights or alarms—it's the fact that I might not see Willow again for a long, long time.

I wrap my arms around myself.

"Fern?" Detective Brookes says. "Are you all right?"

I shake my head and start to rock. There is another police officer with Detective Brookes now, this one in uniform. He remains at the doorway, while Detective Brookes slowly enters the room.

"I'm sorry. I didn't mean to upset you. I just need to have a word to you about something."

"The kidnapping?"

"Fern, Willow is your daughter. I cannot arrest you for taking her to the library."

I frown. "You can't?"

"No."

I am perplexed. "Then . . . why did the police come after me? Why did they take Willow?"

"My understanding is that your sister called to report you and your baby's sudden departure from the hospital. This would have prompted a welfare check from the police. As you were distressed when they found you, a request for psych assessment would have been made, and I'm not privy to those. But there is no suggestion that you kidnapped your daughter, Fern."

"Really?"

"Really."

I take a minute to process this.

"Then . . . why are you here?" I ask.

Detective Brookes takes a seat by the bed. "It's to do with your mother."

"My mother? What about her?"

"We have the autopsy report. It shows two hypodermic injection sites just under your mother's hairline. This indicates foul play."

"Foul play?"

"It indicates someone may have poisoned your mother. But there were no traces of poison in your mother's blood."

"That's strange."

"Yes, it had us a little baffled too until you mentioned your sister was a diabetic. You see, one trend we've started seeing a bit of in nursing homes is insulin overdosing. It's popular because in general insulin degrades quickly in a body. With your sister being a diabetic, she would obviously have access to insulin and be experienced in giving injections. In addition to this, we found a bracelet, identical to yours but with a rose on it, in your mother's room. And given the fact that their relationship was troubled, and your mother was trying to convince you not to give her your baby . . . that's a motive."

I blink. "You think Rose murdered Mum?"

She shrugs. "I'd say it's not looking good for her."

"No," I say. "I don't believe it."

But maybe I do believe it. I think about the way Rose felt about Mum. Even the mention of her name was enough to infuriate her. And Rose had done so many things that I'd never thought she would do. Go behind my back with Wally. Lie about Owen. Accuse me of being dangerous. Take my baby from me.

"It's a lot of compelling evidence. Enough to rule your mother's death a murder. And enough that your sister is the prime suspect."

I stare at her. I'm about to ask where Rose is, but halfway through I realize it's the wrong question. I have a new priority now. A more important question.

"Willow," I say. "Where is Willow?"

I lie on my hospital bed and stare at the closed door. It's all too much to take in.

Detective Brookes told me that Rose will be formally charged and then most likely remanded in custody until trial. The idea makes me nervous. Rose won't be happy about any of that.

On her way out, Detective Brookes told me that she would find Willow, but that was twenty minutes ago, and I've heard nothing since. She told me to stay in my room, so they can find me easily, but it is torture. I'm not in any trouble for taking Willow, Detective Brookes stressed. She is my baby; I'm free to take her anywhere I want. I like the sound of that, even if I'm not sure I trust it.

Finally, there is a knock at the door. I lurch upright as the door opens. It's not Willow.

"Wally?"

He pushes his glasses up his nose and smiles. He's dressed in the first outfit I ever saw him in—jeans, the flannelette shirt, the bobble hat.

"How did you find me?" I ask as he comes in. He closes the door behind him and takes a seat beside my bed.

"Carmel called me, eventually. She said you would be here. I'd been back to maternity but you weren't there and no one would give me any information. It's taken me hours to find you."

I take a minute to marvel at this. Wally, looking all over the hospital . . . for me.

"Wally, I have to tell you something," I say, when I realize I can't wait a moment longer to tell him.

His gaze slides from over my shoulder to meet my eye. It calms me. "What is it?"

"The baby is yours," I tell him.

He closes his eyes and drops his chin to his chest. He is silent for so long I wonder if he hasn't heard me. But when he lifts his head, his face is covered in tears.

"Why didn't you tell me?"

"I wanted to. I should have. But I didn't think I was capable of raising a baby . . . you know, after what happened with Billy. And you . . . you said you didn't want a baby."

"I did say that, didn't I? I don't know why. I guess because it was a theoretical answer. I enjoy answering theoretical questions. But if you'd told me you wanted a baby . . . or that you were pregnant . . . I promise you would have got a very different answer."

"I would?"

He nods. I feel something, actually *feel* it, shift inside my chest. I'm about to ask what the answer would have been when someone comes to the door.

"Knock, knock?"

A woman in black slacks and a pale blue blouse is standing there. She's wearing black orthopedic sneakers. "I apologize for interrupting. My name is Nadine Riley—I'm an administrator here. I understand your daughter has been up in our pediatric unit in the care of your sister, but that your sister has been unexpectedly . . . called away?"

"That's right," I say.

"I see, well, as your adoption paperwork hasn't been finalized, the hospital policy is to keep the baby here in the room with you. I'm told you will be moving back to the maternity ward shortly, but in the meantime, one of the nurses is bringing your daughter here to you. . . . Ah, here they are now."

I stop breathing. Nadine Riley moves to the side and a young nurse enters the room, pushing a crib on wheels. My hands begin to shake. I see the top of her head through the clear plastic crib. Someone has removed her little hat.

"I have a little girl here who would like to see her mother," the nurse says, strolling into the room smiling widely. She is the perky sort of nurse—young and blond, with a high ponytail, white teeth, and fresh, clean skin. She parks the crib beside my bed and applies the brake before reaching for her. Neither Wally nor I speaks, or even moves. My heart beats so fast and hard I contemplate whether I might be having a heart attack.

"Ooh, is this Dad?" the nurse says, gesturing to Wally. "Of course it is, silly me, she's got your hair. She really is just a darling little thing. Who wants to take her?"

She gathers her up with the ease of someone who spends much time around newborns, and then glances from me to Wally, as if expecting a tussle. She doesn't get one. We are both too shell-shocked. Wally is so still I think he may have ceased to breathe.

"Give her to him," I say, finally. "He's got some time to make up for."

Wally remains frozen for just another second. Then he nods, visibly relaxes a little, and opens his arms.

Wally stays in the chair beside my bed for twenty-four hours. When he's not tending to Willow or checking on me, he's downloading parenting books onto his phone and reading them furiously. He introduces me to an app for my every parenting need—a tracker for feeds, sleep times, and nappy changes; a white-noise maker; a height and growth chart. Rather than feeling overwhelmed by this, I find the ritual of entering information into the different fields surprisingly soothing. I am hopeful that soon the new rituals and routines will become a new kind of normal.

For someone who didn't want children, Wally certainly appears enamored with Willow. He holds her like one might hold hot tea in a fine china cup and looks at her the way one might admire a favorite painting or sculpture. In the middle of the night, I wake to find Willow in his arms and him looking down at her like this. I watch for an indeterminable amount of time. The sight of them nearly overwhelms me.

"I'm glad," I say, startling him, "that you are my person."

He looks up at me and smiles. "I think a few people might fight me for that role."

My face must convey my confusion.

"I don't think you realize how many *people* you have, Fern. Carmel. Gayle and your library colleagues. Owen. And yes, me. And don't forget Willow."

I take a minute to consider that. While I'm doing so, Wally says, "Rose said you weren't capable of raising a child. I suspect she may have convinced you of that too, right?"

I shrug.

"Is it just the Billy thing that worries you?"

"It's mostly that. But also my sensory issues. You have to admit, I'm not the ideal mother. What if the baby wants to watch fireworks? Or have a birthday party? I couldn't even handle school pickup or drop-off with all those shrieking children and swarms of mothers in puffer jackets, making small talk."

Wally thinks about this. "Okay," he says. "Well, *I'll* do the school pickups and drop-offs and the birthday parties."

"You? *When?* When would you do the school drop-off? When you're in your van creating your app? When you are traveling around the world promoting FollowUp?"

"I sold FollowUp, Fern."

I blink. "You sold it? Already?"

He nods. "For a lot of money. It makes the deal for Shout! look cheap. So I can do the school run every day, if you like. And you can stay home, or go work in the library, or come to school pickup with me and wait in the car. You can do whatever you like!"

But it can't be that easy. Nothing in life is that easy.

Willow chooses that moment to start fussing.

"Is she due for a feed?" I ask.

Wally checks the app and determines that she is. He brings her to me. As she latches on, he enters the feed time into the app. The ritual of this, even over the past twelve hours, is one I've come to quite enjoy. As she feeds, we watch her. It's surprisingly satisfying. I've never found watching an adult eat enjoyable.

"She's a miracle," Wally says.

I think about that. "Well, no, not really. Pregnancies are actually biologically quite straightforward."

He rolls his eyes. "Sure, but . . . you were on birth control. Which means, what were the chances? Point zero three percent or something?"

I look at him. "I wasn't on birth control."

He blinks. "But you told me you were."

"No, I didn't. Why would I say that?"

"I don't know, but you did say it," he says emphatically. "The first night. I remember it clearly. You told me it was safe."

I frown. "It *was* safe. But what does that have to do with birth control?"

Wally closes his eyes for a moment; then he exhales and smiles. "Well, I guess that solves that part of the mystery."

"What do you mean?"

"I mean . . . it explains how you mysteriously became pregnant."

If Wally is bothered by this, he is keeping it well hidden. But his proclamation about "mysteriously" becoming pregnant triggers a realization that there is something I haven't been clear about.

"There's something else I have to tell you, Wally," I say. "The pregnancy wasn't an accident."

Wally frowns. "What do you mean?"

"Rose couldn't have a baby. She confessed this to me when I found prenatal vitamins in her bag and assumed she was pregnant.

It turned out she'd been trying for a baby for a while and couldn't have one. So . . . I decided to have a baby for her. It sounds crazy, I know. I just thought . . . I can have a baby and Rose can't. Why wouldn't I help her out? It seemed so simple. Then . . . I met you and . . . and . . ."

". . . and you asked me on a date so you could become pregnant with a baby for your sister?"

"Yes."

Wally places both hands on his temples. "Wow."

"But by the time we had sex, I wasn't even thinking about that anymore. I wasn't thinking about—"

Wally walks to the corner of the room, shaking his head. "Wow," he says again. "It's genius."

"What is?"

"Rose," he says.

"What do you mean?"

"She must have known what you would do if you found out she couldn't have a baby."

I shake my head. "But she didn't even tell me she wanted a baby, I found her prenatal vitamins."

"Which she just happened to leave lying around?"

I think about this. But I don't believe it. "You think she did that on purpose? So I would realize she wanted a baby and try to have one for her?"

He shrugs. "I wouldn't be surprised."

"Well," I say. "In any case. I'm sorry."

Wally walks back to my bedside. He looks down at Willow. I'll never get tired of the way he looks at her.

"You know what's funny," he says. "I'm not."

When I'm released from hospital, we go back to Wally's new flat, stopping by Rose's on route to collect Alfie. Wally's flat is in an older-style building that reminds me a lot of my old place. He rented it a few months back—things got so busy with FollowUp that he decided he needed a more permanent base. It still looks like he hasn't properly moved in. He says it's just a stopgap until we buy something bigger, but honestly, I quite like it. I loved my little flat.

Willow and I don't leave the flat for the next forty-eight hours, and Wally only leaves to walk Alfie. Carmel is our only visitor, coming by to drop off a pile of books for me, a couple of takeaway hot chocolates, and an adorable pink onesie for Willow. She said if I needed anything, she was just at the end of the "line." I wasn't sure what line she was referring to, but when I told her this, she just laughed and said she'd check in with me tomorrow.

Both Wally and I try to sleep when Willow sleeps, but we find, frustratingly, that we cannot tune our body clocks to the bizarre schedule of round-the-clock forty-five-minute naps, so we make do with merely resting while she sleeps. Sometimes we read or play a game of sudoku. They're lovely, those little pockets of time we have together.

Two days after we get home from the hospital is a Thursday. My first Thursday, I realize, as a mother, and *without* a mother. The fact that I'm not visiting Mum is made both better and worse by Willow's existence . . . though I can't help but think what a magnificent Thursday it would have been if I could have taken my daughter to meet my mother.

Throughout the days, my thoughts drift indeterminately to and from Rose. Detective Brookes has kept me in the loop. After Rose's arrest, she was remanded in custody and is now awaiting arraignment. She has been asking to see me, apparently. I tell Detective Brookes that I *will* see her, at some point. And I will. But for now, it's a relief to keep my mind busy caring for Willow.

I've been at home for a week when Detective Brookes calls to tell me she'd like to see me at the police station. It's not the usual first outing with a baby, which according to my baby book is generally to the doctor's office or the maternal health clinic. Still, I feel okay about it, as I was given reasonable notice and was able to plan the best route to take and to ensure there will be ample parking for Wally's van. As the baby book instructs, I allow extra time to account for baby-related mishaps, but even so, we pull up to the police station five minutes late.

Detective Brookes is waiting for us outside, as planned. She doesn't appear to be upset about our tardiness. "Follow me. I've reserved a visitor's parking spot for you so you don't have to walk far. And I've found us a quiet room on the first floor."

It was Wally who suggested I tell her about my sensory issues in advance. As it turns out, her son has similar issues and she is happy to make accommodations so I will be more comfortable. I've found that a lot of people have been happy to accommodate me, actually, once they realize my challenges. All this time, I'd thought that Rose was the only person who understood how to care for me. How wrong I was.

We park the van and follow Detective Brookes into a small interview room with three chairs, a table, and a potted plant. Cream floor-to-ceiling horizontal blinds obscure the view of a fire extinguisher outside.

"Take a seat," she says, and I do. Wally declines, instead standing in the corner. Willow is expertly strapped to his chest by a long piece of cloth and he is bouncing even though she is fast asleep. We have both bounced a lot this past week. Sometimes I find myself standing in the shower, bouncing, even though Willow is asleep in the next room.

"The reason I asked you to come in today," Detective Brookes says, sitting down in the chair opposite me, "is that I wanted to show you something."

She places a notebook in front of me. It's pale pink, embossed with gold flowers and the words "A penny for your thoughts" in gold leaf.

"Have you seen this before?"

I reach out and touch the hard cover. "No. I don't think so."

"It's Rose's diary."

I frown. "Rose doesn't keep a diary."

Detective Brookes shrugs. Clearly, it's one more thing I didn't know about my sister.

"Would you like to read it?"

I hesitate. "But . . . you're not supposed to read other people's diaries."

"Rose gave me the diary," Detective Brookes says. "Trust me. She wants us to read it."

I don't get it. "Why?"

Again, she shrugs. But there is something about her expression that makes me think she has her suspicions. "Open it," she says, and I do, flicking it open in the middle and then leafing the pages backward.

"Have a read. Let me know if you have any comments about anything in there."

There's a lot in there. Page after page of Rose's handwriting. I scan the page in front of me. It's about the time I drew on the coffee table when I was little. It surprises me that Rose would write about this. She was always so reluctant to talk about anything in our past. I'm about to turn the page when something catches my eye.

"Wait," I say.

Detective Brookes leans in. "What is it?"

I scan the page again. I remember that day very clearly, because of the drama that followed. I didn't know Mum meant that I should do my homework *in the book on top of the coffee table* and I'd been embarrassed when I realized my mistake. But Mum wasn't mad with me. "Thank god the coffee table was cheap," she'd said with a laugh.

I think it was the laugh that set Rose off. She said Mum would never have laughed if she did something like that. She got so mad she stormed into the bedroom and broke every single one of my toys. It was one of the biggest meltdowns I'd ever seen her have.

But Rose's diary tells a different story.

I flick to the next page. It's about our ninth birthday, when Mum made us that amazing unicorn cake. Rose had been in such a strange mood that day. I'd stayed away from her when she was like that, but this time we had to sing "Happy Birthday." Mum got out the "good plates" because it was a special occasion. I'm not sure why, but this seemed to be the wrong decision and Rose stormed out of the house. Mum looked everywhere but couldn't find her. She was gone all night long. I remember Mum and me waiting in the hallway through the night for her to come home.

But Rose's version of this is different too.

"This isn't right," I say. "This diary, it's . . . not how things happened."

I flick the page. Another story. I don't understand. Why has Rose done this?

There's only one entry that causes me to pause. It's the one entry about Mum's boyfriend Gary. I read that one twice.

"There are two particular entries that we are interested in," Detective Brookes says. "I've earmarked them. Both are to do with a boy called Billy . . ."

I look up, stunned. Rose wrote about Billy *in a diary*? She'd always been so insistent that we never even *talk* about Billy. Unless . . . unless she's created a fictional story for it too.

I flick to the pages that Detective Brookes has dog-eared and read the entries, once, and then again. Then, a third time. I can't believe it.

My eyes find Wally and Willow.

"This isn't what happened," I say. "Rose made this up! I swear, this is not—"

"It's all right, Fern," Detective Brookes says. "We know."

I stare at her. "You *know*?"

"Of course we know. Your sister isn't the first master manipulator we've come across."

"But I don't understand. Why did she write a diary? What is the point of it?"

Detective Brookes sits back in her chair. "It seems to me she was laying the groundwork to claim that you couldn't care for a baby, in case anyone questioned her adoption of your daughter. And, the way she portrays you here, you'd make a prime suspect in your mother's murder, taking the heat off her."

I shake my head. It's too crazy to contemplate. I look down at the diary. Entry upon entry about our childhood. It couldn't have been a spur-of-the-moment plan. This would have taken her *months* to compile. All to make me look unfit and secure her rights to my baby. My heart hurts.

"But why give it to you now?" I ask. "She's in jail, no one is going to give her a baby now. Surely she doesn't want the baby taken away from me and given to a *stranger.*"

Wally keeps his gaze firmly away from mine, but he stiffens slightly. I've become more in tune with his nonverbal communication these past weeks. Perhaps just sharing space with someone does that.

"Why?" I ask. "Why would she want to hurt me like that?"

Detective Brookes smiles ever so slightly. There's a sad edge to it. "I don't know," she admits. "But I have a feeling it's a sister thing."

Wally and I lie on the bed, side by side, staring up at the ceiling. Willow's bassinet is in the corner, but she is snuggled into Wally's chest—her favorite place to be. The flat is quiet and calm, but still my head is spinning. On the way home from the police station, Wally spoke to a lawyer to ask for advice on the Billy situation. The lawyer advised that it would be highly unlikely for Rose's testimony to reopen inquiries into Billy's death nearly twenty years after the fact, particularly with no witnesses to corroborate her story. At this point, everyone seems to have accepted that Billy had drowned by accident and that was the end of the story. It seemed the other part of the story would remain forever buried.

Wally turns his head to face me, and his glasses slide down his nose. "So your mother really never did those things in Rose's diary?"

"No." I think about that. "I mean . . . there were moments of truth in there . . . but they weren't to do with Mum. It's as if Rose just unearthed all our memories and recast them so she was the victim. Mum never broke our things or left us overnight or locked Rose in her room."

"They were all lies," Wally says.

"Yes," I say. Then I hesitate. "Or maybe it's the way Rose thinks it happened? I know that when we have recollected things together, her versions are always a little bit different to mine. Bigger, more dramatic. And she always adds things she couldn't possibly know, like why people did what they did. But the way she tells them, it feels like she believes it is true." I pause.

"What is it?" Wally asks.

"There was another part of the diary that I wondered about. About one of Mum's boyfriends. Gary. She said he did something to her in the swimming pool. I think that part might be true."

Wally frowns. "Why do you say that?"

"Because he tried something similar with me."

Wally rises up onto an elbow, balancing Willow between his chest and other arm. "Your mum's boyfriend—"

I hold up a hand. "He didn't hurt me. I gave him a knee to the groin and he didn't try it again. It never occurred to me that he might try it on Rose. I should have looked out for her better. I hate the idea of something bad happening to Rose. Even now, I hate it."

"Unfortunately, that sentiment isn't reciprocated," Wally says. "If it were, Rose wouldn't have falsified a diary intended to keep Willow from you." He stands up and carries Willow over to the bassinet.

"The part I don't understand is why she lied about what happened the night Billy died. She didn't need to lie about that. I *did* drown Billy! Why did she need to say that she wasn't there when he died?"

Wally frowns. "That is weird." He puts Willow down. Standing upright again, he becomes very still. "You said it was Rose's idea to hold him under," he says slowly. "And she kept time while you held Billy down?"

"Yes."

"And didn't you say if felt like a long time? Maybe it *was* a long time?"

It takes me a minute to understand where Wally is leading me. Rose told me to hold Billy down. She told me how long to hold him. And then she made up a story saying she wasn't there.

"It makes sense. Why else would she need to make up a story about it?" Wally says.

"No," I say. "I don't think Rose would do that."

"I'm sorry, Fern," Wally says. "But I think she would."

It takes me a minute to realize the ramifications of this. "So I didn't kill Billy?"

Wally shakes his head. "I don't think you did."

Before I know it, tears are streaming down my cheeks. "If this is true, Wally . . . it means I can be trusted with my baby! Doesn't it?"

"Yes, Fern." Wally wipes a tear from my cheek. "It does."

I let out a sob. Wally comes to my side and I allow him to hold me for the longest time. It doesn't even bother me the tiniest bit.

I can be trusted with my baby, I tell myself. *I can be trusted with my baby!*

I understand it's true. It's just that, after all these years, it's going to take me a little longer to believe it.

Three months later . . .

I sit on the floor with my legs crossed and Willow in my lap. Linda stands in front of me wearing a pair of giant white underpants over the top of her clothes, and a bright red cape—Captain Underpants. She zooms around the room, her cape flapping behind her.

We're at Baby Rhyme Time. Sixteen mothers sit on the floor cross-legged with their babies balanced in their laps. An additional four mothers sit on chairs at the back, breast-feeding or pushing their strollers vigorously, trying to get their babies to settle. Wally sits on the floor beside me, watching Linda curiously.

"Tra-la-LAAAAA," Linda cries, taking off across the room again.

I have to lip-read, because I'm wearing my noise-canceling headphones. They're big ones—the ones that look like earmuffs—and I'm wearing them over the straps of my black-tinted goggles. Wally is also wearing headphones and goggles, as he doesn't like to be left out. We've been coming to Rhyme Time every week for three months now. Willow enjoys it and it's one of the few places where no one stares at our accessories. *In fact,* a few weeks ago, the funniest thing started happening. A little boy, the older brother of one of the babies, had come in wearing a little pair of headphones and goggles too. His mother told Wally he'd always found the music a bit loud and our solution, she thought, was genius. The following week, another child was wearing them. This week, half a dozen babies and toddlers have them on.

Last week, Carmel had asked if I'd consider facilitating a sensory rhyme time session, where the music would be soft and the lights kept low. I'd agreed before she'd finished asking the question. Since Willow and I were released from hospital, Wally and I have divided our time between staring at Willow and frantically reading books about how to raise a baby, and while it hasn't been a bad existence, I'm missing my routine. Besides, Carmel has told me that Wally is welcome to bring Willow any time we like. I'm glad, because I think Mum was right when she said that taking a child to the library is the very best education you could give a child. Willow is going to be very well educated.

I still haven't visited Rose. I've felt the pull, definitely felt it, but for now I'm ignoring this particular pull. At Wally's urging, I've had a few sessions with a very nice therapist named Kevin. He wouldn't comment on Rose's mental health without seeing her, but last week he did pose a couple of interesting questions that I'm still ruminating on a week later.

How does your relationship with Rose serve you? How has it ever served you?

Until I have an answer, he said, perhaps hold off visiting.

So I am. Until I have an answer.

"All right, mums," Linda says. "Are we ready to fly?"

Linda is affixing an imaginary cape onto Wally's back when I realize it is time to take my leave. I may have been making improvements in recent weeks but pretending to fly in an imaginary cape is beyond even my new capabilities. I hand Willow to Wally and retire to the secret cupboard for a couple of minutes of quiet reading instead.

I'm beginning to think Wally was right when he said I was normal and everyone else was a weirdo.

• • •

JOURNAL OF ROSE INGRID CASTLE

It's been three months since I was remanded in custody, awaiting trial. Now, *there's* a sentence I never expected to write. I keep expecting to wake up and find that this was all a bad dream. No such luck. It seems this will be my life. Bookends of horror, surrounding a too-brief, happyish middle.

As a remand prisoner, I have privileges that a sentenced prisoner doesn't have. For example, I can wear my own clothes rather than the prison garb—though, I'm not sure if this small freedom is a kindness or not, as it makes me stand out to my fellow inmates. I also have more flexibility around visitors—they can come as often as they like. But no one has come. Three months and no visitors. Not Owen. Not even Fern.

All I have, it seems, is my journal.

My prison psychologist suggested it might be enlightening to write in it. To get really honest with myself, he said. I've avoided it for a while, but now I figure . . . why not? It's not like I have anything else to do.

As far as I'm concerned, Billy got what he deserved. Flirting with me all week, and then taking Fern down to the river and *kissing* her?

It was clear Fern wasn't his peer. She was vulnerable. Billy was no better than Gary.

Poor Fern didn't even seem to realize she'd been taken advantage of. She continued to swim around the river with Billy like a fool while they tried to see who could hold their breath the longest.

"Why can't I beat you?" Billy kept crying.

All right, I thought. *If Billy wants to beat you, he can beat you.*

It wasn't hard to orchestrate. "Just let him beat you," I told Fern. And Fern did exactly as she was told, as usual. I kept time, making sure he was under there long enough to finish him off. It worked like a charm... until Mum showed up.

Fern told her it was all her fault, so of course Mum was quick to concoct a cover-up. But afterward, she wouldn't let it go. She started saying things to me like "What really happened?" and "Fern would never..." and "Tell me the truth." She'd become so despondent she had to go to the doctor for sedatives, which made her even more useless than normal. Sixteen years ago, it was easy for a twelve-year-old like me to google how to administer insulin to the hairline, so once Mum was out for the count on Valium, I had no trouble at all. I was hoping she'd die, but a brain injury wasn't a bad result. I thought that would be the end of it.

But when Mum started talking again, telling Fern not to give me her baby, I realized I'd have to finish the job. I'd kept an eye on her from afar, so I was aware she was making advancements even before Fern told me. Who could blame me for trying to defend myself?

By then I'd already started the journal, ostensibly about my marriage. In truth, that had been a surprise—Owen announcing out of the blue that he was leaving because he felt like he didn't know who I was. I tried to convince him to stay, but he was adamant, so I wished him good riddance. I didn't need him anyway. I knew Fern would have a baby for me. Sisters do these kinds of things for each other.

The best thing is . . . I didn't even have to *ask*. All I had to do was leave the Elevit lying around and the rest was history. Fern would do it; I had no doubts about that. She always did what I wanted her to. Of course she did, I'd spent a lifetime making her reliant on me. Planting the idea that she couldn't be relied on—telling her she forgot to pick up milk or left the oven on. Telling her she was supposed to feed Alfie. That one had really got into her head. The result was that she did everything I asked, single-mindedly and perfectly. It was what made her such a great sister. And she didn't let me down; it only took a ten-day staycation just outside of Melbourne (a.k.a. London) to get the job done.

Admittedly, I'd panicked when I thought the father of my future child was homeless, but I hadn't given my sister enough credit. Trust Fern to find the only homeless multimillionaire! The baby would be smart, most likely. And one day, if I allowed her to track down her real dad, he'd owe us child support in the millions! I had it all worked out. It was what made it so painful when Fern decided to turn on me. I don't know why I was so surprised. One by one, everyone seemed to turn on me. Dad. Mum. Owen. Why not Fern too?

The night before she died, I took my journal to Mum, to show her what would happen if she decided to tell Fern not to give me her baby. It was the first time I'd seen her in ten years. Ten *years*! It had started out well. Mum had seemed overwhelmed to see me. Her eyes had filled with tears and she'd actually gasped. That had been nice.

This is your chance, I'd thought. *Make up for lost time, Mum. Show me that your brain injury knocked some sense into you.*

I would have forgiven her. I would have let bygones be bygones.

But you know what she said?

"Don't take Fern's baby."

Ten years. *That's* what she said.

Can anyone blame me for what I did?

She didn't fight me. Why would she? The last time I'd tried to kill her, she'd only ended up with a brain injury. We both knew I wouldn't make that mistake again.

I sit back in my chair and read over the journal entry I have just written. This is what they want, obviously. Everyone. The police. Fern and Wally. My prison psychologist. Documented proof that I am to blame for everything. Good luck with that.

I rip out the pages and tear them into confetti. On a whim, I throw the pieces up and let them rain down on me. *Poof.* I'm not an idiot. I'm not going to provide them with documented proof to collude against me. For what? I did everyone a favor. Billy was a pervert and Mum should have been dead sixteen years ago.

And as for Fern's baby—I'm the only one who cares enough about her to not want her to be raised by an imbecile. A pair of imbeciles! Time and time again, people have rallied against me. Now I know I have no one. Not even Fern. Fine by me.

I open my diary on a fresh page and poise my prison-issued suicide-proof pen. I have another entry to make. I'll start with Fern's recent interest in my insulin dosage and how I administer it. I'll say how she and Mum hadn't been getting along and she'd been resenting having to visit her every week. Then I'll mention how Fern had always loved my bracelet. And how, finally, a few months ago, I'd agreed to lend it to her. *What do you think of that, Fern?*

I smile. I hope she's enjoying her time with my baby. Because once this journal is in circulation, she won't have her long. I'm telling you, Fern might be the librarian . . . but I'm the one who can spin a tale.

ACKNOWLEDGMENTS

I was watching my little girls play together when the seed was planted for this novel. The two of them were rolling around on the grass hugging and giggling, so I took the opportunity to dash back into the house for a moment. But I'd barely crossed the threshold before the moment of harmony turned to blood-curdling screams.

"She bit me," my older daughter howled. Upon inspection I did find a perfect semi-circle of teeth marks.

"Why did you bite her?" I asked my younger daughter (who was worryingly indifferent to her sister's pain.)

"Because she annoys me sometimes."

Sometimes. Not that particular moment. Just sometimes.

The obvious thing to do was to reprimand the younger daughter for biting. But when I tried, my older daughter was indignant.

"Leave her alone! She's my baby sister and I love her! Anyway," she added conspiratorially, "I'll bite her back later when she's not expecting it."

The next minute they were hugging again.

If there isn't a book in that kind of relationship, I thought, my name isn't Sally Hepworth.

But I didn't do it alone. As always I owe everything to my favourite literary agent, Rob Weisbach, who always answers my questions in record speed (even on weekends) and then insists it wasn't a stupid or annoying question. We both know the truth. Thank you for lying.

I am indebted to everyone at St. Martin's, particularly Jen Enderlin, who gave me my confidence back when I lost it; Katie Bassel, who manages to get me publicity in spite of my terrible penchant for blurting out inappropriate things at inopportune times; Olga Grlic, for creating the best covers in the world; and Lisa Senz and Brant Janeway, for somehow getting people to know who I am and to buy my books—no mean feat. Also to the rest of the gang at St. Martin's, who are just so awesome.

To the team at Pan Macmillan, especially publisher Cate Paterson for her patient calming of my neuroses; my sensei-editor Alex Lloyd for his karate wisdom and editorial guidance, and my copyeditor Emma Rafferty for making me seem like a much better writer than I am.

To my other publishers around the world, thank you for everything you do.

To my police detectives (who allow me to call them that)—Kerryn Merrett, Andria Richardson, and Meghan McInness, for checking my police details and making sure I get them right.

To my writer-gang—Lisa Ireland, Jane Cockram, Kirsty Manning, Rachael Johns, Kelly Rimmer—drinking wine with you all is my favourite thing about writing.

On the home front, thank you to my family for putting up with me staring into space a lot, and only half-listening to most of what you say. You know I'm listening to the voices in my head and you have learned to be okay with it. I've learned to be okay with the fact that you all leave your shoes all over the house (honestly, though—would it *kill* you to put them away? Just once?). Let's call it even.

Finally to the readers, who read my books, spread the word, and keep me in a job. This book, and every book, is for you.